To Mom and Dad,
for always running with me

For my daughter, with love

Sophie had only ever stolen one dream.

She'd been six and curious, two not unrelated traits. The dream had been stored in a brilliant blue bottle with a gold-flecked stopper. It was the only unlabeled bottle in the batch, and she'd thought that meant it wouldn't be missed.

She'd spotted it on the top shelf after her parents left (one to the grocery store and one to tend to a customer). She had to haul books downstairs from the shop and pile them on top of a stool before she could reach it. Stretching, she touched the bottle with her fingertips, knocked it off the shelf, and then caught it before it could shatter on the old stained counter below. It took precious seconds to wiggle the stopper out, and she chugged it down without hesitating.

It tasted like fresh melon.

She'd thought she'd see a swirl of mist first, like the squiggly fog that always came before a dream in a TV show, but instead she plunged instantly into the dream. One second she was in her parents' workroom beneath the bookshop, and the next she was tucked into a bed with cupcake-pink ruffled sheets. For an instant, she thought it was her bed, even though she didn't have pink sheets, but then she remembered who and where she was.

Sitting up, Sophie looked around curiously at the cotton-candy wallpaper and the shelves of toys. The owner of this room had a Barbie Dreamhouse and liked horses. A night-light in the shape of a pink unicorn cast a rosy glow over the room. Pink shadows stretched.

One of the shadows twitched.

And a shadowy monster crept out of the closet.

Sophie felt her heart beat deliciously faster. Slowly, so she wouldn't startle the monster, Sophie scooted out from under the sheets. She waited.

The monster skittered left. It dodged right. Sophie pretended to look out the window at the moon, stuck between the pale branches of a tree. Out of the corner of her eye, she noted that the monster seemed to have several tentacles. She looked at it, wanting to count them, and the monster dived beneath the bed.

Lying flat on her stomach, Sophie leaned over the edge of the bed. She lifted up the dust ruffle. Moonlight swept under the bed. The monster huddled in the shadows. Its fur bristled like a cat's.

"Hi. I'm Sophie," she said.

It bared its teeth, three rows of shiny, sharp, shark-like teeth, and growled.

"Shh. It's okay. I won't hurt you." She felt her heart patter inside her rib cage and wondered if it would hurt if the monster bit her dream self with those teeth. She guessed it would, but only until she woke up. "Come on out."

The monster snapped its tentacles like whips, and Sophie scrambled back. Retreating to the pillows, she took several deep breaths. She told herself firmly that she shouldn't be scared. This was what she'd wanted, after all, her very own dream.

Inching forward, she again leaned over the side of the bed. The monster waved its tentacles at her. "You have lovely tentacles," Sophie said. "Like a furry octopus. Did you know that an octopus can open a jar with its tentacles? I read that once. I like books. Do you like books? My parents own a bookstore. It's nice. We have lots and lots of books." She kept her voice soft and even, as if she were luring out a stray cat. The monster lowered its tentacles. "That's a good monster. You can come out."

The monster scooted forward. Sticking its head out from beneath the dust ruffle, it looked up at her. It had overly large eyes like a lemur's. Its pupils were the size of Sophie's fists and ringed with gold.

"Are you a girl monster?"

It snorted.

"A boy monster?"

It blinked at her. She decided that meant it was a boy monster. He inched out from under the bed. She counted six tentacles. He also had four tiny legs with sharp, curved claws. Squatting beside the bed, he kneaded the carpet with his claws.

"Are you an in-the-closet monster or an under-the-bed monster? The dream bottle wasn't labeled, and we have lots of both. We even have a few on-the-ceiling monster dreams, but those aren't as common." She wasn't supposed to talk about her parents' dream collection. But since she was in a dream, talking to a dream creature, she decided the normal rules didn't apply.

The monster crept farther into the moonlight. His fur was black with hints of red and blue in it. She thought he was iridescent black. She liked the word *iridescent*. She'd learned it just the other week.

"You have beautiful iridescent fur. That means you shine with different colors," Sophie said. "You're a very handsome monster."

The monster purred.

"It's nice that you don't have any slime. So many dream monsters are coated in goo." She patted the blanket next to her. "Do you want to come up?"

He hopped onto the bed. He was about half her size, though if he stretched out his tentacles, she bet he'd be larger. Instead, he curled his tentacles underneath him in coils of fur. She wanted to pet his fur. She wasn't sure she dared. He continued to watch her with his large lemur eyes.

"I bet the dreamer who thought you up was scared of cats," Sophie said. "I've never had a cat. Or dog. Or any kind of pet. I've always wanted a pet. I wish you could be my pet."

The monster nudged her hand with his nose. She felt her breath catch in her throat. He had so many sharp teeth that they couldn't all fit in his mouth. A row of teeth stuck out beyond his gums. He wormed his head under her hand. His fur felt softer than cotton and smoother than silk. Sophie stroked his head and scratched behind his ears.

Sighing happily, the monster closed his eyes.

She lay down next to him, continuing to pet him. He began to snore, and Sophie bit back a laugh that bubbled up inside her. His snore sounded like a toy train. After a while, she fell asleep.

She woke to her parents' screams.

Uh-oh, she thought. Sophie opened one eye and then the other. Her mother was, oddly, perched on top of a table next to the dream distiller. She held a broom and was brandishing it like a sword. Her father held a fire extinguisher with the nozzle pointed at her.

"Don't move, Sophie," Dad said.

"It's okay, baby, don't be scared." Mom's face was chalky, as if she'd used powder instead of blush on her cheeks. Her voice sounded unusually shrill.

Sophie didn't move.

She was lying on the floor. Her head rested against a cabinet, and her feet were stuck in a pile of sponges and mops. She had the open and empty blue bottle in her left hand. Curled against her right side was a furry warmth.

Her mom tightened her grip on the broomstick. "Kenneth, what is it?"

"Some sort of badger," Dad said.

"It has six tails," Mom pointed out.

Sophie shifted her head slightly. Her monster was curled up beside her, still snoring, but the cupcake-pink sheets and the rose-wallpapered bedroom were gone. She was home in her parents' dream shop beneath the bookstore. "They're tentacles, not tails."

"Badgers don't have tentacles," Dad said.

"Sweetie, you know it's not a badger," Mom said to him.

"It looks like a badger," Dad insisted. He inched closer. The floorboards creaked under his feet. He stopped as the monster gave a whistle-like snort in his sleep.

"It looks nothing like a badger. Sophie, did it hurt you?"

"It's a he," Sophie said. "And he's really very sweet. Can I keep him? Please?" She shifted so she could look at the slumbering dream monster. If you ignored all the tentacles and the sharp teeth and the sheer size of him, he could almost pass for a housecat. Maybe a housecat with an enormous appetite.

"Absolutely not," Mom said.

"I think it's a wombat," Dad said. "Or a wolverine. Some *w* animal. Sophie, if you can inch away, I'll spray it with the fire extinguisher, your mother will incapacitate it with the broom, and then we can look up what it is." His voice was light, but Sophie saw that his hands were shaking. Her parents were scared, and they were trying not to scare her.

Sophie wrapped her arms around the monster. "Don't hurt him!"

The monster woke up.

Lashing out with his tentacles, he snapped his jaws and snarled. Her parents rushed forward, but Sophie jumped up to block them. "Stop!" She shook her finger at the monster. "You stop too!"

Cringing, the monster whimpered.

"Sophie, what's in your hand?" Mom was frowning at the blue bottle that Sophie still had clutched in her hand. "Did you . . . Oh, Sophie."

"I'm sorry!" Sophie stared down at her sneakers, unable to meet her parents' eyes. They had told her time and again to leave the bottles alone. "It was only a monster-in-the-closet dream."

Both of her parents were silent.

The monster growled softly and leaned against her ankles. She bent and scratched behind his ears. He bared his teeth at her parents. "Be nice," she told him. She risked a glance up at them.

Her parents didn't look angry, but they did look extremely worried. Sophie felt her heart thump faster, and not in the pleasant way that it had within the dream. Her father set down the fire extinguisher. Her mother laid down the broom. "Tell me the dream," Dad said quietly.

Sophie described the room and how the monster had emerged from the closet. She told them how she'd spoken to him and how they'd fallen asleep. "And that was it," she said. "It was a nice dream."

"You made it a nice dream," Mom said. "I doubt it started out that way. This monster was undoubtedly meant to eat you."

The monster made a chirping sound, as if to deny he would ever do such a thing, and he pressed closer to Sophie's ankles. She caught her balance on the counter. He was heavy. "See, he's sweet!" she said.

Mom sighed. Sophie looked at her hopefully. She knew that sigh. It meant that Mom was about to cave. "Sophie, we won't hurt your new . . . friend. But we will need you to step away from him so we can turn him back into his dream self. Kenneth, pass me one of those dreamcatchers."

"No!" Sophie shrieked. She threw her arms around the monster's neck. "Please, I promise I'll take care of him. You won't even know he's here."

Her father climbed a stepladder and took down a dreamcatcher. It was a pretty one, a circle of soft wood with a spiderweb-like tangle of string in the center. Charms and crystals hung from the strings, and feathers dangled from the bottom. He handed it to Mom.

The monster shrank back and bared his teeth.

"Give him a chance," Sophie said. "He doesn't deserve to be sent away. He's special. Can't you see? And he likes me."

"Sophie, dreams don't belong in the real world," Mom said gently. "He shouldn't be here." Holding the dreamcatcher, she stepped toward Sophie and the monster.

"But he is!" Sophie cried. "Maybe he's here for a reason! Maybe he's supposed to be my friend! I want a friend! You never let me have friends!"

Mom halted. She looked pained, as if Sophie's

words had jabbed her. "That's not true. You have friends at school."

"Friends have playdates! Friends don't keep secrets from each other!"

Her parents exchanged glances.

"And you think this . . . thing will be your friend?" Dad asked. "He's a monster. He could decide you're his midnight snack. He could rampage through town. Last thing this town needs is a rampaging monster." He didn't say it with much conviction. Sophie sensed she might be winning.

Sophie squatted beside the monster. "If you stay, will you be my friend?"

The monster licked her cheek. He then looked directly in her eyes with his wide lemur eyes and said in a gravelly voice, "Yes. I will be an excellent friend for you, Sophie."

Mom dropped the dreamcatcher. "He talks!"

Sophie patted the monster's head. "He's a very clever monster. Please, please let him stay!" The monster lolled his tongue out and tucked his extra tentacles behind him so he looked more like a cat or a stuffed animal than a monster. He turned his wide eyes on Sophie's parents.

"Oh . . . well . . ." Dad said. "We want you to have friends. Real friends. But . . ."

Mom knelt in front of the monster. "If you mean my daughter any harm, I will personally skin you before shoving you back into a dream. Understood?"

The monster managed to look solemn as he nodded.

Mom fixed her gaze on Sophie. Sophie had never seen her look so serious. "If we keep him—and I said *if*—you must make three promises to me. One, you will never drink another dream. Two, you will not let anyone see your monster. And three, you will never, ever, ever tell anyone that what you dream can become real."

Sophie nodded vigorously. She wrapped her arms around her monster's neck. He wound his tentacles around her waist. One of his tentacles patted her shoulder.

Dad took Sophie's hand in his. "Repeat the promises."

"I'll never drink another dream. I'll never let anyone see Monster. And I'll never tell. Can I keep him, please, please, please?"

"There are people out there who might . . ." Dad began.

"Don't scare her," Mom said.

"She should be scared," Dad said. "This is serious. We are taking a risk we might regret, and she must understand the consequences."

The monster spoke again for a second time. "I will protect her." He wound his tentacles tighter around her, comfortingly warm.

"Very well." Mom stood and straightened her skirt. Now that this was resolved, Sophie could tell she was moving on. "We're having fish for dinner. What do you eat, Monster?"

"Small children," he said hopefully.

Mom recoiled.

"Joking," the monster said. "I am telling a joke. I am a funny monster, aren't I?"

"Hilarious," Dad said drily.

Monster untangled himself from Sophie and trotted after Mom. "Just a few hamsters would be fine. Or mice. I like mice."

And that was how Monster came to join Sophie's family.

SOPHIE LIVED IN A PALE YELLOW THREE-STORY house that her mother called "charming" and her father called "in danger of collapsing if a bird sneezes." On the third floor, which used to be the attic, were two bedrooms, one for her and one for her parents, plus a tiny bathroom. Both bedrooms had plenty of skylights so you could see the stars (and plenty of buckets under the skylights to catch the rain that dripped in). Her mother liked to keep cut flowers in the buckets. Both rooms also had plenty of books, which were kept away from the drips, and homemade pillows everywhere so you could curl up and read the instant the reading mood struck you.

On the second floor were the kitchen, dining room, and living room, all stuffed with books too. There were so many stacks of books, in fact, that

Sophie could cross from the stairs to the kitchen without touching the floor once. She usually went barefoot so she wouldn't dirty the books as she clambered over them.

Downstairs, on the first floor, was her parents' bookstore, the Dreamcatcher Bookshop. Sophie loved the bookshop. It was a labyrinth of ceiling-high bookshelves that were crammed with new and used books. It smelled of warm dust and fresh cupcakes. The cupcakes were baked every morning by their newest neighbor, a woman who had always dreamed of owning a bakery, and were sold from trays by the cash register. The shop had a bay window with a window seat where you could sit, read a book, and eat your cupcake. It also had three or four red velvet chairs with worn upholstery, tucked between the shelves. After closing, Sophie would intercept the unsold cupcakes on their way to the trash, and she and Monster would curl up on one of the red chairs. She'd eat one cupcake, and Monster would inhale ten. Monster had a sweet tooth, or several.

One of their favorite games was for Sophie to stand at the bay window (shades down so no one could see in) and toss cupcakes across the bookstore. Monster would run, leap, and catch them in midair.

This often led to cascades of books crashing to the ground. Luckily, with his six tentacles, Monster was also skilled at restocking shelves.

But even better than the bookshop with its cupcakes and overflowing bookshelves was the basement. Hidden from ordinary customers was her parents' secret shop, the Dream Shop.

This was where her parents bought and sold dreams.

Sophie loved the Dream Shop more than any place in the world. Dozens of shelves lined the walls, each filled with bottles, sorted by the type of dream they held. There were beach dreams and outer-space dreams and falling-through-empty-air dreams, lost-loved-ones dreams and first-love dreams, ordinary-life dreams and late-for-the-bus dreams, and of course, monster dreams. Each dream was stored in a bottle and labeled with a number and date, and every dream was tracked in a massive leather-bound ledger where her parents recorded notes on the dream's contents, as well as details of every transaction with every supplier and buyer.

Her parents bought the dreams in their raw form, caught in a web of threads called a dream-catcher. Sophie's whole family (minus Monster) made dreamcatchers. Dad would purchase bendable wood to make the circle frame. Mom would weave spider-web-like patterns inside. Sophie would decorate them with crystals and beads and feathers. They then hung them in the windows of the bookstore, filling the entire bay window with sparkles. They'd become the book-store's gimmick. Buy a book, get a dreamcatcher. Buy a cupcake, get a dreamcatcher. Want an extra? Fine, it's yours. But if it becomes worn, if the strings fray or sag, return it and take a new one. Often enough, these same dreamcatchers came back, either brought in by the customer or "found" by a supplier.

Her parents then took the raw dreams and put them into the distiller, a complex contraption of intertwining glass tubes, valves, and levers that sat on a table at one end of the workroom. The distiller extracted dreams from dreamcatchers, transform-ing them into liquid, which would drip into bottles. Sophie had never used the distiller on her own, but she had watched her parents countless times and prac-ticed (without an actual dream) when they weren't looking. She hoped that someday her parents would let her use it for real. She'd tried pleading, crying, beg-ging, demanding, and simply asking, but they always said, "When you're older." They had been saying that for pretty much all of the nearly twelve years of Sophie's life. For now, her daily chore was to dust the distiller. It was boring, but even without ever having worked the distiller herself, she knew it was important to avoid specks of dust in the dreams. Producing a clear dream was a tricky process.

On the opposite side of the room, beneath the stairs, was the somnium. Also made of glass tubes, the somnium was a dream viewer. If you poured a liquid dream into the funnel at the top, the dream would appear in the bulge of glass in the center. It then could be collected again into a bottle for reuse. The somnium was an essential tool for sorting the dreams. They wouldn't know what kind of dream they had until they'd poured it into the somnium.

Sophie liked to wake early and spend an hour or even two before school at the somnium, watching other people's dreams. She never tired of it. She'd tuck herself under the stairs, out of sight, and she'd watch dream after dream. Often Monster watched with her. Sometimes he read books instead.

She loved all sorts of dreams: scary dreams, funny dreams, bizarre dreams. She especially loved the ones that featured improbable creatures like her monster or talking clocks or rabbits in waistcoats.

Watching them almost made up for never having any dreams of her own.

★★★

Except for the dream she stole, Sophie had never had a dream. She'd tried everything: warm milk and cookies before bed, no food or drink before bed, a scary movie in the dark late at night, a book under the covers with a flashlight, inventing elaborate stories before she fell asleep, picturing the best images from other people's dreams. But every night, she laid her head down on her favorite pillow, curled up under the quilt, and closed her eyes. And boom, it would be morning again.

After twelve years of no dreams (except the stolen one), she had given up trying. Almost.

"Good night, Monster," she said on the night before her twelfth birthday.

"*Boa noite,* Sophie," Monster said from the floor beside her bed. He slept in a dog bed fluffed with extra pillows.

She leaned over the bed to look at him. "What?"

"It is Portuguese for 'good night,'" Monster said. "I am learning Portuguese."

"Oh." She lay back down and pulled her blankets

up to her chin. The window next to her had a draft, or more accurately, a gap around the frame. A few fallen leaves had drifted inside and littered the floor. "Um, Monster, why are you learning Portuguese? We don't know anyone who speaks Portuguese."

"In case I ever encounter a Portuguese man-of-war," he said. "I would like to dissuade him from stinging me. They leave welts so painful that they last for two or three days."

"I don't think jellyfish speak Portuguese," Sophie said. "Or any language."

"Men-of-war are colonies of multiple organisms," Monster said. "They have to communicate with each other."

"You need to stay out of the biology shelves." Sophie curled up on her side. Through the window, the street lamp lit the bare branches of a tree. A few golden leaves swayed in the wind. She listened to the wind whistle down the chimney. "It's my birthday tomorrow."

"You may have the extra cupcakes," Monster said graciously.

"That means it's a special night," Sophie said. "A change night. I wake up someone different, a twelve-year-old."

She heard the rustle of blankets. Reaching up, Monster patted her cheek with a tentacle. Monster's fur was softer than any teddy bear. "You are always special, Sophie. You do not need nighttime wonders to make you so."

Sophie sighed. "I know."

"Fill your days with wonder instead."

"You sound like a fortune cookie."

He withdrew. She heard him circle like a cat to find a comfortable position. He settled down and kneaded the pillows with his claws. "I value what you are, not what you are not."

"One dream," Sophie said. "I don't think that's a lot to ask for a birthday present."

"You had your one dream," Monster said. "You birthed me."

"Ew, you make it sound like you're my baby."

In a falsetto voice, Monster chirped, "Mama! Mama!"

Sophie laughed.

From the other room, Sophie's father called, "Go to sleep, Sophie. If you aren't asleep, the birthday fairy won't come and leave you presents!"

"I don't believe in the birthday fairy," Sophie called back.

"Oh no, you've hurt her feelings!" Dad said. "She's crying. Sobbing! I hate dealing with morose fairies. You apologize right now, young lady."

"Sorry, Birthday Fairy," Sophie called.

"I forgive you," Mom said in a pseudo-quivery voice. "But my magic has been so diminished by your lack of belief that I don't know if I can fly anymore."

Monster looked quizzically at the door between bedrooms. "Your mother can fly? I have never seen her do so."

"I'm not her mother," Mom said in the same fake voice. "I'm the birthday fairy. My blood is streamers, my heart is a balloon, my flesh is made of cake . . ."

"Yum, yum, yum," Dad said.

Sophie heard her mother laugh and then a muffled squeak.

"You know, your parents are very strange," Monster observed.

"So says the six-tentacled monster," Sophie said.

"Good night, Sophie," Mom called in her own voice. "Happy almost-birthday!"

Dad echoed her. "Happy almost-birthday, sweetheart!"

With a smile on her face, Sophie closed her eyes.

She listened to her parents' voices, too soft for her to hear words, continue in the other bedroom. Outside, the wind tapped on the window, and Sophie fell asleep.

She woke dreamless, twelve years old.

3

THE SUN WASN'T AWAKE YET, THOUGH SOPHIE WAS.
Sitting up, she poked Monster with her foot. Per
usual, he'd crawled up onto her bed during the night.
He claimed he did it in his sleep. He was now a warm
weight at the foot of the bed. "Hey! Wake up!"

Groaning, Monster flopped his tentacles over his
head.

"It's morning!"

"Not morning."

"Almost morning, sort of." Lifting the shade a
few inches, Sophie peeked outside. The streetlights
were still on, but the sky had that expectant, about-
to-brighten look. The stars were pale, and the moon
was fading. She let the shade flop down again so no
one could see inside, and she flipped on the light.

"Gah!" Monster cried. "I'm blinded!" He waved all his tentacles in the air.

She threw a pillow at him. "Stop it. Mom and Dad said we could sort the new dreams before school if we woke extra early, remember? Special birthday treat." Having a dream shop meant keeping odd hours. You couldn't risk ordinary book customers finding out about it, so most of the work had to happen before dawn or late at night. Sophie was used to waking up hours before the bus came. Monster always whined, though.

He opened one eye. "Do you think there will be more wolf dreams? I like those."

Wolf dreams usually featured exciting chase scenes through dark woods. Sophie liked them too, except when they ended with munching on a rabbit. She'd always had a soft spot for rabbits. "Maybe there will be mermaid dreams."

Sitting up, Monster licked his fur clean like a cat. He had a golden tongue. "I do not understand why anyone would want to be half fish. Eat fish, yes. Be a fish . . . no."

"You could swim with dolphins."

"If you want to swim with dolphins, then be a

dolphin. At least then you'll still be a mammal instead of half mammal and half mackerel."

"But mermaids sing catchy songs about seaweed."

"Technically, the crab sings; the mermaid is an unwilling audience." Snagging Sophie's hairbrush with a tentacle, Monster pretended it was a microphone and whisper-sang "Under the Sea." Sophie drummed in the air, silently so her parents wouldn't hear. In the middle of a lyric about a fish on a plate, Monster's stomach growled, and he broke off singing. "Speaking of special birthday treats . . . cupcakes for breakfast?" Monster widened his eyes hopefully.

Ms. Lee had baked a fresh batch in honor of Sophie's birthday. Imagining them, Sophie could practically taste the frosting. They never got to eat them fresh, but today *was* a special day, and they were baked in her honor . . . "Mom and Dad won't like it . . ."

Monster inched toward the bedroom door. "There might be some with pink frosting. And sprinkles. Special birthday sprinkles. Mmm."

Lunging forward, she caught him around the waist. "I'll get them."

He wiggled free. "I will be sneaky. I am the sneakiest monster. I did your homework for you last night, and you didn't even notice. Special birthday surprise!"

"Uh-oh." Releasing him, Sophie crossed to her backpack. She'd intended to do it on the bus. It kept the other kids from talking to her.

"Why 'uh-oh'?" He bounded after her.

"Last time you wrote every letter upside down. I had to claim it was an artistic experiment." She pulled out her homework. He hadn't touched history, but her science worksheet was complete. She scanned it. Instead of drawing a plant cell, Monster had drawn in minute detail the circulatory system of a rodent. He'd also answered every multiple choice question with C. "Oh, Monster."

"Cupcake?" He wagged his tentacles like a dog with six tails.

She gave up. "Stay," she ordered.

Unlocking her bedroom door, she sneaked past her parents' room and down the stairs. She knew exactly which boards squeaked, and she eased over them, gingerly placing toe first and then heel as she crept down two flights to the bookshop.

There, on the counter, under a glass dome lid, was the tray of cupcakes. It was near the window, and light from the street lamp shone in, illuminating the tray as if it were in a spotlight. She crossed to it and lifted the lid.

Behind her, the bell over the door rang.

She froze.

"Good morning." A voice drifted over the book-shelves. It was male, smooth, and deep. She thought she heard a hint of an accent, maybe British. She liked accents. When people with accents came into the shop, she often hid between the bookshelves and eavesdropped. People with accents tended to know different stories and have different dreams. But nice voice or not, it was too early for customers. The door should have been locked.

She thought about pretending she wasn't here, but she couldn't just leave him wandering freely. She wished her parents were downstairs. "I'm sorry, but we're not open yet." Craning her neck, she tried to see him around the bookshelves without him seeing her. The door had already swung shut, and he wasn't in view.

"My apologies. I'm early for my appointment. Please convey to the owners of this establishment that I'm here to make a purchase from their *downstairs* collection."

Oh no, Sophie thought. This was a dream buyer. She wasn't supposed to talk to buyers or suppliers. In fact, they weren't even supposed to know she lived here. Her parents had a system to avoid situations like this. Every morning as she packed her lunch, Sophie was supposed to check the calendar on the refrigerator. Days she had to hide herself and Monster were marked in black, and days she had to take the recycling out to the curb were marked in green. Today, she hadn't gone to the kitchen to check the calendar. "I'm Betty from next door. But I'm sure I can find them for you."

"Very well, Betty from Next Door."

She bolted toward the stairs. As she did, she saw the buyer sit in one of the red velvet chairs by the bay window. He wore a hat that shaded his eyes so that they looked like black smudges. His chin had a tiny beard, the kind that is as meticulously trimmed as if it were a topiary. He wore a trench coat and carried a briefcase. Except for the fact that she couldn't really see his eyes, he didn't look so scary. He looked like countless others who came into the shop looking for books.

She met her mother halfway across the shop. Mom frowned at her. "Sophie, you should be upstairs. We're expecting a buyer in about fifteen minutes. I've already unlocked the door for him. Didn't you check the calendar?"

Sophie wished Mom had spoken softer. She was certain that the man had heard her name wasn't Betty. Also, he could now guess that she belonged here. "He's here."

Mom's face whitened. Her lips pursed tight. "Go."

Sophie fled toward the stairs as she heard Monster cry, "Sophie, come back! The calendar's marked black. It's not safe!" A streak of fur sailed over the books. He collided with her stomach, and she was propelled backward. They smacked into a bookshelf. Books flew off the shelf and crashed down on either side of them. Monster shielded her from them, and several smacked into his back.

"Sophie! Are you okay?" Mom rushed toward her.

The man in the trench coat approached as well.

"He's the buyer," Sophie whispered to Monster. He twisted his neck to look at Sophie's mother and the man. His lemur eyes opened impossibly wide, and then he bounded toward the stairs. His tentacles pawed the floor, propelling him faster. In seconds, he was out of sight.

The man in the trench coat watched it all.

"I'm fine," Sophie said. "Just . . . my cat. He loves to cuddle."

Kneeling, the man picked up several books. He handed the stack to Sophie. "Unusual cat, Betty."

Sophie forced a laugh. "He's . . ."

"Mutation," Mom interrupted. "Owners were going to have him put down. But other than the extra appendages, he was perfectly healthy. If you'll follow me downstairs, please . . . ?"

"Of course." The man didn't take his eyes off Sophie as he passed her. She froze and wished she could melt into the bookshelf. Her rib cage felt tight, as if it were squeezing her lungs. Closer, she could now see the man's eyes, and she preferred when they were shadowed. The whites were streaked with red as if he hadn't slept in days, and the skin underneath them sagged into wrinkled pouches. He tipped his hat toward her, and then he followed her mother downstairs.

Monster poked his head around the corner of the stairs. "Sophie?"

"It's safe now," Sophie said. "I think."

"I failed you," Monster said.

"It was an accident."

All six tentacles drooped. He slunk down the stairs to curl around her ankles. "I'm supposed to protect you."

She scooped him into her arms, staggering back from the weight. "Don't blame yourself. I'm the one who forgot to check. It's my fault. I'll tell them they shouldn't yell at you."

"I don't care if they yell or yodel; I just want you safe."

But her parents didn't yell at either of them. In fact, they didn't speak to them at all. After the buyer left, they retreated back down to the basement, shutting the door behind them. Monster pressed his ear to the door. Sophie tried to hear through the crack beneath it.

". . . like Abril's farm." Mom's voice drifted up the stairs and through the door. "It's a good place for a girl to grow up. Chickens and so forth. Streams to jump in. Fresh air. Lousy school district, but Sophie is smart enough on her own."

"It may not be a problem," Dad said soothingly.

"He saw Monster! There was no disguising him. Or Monster's connection to Sophie. It was clear he belongs to her."

"But it is unlikely he'll guess Monster's origin," Dad said. "More likely, he'll think we found Monster. Or bought him. There's no reason for him to assume—"

"And what if he does? Are you willing to take that risk? With Sophie? If he tells the Night Watchmen . . . I don't know what they'll do if they find out about her, and I don't want to ever find out."

"Why would he? He'd have to admit he was here and why."

"But what if the Watchmen—" Mom cut herself off, then said loudly and clearly, "Sophie and Monster, if you are up there listening by the door, I will revoke all book privileges so fast, you will have whiplash."

Sophie and Monster scrambled away from the door.

"Get ready for school. Upstairs, both of you. *Now.*"

Sophie and Monster ran upstairs.

Monster took the steps three at a time, reaching with his tentacles, and Sophie bounded behind him, up to the living room and all the way up to the bedrooms. She slammed her bedroom door shut. She then dived onto her bed and wrapped her blankets around her. Monster curled against her back.

"Do you think he'll tell the Night Watchmen about me?" Sophie asked.

"He'd have to admit he was buying dreams," Monster pointed out. "The Watchmen won't like that.

Plus if he tells, the Watchmen will come and destroy the shop, and he'll lose his source of dreams."

"Not helpful, Monster." Her eyes felt hot. She was going to cry. She hated crying. It made her insides feel squishy, like she'd swallowed a jellyfish and it had lodged itself in her throat. All her life she'd heard about the Night Watchmen— "vigilantes," Dad called them. Really dangerous, really organized, really determined fanatics who wanted to stamp out the dream trade and anything to do with bottled dreams. If she could have nightmares, they'd be star players. "Do you think Mom and Dad will really send me away?"

"They're scared for you, as am I," Monster said.

"I don't want to live on a farm," Sophie said. "I want to stay here!"

"Me too." His voice was tiny, as if he'd shrunk.

She twisted to look at him. She realized she hadn't heard them say "Sophie and Monster." They might not intend to send Monster with her. They could decide it's too risky. He'd hidden every time Aunt Abril had come to visit, and he'd stayed home the one time they'd visited her. By the time they got back, he'd eaten all the food in the refrigerator, plus a few forks and plates. "You'll come with me if I go, won't you?"

"I go wherever you go—to the ends of the earth, even if that phrase doesn't make any sense because the earth is round," he said. "You're my friend."

"You're my best friend," Sophie said.

"My best friend," Monster repeated. He laid his snout on her shoulder and purred.

Throwing her arms around him, she said into his fur, "And this is officially the worst birthday ever."

"I didn't even eat any cupcakes," he said mournfully.

She laughed—a tiny, barely there laugh, but it still counted.

Outside, the sun began to rise. Yellow light seeped in around the shades and streamed through the skylights. Sophie dressed slowly, brushed her teeth, and tied her hair back into a ponytail. As she was finishing, her dad called up the stairs, "Sophie? Monster? You can come downstairs now."

She and Monster looked at each other. He kneaded the carpet with his claws, nervous. Neither of them said anything as they headed down to the Dream Shop.

She found her parents by the somnium. Quietly, she tucked herself under the stairs beside them. Dad poured a bottle of shimmering yellow into the silver funnel at the top. The liquid dream dribbled down the tube, lighting up the glass with a soft glow. It twisted and stretched as the tubes narrowed and turned, forcing the dream to lengthen and separate. At last, the dream slid into the glass chamber at the heart of the somnium, where it dispersed in the steamlike solution. All four of them pressed their faces closer to the glass.

"Get the bingo cards, Sophie," Dad said without looking at her.

Sophie raced to a drawer and pulled out the cards. They'd invented their own bingo game a few years ago. Each square showed a different theme or event or object commonly seen in dreams. Get five in a row and you won. She handed her parents their cards, and one to Monster. Several squares were already marked off from last time.

Maybe they aren't going to send me away, she thought. *Maybe they changed their minds.* She waited for them to say anything, but they merely watched the somnium. Slowly, an image materialized.

It was a girl. Sophie squinted at her. She thought she maybe recognized her, perhaps from school? She wasn't sure. It was difficult to see the girl's face as she swooped between the mists of the somnium as if they were puffs of clouds.

"A flying dream," Dad said. He checked his card. "Nope."

"Got it," Mom said. She marked a square on her card.

From the bottom of the somnium, waves of blue lapped at the glass. Sophie pointed at a loglike shape that surfaced. It was covered in bumps. It opened its jaws. "Crocodile," she said. She checked her card for wild animals. She had a square for pets but none for predators.

The girl screamed, her mouth wide but the scream silent in the glass tubes. There was never any sound in the somnium. She plummeted through the darkening clouds toward the crocodile-infested water.

"I have *falling*!" Sophie said. "Oh, wait, got that already."

Before the girl could smash into the water, she landed in a pile of leaves. A circle of kids stood around her, laughing and pointing. The girl curled into a ball.

"Highly generic dream," Mom observed.

"I have *humiliation*." Dad peeked at their cards. "Better watch out. I might win this round." He sounded like himself. Was neither of them going to mention the buyer? She wasn't sure she dared ask, but she couldn't stand not knowing. Not knowing felt like being pricked with a dozen needles.

"I already have three in a row." Sophie held up her card for them to see.

Dad held up his. "Three on a diagonal, plus the free space in the center. I only need"—he checked the square—"a historical anachronism."

Sophie wrinkled her nose. "What's that?"

"It is a contradiction in times," Monster said. He had chewed his own card to shreds. "For example, a phone rings in medieval England. Or a knight jousts in Times Square. Something that doesn't belong."

Taking a deep breath, Sophie said, "I don't belong on a farm."

Mom and Dad exchanged glances.

"We know," Dad said quietly. "You belong with us."

Sophie hugged her parents, and Monster wrapped his tentacles around them all.

4

In a cheerful voice, Mom announced it was time to face the day. Dad put away the bottled dreams, Sophie returned the bingo cards to their drawer, and they all trooped up two flights to the kitchen to prepare for school and work as if nothing out of the ordinary had happened.

Sophie checked the clock. She wasn't late yet. No damage done. She hoped. Getting supplies from the cabinets, she smeared peanut butter onto a slice of bread and then cut the crusts off the sandwich. Raiding the fridge, she added an apple and a cold tamale to her lunch bag.

Side by side, her parents eyed the kitchen sink. It was stacked with plates from last night's dinner — Dad had cooked. Strands of spaghetti were stuck to the plates, and the sauce had congealed in clumps.

"I'll open the store today if you wash the dishes," Mom said to Dad.

"Deal." Dad spat on his hand and held it out. Mom spat on her hand and shook his.

"You know that is both disgusting and unsanitary," Monster said from atop the refrigerator. He had wedged himself in between two soda bottles and a loaf of bread.

"Street kids in medieval London did it all the time," Dad said.

"Sure," Monster said, "before they all died of plague."

"Spitting three times to ward off the Evil Eye is traditional in many cultures." Mom grinned and leaned toward Sophie, ready to spit. "In honor of your birthday . . ."

Sophie scooted out of range.

Her parents both laughed and then set about their various tasks. Sophie stowed her lunch in her backpack and checked to be sure she had her homework (though she wasn't sure she dared turn it in) and a bunch of new dreamcatchers.

"Anything special planned at school today?" Mom asked.

Sophie heard the hope in her voice. Mom was

always hoping Sophie would make friends. "I'm giving Madison and Lucy fresh dreamcatchers," Sophie said.

"Oh. You should tell them it's your birthday."

"Yeah, maybe I will." She knew she wouldn't, but her saying it made Mom smile. This school year, Sophie had met two girls who had horrific, wake-up-screaming nightmares. Every week or so, she delivered fresh dreamcatchers to them and collected their used ones. She'd then give the used dreamcatchers to her parents so they could harvest the nightmares and sell them in their secret shop. It was a win-win for everybody: the girls were nightmare-free and her parents had more fresh dreams to sell to people who desperately needed a little escape from their lives. But Sophie didn't exactly have the kind of relationship with Madison or Lucy that included telling them her birthday, or anything else about her for that matter. She tried changing the subject. "I think I may have found someone else who needs dreamcatchers."

Mom smiled wider. "That's wonderful, darling! What's her name?"

"His name is Ethan." He was the new boy in her history class. She'd been watching him for a while, and she was (reasonably) sure he suffered from serious nightmares. She was planning to talk to him today, if she could catch him alone. She'd made an extra dreamcatcher, a nice one with black beads and dark blue feathers.

"Ooh, a boyfriend?" Mom teased.

"Let me know when I should build the Rapunzel tower," Dad said.

Sophie felt her face blush bright red. "Are you two taking lessons on how to be embarrassing? I'm leaving now."

"Aw, Sophie . . ." Dad began.

Sophie pointed at the clock. "Time for the bus." Swinging her backpack over her shoulder, she waved goodbye to Monster and her parents.

"Love you, Pumpkin!" Dad called after her.

"Love you, Melon!" Sophie called back.

As she hurried downstairs, she heard Monster add, "Love you, Brussels Sprouts!" Smiling, she headed out the door and raced to the bus stop.

As always, she sat alone on the bus. She ignored the chatter around her and instead stared out the window. The town flashed by like moments in the somnium—a man getting into a car, a toddler being carted down the street, a neon *Open* sign switching on in a store window. Eventually, the ride ended, and the world assumed normal speed. She climbed out of the bus and was swept into the school with the chattering swarm.

She stowed her coat and backpack in her locker, and she slid a dreamcatcher into one of her folders. It bulged a little, but if she held her books against her, she didn't think anyone would notice. No one ever noticed her anyway. Certainly no one knew it was her birthday. She told herself that she didn't mind. Really, she didn't. She had plenty of other things to do today: dreamcatchers to deliver, a boy to talk to, and a history test to pass—which, considering that she hadn't studied, was as close as she could get to having her own nightmare.

★★★

Delivering a dreamcatcher to Madison Moore was never easy, even though they had first period together and second period free. Madison didn't want anyone to find out about her nightmares, which meant no one could ever see her taking a dreamcatcher from Sophie . . . which meant Sophie couldn't simply hand it to her in class or in the hall. It was, Sophie thought, kind of silly. But Madison didn't want anyone to know she had dreams choked with fire and filled with floods. Also, sometimes giant bugs. Or giant bugs that breathed fire.

Sophie had met Madison in the janitor's closet back in September. She'd ducked inside to avoid being caught by Principal Harris for skipping class (she was supposed to give an oral presentation that day and couldn't face being stared at by that many kids) and found Madison behind a trash can full of mops. She'd been crying so hard that she'd stuffed her fist into her mouth to keep from being heard. Her fist was red and soft, as if she'd had it in her mouth for a long time.

Sophie recognized her immediately, though they'd never spoken before. Madison was the sort of person you noticed. She had hair as straight as straw, cut on a sharp diagonal, and a chin and nose that came to points. Her voice was piercingly loud, and she never walked when she could parade.

Madison had sworn her to secrecy, promising that she'd make Sophie's life a living nightmare if Sophie breathed a word to anyone about how Madison had been crying in the janitor's closet. It wasn't hard to agree. After all, what was one more secret to carry? Besides, Madison had said the word *nightmare*, and Sophie couldn't help but ask, "Do you have nightmares?" Madison hadn't answered, but Sophie had offered her a dreamcatcher anyway. "It eases nightmares," she told her, exactly as her parents told customers in the bookstore. "Just bring it back next week, and I'll give you a fresh one." Sophie could tell that Madison thought it was nonsense. But she'd brought the dreamcatcher back the next week and asked for another . . . and Sophie tried not to be bothered by the fact that a person with serious personality flaws got to have such magnificently vivid dreams.

Sophie knew better than to smile at Madison as she slid into the seat behind the scowling girl. Madison always scowled. It was her at-rest expression. Anyone who came into her line of sight was subjected to it. Safest to avoid eye contact altogether.

She spent the class wondering where Madison was going to want to meet for the exchange. Under the bleachers? Usually that was packed with kids who liked to pretend they were tough, but Madison always cleared it out before Sophie arrived. Sophie had once asked how she did it, and she'd shrugged and said, "Sprayed the place with Wannabe-Be-Gone."

Another time, they'd met behind the dumpsters. Madison had sworn never to do that again, and Sophie had agreed. Leftover milk containers stank worse than

Aunt Abril's perfume—and Monster claimed her perfume was bad enough to disgust a dolphin. Dolphins, he said, had no sense of smell. That was the joke.

At the end of class, Madison stood abruptly, knocking her textbook onto the floor. She shot Sophie either a glare or a significant look. With Madison, the two were the same. Sighing, Sophie slid out of her seat to pick up the textbook as Madison bent to retrieve it.

"That's mine, Freak Girl," Madison snarled, loud enough for others to hear. Under her breath she said, "Library, four minutes." She strutted out of the classroom without a backward glance. Three of her friends with matching ponytails closed ranks around her. Their hair bounced as they walked.

Sophie trailed behind them out the door. She then wove through the crowded hallway, bypassing Madison and her flock of friends and ducking into a side hall—a shortcut to the library. This hall was mostly empty, and she breathed deeper, as if there was more air here.

She didn't know how a place could be so crowded and lonely at the same time.

She made it to the library with two and a half minutes to spare. A few students were bent over books at a table by the window. One looked up as she came in, checked out Sophie's outfit, then returned to her book without meeting her eyes. The others didn't even bother looking up, as if Sophie were invisible.

At the circulation desk, the librarian beamed at Sophie, and Sophie wished she actually were invisible. The librarian always made a fuss when she saw her, as if she was on a personal crusade to crack Sophie out of her shell. Sophie wasn't interested in being cracked.

"Sophie! Can I help you find anything?" The librarian was as loud and bouncy as a cheerleader at a championship game.

"I'm fine, thanks." Sophie scooted closer to the door and watched for Madison. She'd probably want to meet in the stacks, where the other students couldn't see them, but she hadn't specified which stacks.

"I've been meaning to come by the bookstore all week," the librarian said. "Your parents always have new old favorites. You know, those books that you read over and over because they make you feel like you've been hugged?" For extra emphasis, she hugged her own arms.

"Uh-huh."

"How is everything at the store? Lots of business?

Ooh, any new kinds of cupcakes?" She rubbed her stomach, and Sophie wondered if she planned to pantomime every sentence.

"Um, not that I know of." She wished the librarian would stop talking to her. She could feel herself starting to blush beet-red.

Two minutes late, Madison sailed into the library, past Sophie. Pausing at the circulation desk, she asked, "Which section has books on how to save the fashion-inept?"

"Hi, Madison! I haven't seen you in a week, and I know you've had free periods. You know, if you socialize too much instead of visiting the library, the books get lonely."

Madison blinked once, slowly. "Fashion?"

The librarian checked her computer. "Seven forty-six is fashion design." She pointed, but Madison didn't wait. She nodded at the students at the table like a queen recognizing her subjects, and then glided between the shelves.

Backing away from the librarian, Sophie said, "I just have to . . . find a book." She fled toward the stacks, picked a different aisle from Madison, and then circled around to meet her by the fashion design books.

"You're pathetic," Madison informed her in a low voice. "You just have to 'find a book'? Really? You couldn't think of a single specific topic out of the entire library?" Before Sophie could respond, Madison shushed her with a hand wave. "Whatever. Do you have it?"

Sophie held out the folder with the fresh dreamcatcher. "Less sparkles this time, like you asked." She'd used an unadorned willow for the ring, steered clear of any beads, and chosen only one black feather.

Madison didn't touch it. "My mom nearly pitched the last one. Said it looked like it was made by a germy kindergartner."

"This one's better," Sophie promised.

"It better be." Madison snatched the folder and shoved a paper bag at her.

Sophie peeked in and saw the used dreamcatcher. It looked intact. So long as the threads weren't snapped, the dream would be fine. It could handle a little jostling. Dreams were sturdier than they seemed. "Does she know about your nightmares? If you told her—" She cut herself off. It was safer if the truth about dreamcatchers stayed a secret. If word got out . . . Just thinking about the Night Watchmen finding out about Sophie and her family made her want

49

to curl into a ball between the library shelves. And if they ever found out about what happened when she drank a dream . . . An image flashed through her mind: shadowy Watchmen bursting into the shop and dragging her away. Definitely better to keep everything a secret.

Madison snorted. "We don't have nightmares in my house. Night is for sleeping. Do you cry to your mommy every time you have a little nightmare? I know you do. She probably sings you a lullaby, tucks you in with your blankie, and gives your teddy bear a kiss. You're such a baby." She peeked into the folder, looking at the dreamcatcher as if she wanted to complain about it but couldn't think of anything wrong with it. "See you next week. Don't talk to me before then. And . . . thanks." The last word was said as if it hurt her.

"You're welcome," Sophie said.

"You better not have made me late." Madison stalked out of the shelves, snagging a random book on her way. Catching a glimpse, Sophie saw it was on guinea pigs. She opened her mouth to tell Madison that it wasn't a fashion book, but Madison strode out of the aisle before Sophie could even form the words.

Sophie waited a few minutes and then emerged

from a different set of shelves. She hurried out of the library before the librarian could try to talk to her again. Returning to the main hallway, she deposited Madison's used dreamcatcher in her backpack and stuffed it in her locker.

★★★

Delivering a dreamcatcher to Lucy Snyder was also difficult, but for different reasons. Lucy was still in elementary school, and Sophie could only exchange dreamcatchers with her on days when Sophie's free period intersected with Lucy's recess.

Sophie checked the clock above the lockers. She had exactly fifteen minutes to cross the street to the elementary school, locate Lucy on the playground, and scoot back before her free period ended. It was doable.

She'd met Lucy two months ago. Her mother had dragged her into the shop and asked for books without any villains in them, because her daughter had night-mares. Sophie's parents had sold the woman a few of their happiest little-kids' books—the kind with pink winged ponies and cheerful mice—and given her a dreamcatcher. The woman had rolled her eyes at the dreamcatcher and muttered about "New Age hippie nonsense," but the little girl wanted it. The next day, Sophie spotted Lucy across the street at recess. When the teachers weren't looking, Sophie crossed the street to the school playground and asked how the dreamcatcher had worked. Lucy burst into tears of relief and said, between sobs, that she hadn't woken up "too scared to pee" for the first time in forever and ever. So Sophie had the idea to set up a secret weekly exchange.

It was tricky at first, since middle-schoolers weren't supposed to just waltz over to the elementary school, but now Sophie had an official pink note with a faded, unreadable date that said she had to deliver a message to the elementary school nurse. She'd obtained the note legitimately a few weeks ago and had been using it ever since.

Taking the note and a fresh dreamcatcher, she strolled out of the school and across the parking lot. It was always important to look purposeful and not sneaky when one was trying to be sneaky. (That was Monster's advice, though he always said it didn't help if you had six tentacles.) The little kids were already on the playground for recess, swarming over the equipment like monkeys.

Lucy, of course, was the one standing next to the

swing set screaming her head off. She would have been noticeable anyway with her strawberry blond hair that liked to point in all directions at once. But the screaming made her unmissable. Her face had already deepened to a rose-like purply red that spread to the tips of her pronounced ears. Sophie didn't bother wondering what had set her off this time. It could have been anything from a spider to a skinned knee. The other kids gave her a wide berth.

Sophie scanned the playground for adults. Normally, she'd wait until Lucy came over to her, but given how loud Lucy was screaming, it could be a while before she calmed down enough, and Sophie didn't have time to wait. She'd take the direct approach today.

She marched across the playground and halted right in front of Lucy. "If you don't stop crying, I'll pour water on your head. We have less than a minute before one of the teachers comes over and asks what I'm doing talking to you."

Lucy hurled herself at Sophie, wrapped her arms around the bigger girl's waist, and sobbed into her shirt. She rubbed her nose against Sophie's sleeve.

"Please, tell me there were no boogers," Sophie said.

"That man s-s-s-cared me!" Lucy howled.

Sophie didn't see any man. "I'm quite sure he regrets it. You know you howl loud enough to wake the dead."

This was not the right thing to say to a girl who had nightmare issues.

Lucy howled louder.

"Maybe people would be nicer and not scare you if you didn't scream so much." All the kids nearby were staring at them, and Sophie wished she'd stayed back at the middle school. She didn't like this many eyes on her. They'd be talking about her, the girl who was friends with Lucy. It wasn't good for people to be talking about her. Maybe she should have waited. Or skipped today and come back tomorrow instead.

"Not *them*," Lucy said. "The nightmare man!"

"What 'nightmare man'?" Sophie asked. Immediately, she wished she hadn't. She didn't have time for lengthy explanations. One of the teachers was homing in on them. Lucy cried so often that the teachers didn't respond quickly anymore, but the sight of an older kid on the playground was enough to catch their attention. "Never mind. I have your dreamcatcher. Want to trade?"

Sniffling, Lucy nodded. She pulled a ribbon out from under her shirt. She'd strung the dreamcatcher on it like a large necklace. The dreamcatcher was about the size of Sophie's palm, small enough to fit in Sophie's pocket but too big for Lucy's. Quickly, Sophie untied the string, slipped off the old dreamcatcher, and slid on a new one. She shielded Lucy from view so that the other kids wouldn't notice, and then Lucy stuffed it back into her shirt. It bulged a little, but her shirt was baggy enough to hide it.

"Do you have a story to tell the teacher?" Sophie asked. "Or do you want me to improvise?"

Lucy sniffed again. "What's 'improvise'?"

Before Sophie could define the word, the teacher was there. "Excuse me. Is everything okay here? Lucy, who's this?"

Lucy hurled herself at the teacher. "A m-m-mean man was b-b-bothering me! She scared him away! She saved me! I was so s-s-scared!" She howled again.

That, Sophie thought, *was improvising.*

"A man? Where?" With narrowed eyes, the teacher scanned the parking lot.

"Just someone passing by, I'm sure. I didn't get a good look at him," Sophie said. "She seemed upset, so

I came over. I was visiting the school nurse, delivering a message." She waved the pink slip. "Have to get back now."

"Can you describe the man, Lucy?" the teacher asked the little girl. She knelt down to be even with Lucy's eye level. "What did he look like? What did he say?"

Sophie retreated while Lucy talked. She trotted across the playground, pretending she didn't hear the teacher call after her. In minutes, she was safely back in the middle school. She stowed the used dreamcatcher inside her locker with Madison's and went to class.

A close call, but a success. Now, if she could only talk Ethan into taking a dreamcatcher, it would be an excellent birthday. Or at least a very good ordinary day.

5

ETHAN WAS IN HER LAST-PERIOD CLASS. SHE'D BEEN watching him since the start of the year, and he had all the hallmarks of a kid with nightmares—circles under the eyes, unusual quietness in the mornings, discreet checking-out of shadowy corners when he thought no one was watching. She was betting on classic monster dreams, and she couldn't wait to dump them into the somnium.

Ethan was new this year. His family had moved here from Iowa or Idaho or India. He'd found a batch of friends immediately, due to sports, and seemed to be one of those well-adjusted kids who are never called to the counselor's office . . . except he was. Once a week, after last period, he slipped away from his friends and trotted down the hall to the counselor's office. Sophie knew because she'd followed him, as she intended to today.

Waiting until the teacher's back was turned, Sophie twisted in her seat to check the clock. Ms. Sherman hated it when students paid more attention to the clock than to her. Class ended with the bell, and they were to give Ms. Sherman their full attention until then. Otherwise, she threatened to break into song and interpretive dance, and no one wanted to see that . . . at least not after the first week, when at least half the class had tested the threat. Ms. Sherman was tone deaf, and she loved show tunes.

When the bell rang, Sophie left the classroom slowly, lagging behind Ethan. His friends circled around him, but he waved them off. She couldn't hear what he said, but she imagined he was making some excuse, most likely not involving an appointment with the school counselor. One of his friends laughed, and Ethan flashed a brilliant grin.

Sophie knew that kind of grin. It was a midday grin . . . hours from waking from a nightmare and hours from plunging back into one. He definitely had nightmares. Bad ones. He needed a dreamcatcher.

She trailed behind him, bypassing her own locker.

She'd pick up her backpack and the used dreamcatchers later. Keeping her eye on Ethan's blond head, she wove through the crowd in the hallway. The conversations melded into a buzz.

Closer to the offices, the hall emptied out. All the students were back, clustered by the lockers. Ethan paused to drink from a water fountain, and Sophie slowed, pretending to look at the announcements pinned on a bulletin board. She started forward when he finished. Up ahead, he turned a corner into the next hall. She hurried.

Rounding the corner, she skidded to a stop.

He was waiting for her.

"You wouldn't make a very good secret agent," he told her.

She felt her face flush red.

"Unless you have secret spy gadgets in your pocket, as well as grappling hooks that extend from your belt," he said. "*That* would impress me."

"I just . . ."

"You're Sophie, aren't you?" he said. "From the bookstore."

She didn't remember him ever coming into the bookstore. If he had, it would have been a lot easier to talk to him then. Plus he would have had a dream-catcher already, simply from being a customer. "I have something to give you." She pulled out a dreamcatcher with dark blue feathers. She'd planned to lead up to this more, but it threw her that he knew her name. She'd always considered herself somewhat invisible and liked it that way. She wanted this conversation to end as quickly as possible so she could return to her anonymity. "Bring it back next week and I'll give you a new one." She held it out to him.

"Um . . . thanks?" Gingerly, he took it by the string. The dreamcatcher spun. Crystals caught the light. "You know, it's not really my kind of thing."

"It will help with the nightmares."

He froze, and she knew in that instant that she'd guessed right. In a soft voice, he said, "How do you know . . ." He clutched the dreamcatcher to his chest as if it were a secret he wanted to hold tight.

Choosing the easiest explanation, Sophie nodded at the counselor's closed door. "Just a guess. Besides, everyone's supposed to have nightmares in middle school. I'm told it's part of the experience." She turned away. "Hang it by your bed and try not to touch the strings too much." She headed back down the hall.

She heard him follow her. "So you really believe this works?"

"Would it hurt to try?" Sophie countered. She'd heard her parents use that argument in the bookstore. It usually worked.

"Guess not," Ethan said.

She kept walking.

"Hey, why me?"

"Sorry?"

"Lots of people have . . . you know. Sleep problems." He held up the dreamcatcher. It spun and twinkled. "Why give this to me? You don't even know me."

She didn't have an answer for that. Maybe because she was curious what his dreams were like? Maybe because he tried so hard to pretend he had no problems? Or maybe it was because some mornings he looked so haunted that she thought someone had to do something. She went with the last option: "Because you need help. And I can help you."

He shifted from foot to foot. "Look, Sophie . . . you won't, you know . . ."

"Tell anyone?" she finished for him. "I never do."

He nodded once and then trotted toward the

counselor's door. She watched him until he reached it, and then she turned and headed back to her locker. That had been easier than she'd hoped. His nightmares must be really bad. Or else he was just being nice. She wondered what the somnium would show of his dreams.

As she walked through the hall, she felt like smiling. She'd done good here, on her birthday. Ethan would never know, but his nightmare would be sold to someone who needed it. His bad dream could be the perfect distraction for someone who wanted to escape his or her own life for a little while. Or it could give someone a safe way to face their own fears. Or serve as inspiration for an artist. That's what Mom and Dad did in their dream shop: turn something unwanted into something wonderful. It was the best kind of recycling.

She reached her locker. The hall was clear of kids now. Everyone had scrambled for the buses. If she hurried, she could still catch hers. She unlocked her locker and opened it to retrieve the used dream-catchers . . .

Both of them were gone.

She shot looks up and down the hallway.

She emptied out her backpack.

A red envelope fluttered out. It was unlabeled. She opened it and pulled out a card. On the front, a fluffy black cat held a bouquet of balloons. She opened the card. In neat black handwriting were the words:

Happy birthday, Betty.

It was signed, *from Mr. Nightmare.*

HER FIRST THOUGHT WAS, *I'M NOT BETTY.*

Her second thought was, *I am Betty.* Or at least she was to this morning's buyer. He'd said, "Unusual cat, Betty," when he'd seen Monster. And now this card . . .

It had to be a joke. A bad, creepy joke. She felt prickles walk up and down her spine, and her hands, holding the birthday card, began to shake. Somehow, he'd put this card in her locker. He could still be here, watching her read his note, waiting for her to laugh. Or scream.

Sophie scooped everything into her backpack, slammed her locker shut, and ran as fast as she could through the hall, out the front door, and toward the school buses.

She threw herself onto her bus. She was the last

one on. Panting, she plopped into the first open seat, next to a sixth-grader she didn't know. The sixth-grader hugged her backpack and scooted closer to the window, steadfastly looking outside and not at Sophie, but Sophie didn't care. She'd made it to the bus. She was safe.

"Wow, was that the first time you've ever run?" It was Madison. Her voice was so loud that Sophie felt like someone was biting her ear.

Other kids snickered.

Sophie ignored her and them. Madison wouldn't be laughing if she knew the dreamcatcher was gone — not that she knew it really held her dream.

Looking out the window instead of at the other kids, Sophie tried to remember if she'd locked her locker before her last class. She always did. It was habit. But she didn't have a specific memory of clicking shut the lock today. Maybe she'd forgotten, and that was how Mr. Nightmare had stolen the dream-catchers. But why had he taken them? You couldn't reuse a dreamcatcher, not without distilling the dream. Maybe it was a mistake, or a misunderstanding. As soon as she was home, she'd ask her parents — there must be a simple, not-creepy explanation for both the card and the missing dreamcatchers.

When she reached her bus stop, Sophie bolted off, brushing past two other kids, who yelped in protest, and ran the entire way down the sidewalk and into the Dreamcatcher Bookshop. The bell over the door tinkled wildly. "Mom?"

Her mother was at the cash register. She waved when she saw Sophie. Beside her was Ms. Lee, the woman who baked the cupcakes for the bookshop. Sophie had liked Ms. Lee from the moment she'd moved in next door. She had a musical voice, a pretty smile, and soft black hair that she wove into intricate braids. Her yard was full of birdfeeders, and in summer, she had flocks of hummingbirds that flitted around her windows. She was known to buy lemonade from every kid who set up a stand, and she volunteered every Saturday at the library. She was the nicest person that Sophie had ever met, but right now Sophie wished she'd leave.

"Look at this!" Mom waved a cupcake in the air. It had a dollop of creamy white frosting and a garnish that looked like cracked leather. "Savory cupcakes. Bits of bacon and . . . What does this one have?"

"Honey bacon cupcake," Ms. Lee said. "And that one is pesto and pepper jack." She smiled shyly at Sophie. "I'm experimenting. Would you like to try one, Sophie?"

"Uh, thanks, but . . . Mom, can I talk to you for a minute?" Sophie asked.

Mom pulled Sophie's hand toward her and dropped the honey bacon cupcake onto her palm. "You'll love it. Try it." Both Mom and Ms. Lee watched her with identical hopeful expressions on their faces, as if their future happiness depended on Sophie's taste buds.

"But I . . ."

Ms. Lee's face fell. "You hate the idea. Pig on a cupcake. You think it sounds disgusting."

"No, no, I'm sure it's great." To prove it, Sophie took a huge bite. The frosting smeared on her lips. She chewed, crushing the bacon as fast as she could. Around half-chewed cupcake, she said, "Delicious!"

Ms. Lee brightened again. "Do you mean that?"

Catching crumbs in her hand, Sophie nodded. It actually was good.

Beaming, Ms. Lee spun to face Mom. "Gabriela, do you think they'll sell? The best bakeries have dozens of recipes. If I can perfect a few more, we can expand . . . but I'm getting ahead of myself."

Mom clasped her hands. "I think you'll sell

hundreds, Jia. You're a fantastic baker. Look at all you've achieved already! You need to believe in yourself. Believe in your dreams!"

Sophie tried not to react to that phrase, even though she knew Mom meant daydreams, not sleeping dreams. Sophie wondered if Ms. Lee dreamed about cupcakes, or maybe singing cupcakes and dancing measuring spoons. The two women hugged, and Ms. Lee left, nearly skipping out the door. Sophie swallowed the wad of cupcake in her mouth as her mom asked, "How was school today, sweetie? Did you have the history test?"

Sophie wiped the frosting off her mouth with the back of her hand. "Mom, that buyer—"

"Use a napkin. Here, let me." Reaching over the counter, Mom dabbed Sophie's face with a stray napkin.

"Mom!"

"I know I baby you, but you're still my baby-waby." Mom curled her lips into a fishy face and made kissing noises at Sophie. She then turned to the cupcake display to add the new savory cupcakes. Every morning, she or Dad artfully arranged them in a pyramid inside a glass dome. Sophie had helped with pictures of leaves and flowers on the calligraphied sign

(*Gourmet Cupcakes $3.00*). "Ms. Lee wants us to add a few tables and chairs. Serve some iced tea in the summer with the cupcakes . . ."

"Mom, he stole my used dreamcatchers and left a note."

Cupcake in hand, Mom froze. Her eyes widened. The words seemed to hang in the air for a moment, like a cartoon coyote about to fall off a cliff. Sophie exhaled. At last she'd gotten Mom's attention. "Who?" Mom asked, her voice calm. She placed the last cupcake on the pyramid and closed the glass dome.

Sophie dug into her backpack and handed her the note with the black cat and balloons.

Mom read it and frowned. "I don't see—"

"I told the buyer this morning that my name's Betty."

The color drained out of Mom's cheeks. She strode over to the bookshop door, locked the deadbolt, and flipped the sign to *Closed*. "Your father is downstairs. Come, and tell us both everything."

Sophie followed her. "Where's Monster?"

On top of one of the bookshelves, something sneezed. Dust plumed into the air. Looking up, Sophie saw a shadow launch itself off the top shelf and call, "Catch me!"

Tentacles out, Monster sailed through the air and slammed into Sophie's chest. She staggered back as Monster wrapped two tentacles around her neck. "Oof! Hi, Monster."

"You're upset. Who upset you?" Monster demanded. "Tell me, and I'll bite him."

"No biting," Sophie and Mom said at the same time.

"Little nibbles?"

"No," they said.

"Ferocious licks?"

"Ew," Sophie said.

Mom unlocked the basement door with a key they kept hidden in a battered copy of *Moby-Dick*. They kept the basement door locked at all times—no one wanted a bookstore customer wandering into the Dream Shop by accident.

"I know what will cheer you up! Honey bacon cupcakes. I know that would cheer *me* up. Honey cheers everyone up. Except bees. But that's because it takes two million flower visits for a bee to make one pound of honey, and they're tired. It's a scientific fact." Listening to Monster prattle on made Sophie feel safer. She hugged his furry body as she carried him downstairs. He patted her cheek with the soft pad of a tentacle. "You still look worried. Please don't worry. Monster is here."

Downstairs, Dad was at the distiller. His forehead was crinkled as he concentrated on hitting the correct levers. The dream dripped fast from tube to tube, and Dad raced ahead of it, adjusting the valves and choosing levers as it sluiced through the turns and twists. He moved like a bird, his elbows flapping and fingers flying. Each choice he made would shape the depth and duration of the dream. He could even cut or blur details, if he wanted.

As the dream picked up speed, it glowed brighter and began to sparkle with purple flecks. Reaching across Dad, Mom twisted a dial and pressed another lever, sending the liquid shooting to the left. At last, it poured into the final tube. As Dad worked the levers, Mom plucked a bottle off a shelf and held it under the spigot. Drop by drop, the essence of the dream filled the bottle.

Watching her parents distill a dream was one of Sophie's favorite things to do. They were artists. Dreams that they distilled were crisp and bright. They prided themselves on that. People who bought their dreams were purchasing a special experience—a story in a bottle, as her dad liked to say, to enrich their lives from the inside out.

Seeing her parents at work, doing what they loved, calmed her. Her parents would figure out what the card meant. Probably it wasn't a big deal, just a man with a warped sense of humor. Or maybe he was trying to be nice, surprising her with a happy birthday wish when no one else did . . . except that he'd also taken the dreamcatchers. She couldn't forget that.

After the final drop, Mom eased the bottle out and capped it. Dad smiled at her. "Excellent timing, my dear, per usual," he said.

"You should have waited for me." The distiller could be worked solo, but their finest dreams were made when they worked together. "But that's not why I came down. Sophie had a little scare at school. She's okay, though. Safe and sound." Mom was smiling as she said it, but it seemed like a painted-on smile. Dad took the card from her.

"I found it in my locker," Sophie supplied. "The buyer from this morning thinks my name is Betty. It has to be from him."

Dad read the note, and then looked at Mom. He swallowed, hard enough for Sophie to see his Adam's apple bob up and down. "Don't let it worry you, Sophie."

She *wanted* to quit worrying, but . . . "I also had two full dreamcatchers in my backpack, and they were gone. And Lucy said she saw a 'nightmare man.'"

"Did you see him?" Mom asked. "Did he talk to you?"

More softly, Dad asked, "Did he hurt you?"

Mom shot him a look.

"Not that he would," Dad said quickly. "But if he did . . ."

"Tell us everything, sweetie," Mom said.

Monster growled. "If he hurt you, I will do more than bite him." He wrapped his tentacles tighter around Sophie, squeezing her waist. It felt like he was superglued to her.

Sophie shook her head. "Just the card. I didn't see him."

Mom sank into a chair. It wobbled under her. She rubbed her forehead as if her head suddenly hurt. "I shouldn't have unlocked the shop door. But buyers don't like to wait outside; it's too conspicuous. If I'd known Sophie was up . . ."

"Don't blame yourself," Dad said.

"Blame me," Monster said, ducking his head

against Sophie's neck. His voice was muffled as he talked into her shirt. "I failed my responsibility. I am deeply ashamed."

"One accident in six years is not terrible," Dad said. "We all should have been more vigilant. It's as much our fault. We didn't remind Sophie."

And she should have checked the calendar and been more careful in the first place, but that didn't matter now. What mattered now was figuring out what the card meant. Cutting off the conversation, Sophie asked, "Who is he? What does he want?"

"He knows you're our daughter," Mom said. "And he saw Monster. If he put two and two together and reported it to the Night Watchmen . . ."

"But he didn't," Sophie said. "He just left a card."

All of them brightened. Monster lifted his head, and his tentacles loosened. "Sophie's right," he said. "If the Watchmen knew about Sophie, they'd come for her. And they haven't."

The Night Watchmen thought drinking another's dream was immoral instead of amazing. If they had any idea that Sophie could bring dreams to life, they'd take her away—and who knew if she'd ever come back? Sophie's parents had drilled it into her: the

Watchmen were her enemy. The fact that they hadn't come was a very, very good sign.

Dad nodded. "We're jumping to conclusions and imagining the worst-case scenario. He couldn't have realized where Monster came from."

"I did tell him the mutant housecat story." Mom hopped to her feet and began to pace. There wasn't much room for pacing in the shop—she took six steps to the somnium, then had to pivot and walk six steps back to the distiller. Her heels clicked on the wooden floor.

Still holding Sophie with four tentacles, Monster waved two in the air. "I don't like that story. I am not a cat. Or a mutant. Frankly, I'm not sure which is more insulting. Can't we say I'm the result of a science experiment that was supposed to result in superintelligent beings?"

"Hush, or we'll say you're a feral wombat," Mom said. "This is serious."

"But nothing to worry about," Dad said quickly. "As you pointed out, we have no proof that he means any harm, or that he would involve the Night Watchmen."

Stopping, Mom reached over Monster and put her

hands on Sophie's shoulders. "Absolutely. You don't need to worry. We'll take care of it." She was trying to radiate confidence, but Sophie could read the concern in her eyes as easily as she could read the label on Dad's newly bottled dream.

"But why did he do it?" Sophie asked. "Was he trying to scare me?"

"It's probably nothing. Just a man trying to show he's clever." Mom hugged Sophie, squishing Monster between them. Monster squeaked. "Why don't you do your homework while Dad and I talk about how to fix this?"

"I'd rather talk with you."

"I'd rather not be squished," Monster said, wriggling.

Stepping back, Mom released them, and Monster sucked in air melodramatically, expanding his chest as if he were a balloon.

"You can't send me away when you're going to talk about important things that have to do with me," Sophie protested.

"Sure we can," Dad said. "That's what parents do all the time."

Mom patted her shoulder. "We were just more

subtle about it when you were younger. Now we expect you to be mature enough to understand. Your father and I need to talk about you behind your back and then decide what to do."

Glaring at them, Sophie plopped on the floor with so much force that the bottles on the shelves rattled. She wasn't leaving. They'd need to drag her upstairs, which would be uncomfortable for everyone. "You can't send me to Aunt Abril's. You said you wouldn't."

"You did say that," Monster put in.

"We're not sending you away." Dad knelt next to her. "But we don't know how serious this is. He approached *you*. Scared *you*. That's not acceptable. We may be overreacting, but it's only because we love you more than any other being in the universe."

"Maybe it was a friendly note," Sophie said. "Maybe he took the dreamcatchers by accident. He could be trying to be polite."

"You don't accidentally follow a child to school, then break into her locker and steal her things to be polite," Mom said. "No, this was to send a message to us."

"What kind of message?" Sophie asked.

Mom and Dad looked at each other. Neither of

them answered. So Monster did. "That they have a weakness. You. If he threatens you, they'll do drastic things to protect you. Like send you to a farm."

"Why would he want me on a farm? Does he like chickens?" Sophie tried to make it sound like a joke, but her voice was shaking too much.

"Maybe he likes sheep," Monster suggested. "And I'm told that many farms keep llamas, to comfort the sheep if they're lonely. Sheep like flocks. They're herd animals. Like dogs. Except you say 'packs' for dogs, not flocks. And 'gaggle' for geese. Pride of lions. Crash of rhinos."

"'Crash of rhinos'?" Sophie repeated, grateful for a chance to make her voice sound calm again. "You made that up."

"Did not. Look it up. There are many interesting names for groups of animals. A quiver of cobras. A charm of finches. A parliament of owls."

Dad smiled broadly. "Hey, you know, hate to interrupt, but I think I forgot to eat lunch." He put his hands over his stomach, and it growled as if on command as loudly as Monster's snore.

"How can you eat—" Mom began, then suddenly stopped. "You're right!" she said brightly. "We'll eat.

Leftovers. Upstairs, all of you." She shooed Sophie, Monster, and Dad up the stairs to the bookstore and up again to the kitchen.

"What do you call a group of monsters?" Sophie asked Monster as they climbed.

"Awesome," Monster said.

Upstairs on the second floor, Mom raided the refrigerator for leftovers: a hamburger and two chicken enchiladas (Mom's best recipe), a few bagels, and a hunk of cheese for Monster. She tossed the cheese at him, and he caught it in his teeth. Taking it out of his mouth with a tentacle, he nibbled at it. Mom shoved the enchiladas in the microwave and the bagels in the toaster. Sophie set the table at the same time, and Dad fluttered from window to window, looking out and then shutting the shades.

They're trying to distract me, Sophie thought. It was Dad's favorite trick: distract with food. Mom had tried to send her away to do homework, and now it was Dad's turn. She bet they planned to talk after Sophie went to bed. "What did you mean, he was 'sending you a message'? The card was for me. What makes you think it was a message to you? And what kind of message?"

"Who?" Mom asked innocently as she poured apple juice into Sophie's glass.

Sophie rolled her eyes. They were so transparent. Did they honestly think she'd forget what they were talking about? "The buyer. Mr. Nightmare. What do you think he wants?"

Mom sighed heavily. "We don't know. We'll have to find out."

Dad nodded. "Tomorrow, we'll meet with him and ask." He cocked his head at Mom as if that was a question, and she nodded.

The microwave beeped. Mom carried the casserole to the table. Cheese had separated into clumps that clung to the pasta. Certainly not appetizing enough to distract Sophie from the conversation. "What if he's dangerous?" Sophie asked.

"Oh, I doubt that," Mom said breezily. "We met him, and he seemed harmless. In fact, he was very polite, though a bit intense."

"Not someone I'd want to have over for a barbecue," Dad said, "but no alarm bells."

Mom nodded. "He said he considers himself a nightmare aficionado, and he'd heard of our work through a colleague. He complimented us for a while, clearly trying to butter us up, and then bought one of our finest nightmares, one that mixed Greek mythology with a cruise ship disaster. And then he said if he liked it, he'd be in touch."

"He's most likely trying to bargain with us," Dad said while he set the table with forks and knives. "Our prices are higher than most, but that's because our quality is higher."

Mom nodded. "Probably thinks he's being clever. We'll explain that if he ever contacts you again, we won't do business with him anymore." The bagels popped up in the toaster, singed around the edges. "By the time you're home from school, this will all be settled."

"I'm going to school tomorrow?" Sophie thought of the note in her locker. Mr. Nightmare had been in her school. He could be there again.

"It's a Tuesday," Dad said. "You usually go to school on Tuesdays."

"But this is different!"

"And that's why Monster will go with you," Mom said.

Monster hopped onto the table and nodded solemnly. "I will."

Sophie felt her jaw drop open. "Wait, what? You want Monster to come to school with me? Are you serious? You're aware he has fur, three rows of teeth, and six tentacles, right? I can't pass him off as an out-of-state cousin here to visit, and we haven't had show-and-tell since kindergarten."

"Monster will hide himself." Calmly, as if this were an ordinary dinner conversation, Mom served the casserole. She scooped some into a cat dish in front of Monster. He stuck his face in it.

Scooping more, Mom dropped a mound on Sophie's plate. Sophie didn't touch it. She couldn't imagine eating right now. "You know this is *Monster* we're talking about, right? There are hundreds of kids in my school. If anyone sees him . . ."

"They won't," Dad said quietly, firmly. "They've never seen him before."

Sophie gaped at Monster. "Before? What do you mean, 'before'? He's never come to school with me."

Monster dropped his head as if embarrassed. Face near his food dish, his nostrils flared. He began eating.

Sophie poked him. "Monster?"

"We've sent him a few times to check on you," Mom explained. "Once when you had a bad cough.

Another time when you were worried about some kids being mean to you . . ." She trailed off.

"But he never said anything about it." Sophie couldn't imagine there were things Monster didn't tell her. She'd thought they had no secrets. Monster didn't meet her eyes.

"We asked him not to," Dad said.

"How often did he follow me? And why?"

"Sometimes we worry," Dad said. "It's a parent thing."

"Sophie, this is not open for discussion." Mom slammed the casserole down on the table. "You can't be here when we talk to Mr. Nightmare, and we aren't letting you out of our sight without knowing you're watched over by someone we trust."

Lifting his face out of his dish, Monster purred. Bits of hamburger stuck to his fur. "They trust me, despite this morning," he said happily.

"Of course we trust you," Mom said. "You've proven yourself time and again."

Monster mimed wiping an imaginary tear from his cheek. "I have succeeded where all other monsters have failed. I have won myself a true family. I am the happiest monster of all." He flounced dramatically onto the counter.

"Besides, if you fail," Mom continued, as if he hadn't spoken, "you know we'll skin you and use you as a new blanket."

"Ouch," Monster said.

"She's kidding," Sophie said quickly.

Monster looked at Sophie with wide, serious eyes, no trace of melodrama. "No, she isn't. Or if she is, she shouldn't be. I will not fail you, Sophie. I will guard you with every hair of my furry body."

Sophie hugged him. "I know you will. But I can't believe you didn't tell me you'd followed me to school before."

"I'd do anything to keep you safe." He wrapped his tentacles around her, and she couldn't be mad at him. "You're my Sophie."

"Before, he sneaked into the school after you arrived, but I think tomorrow he should go in your backpack," Dad said. "Once you're in school, he'll hide."

"I'm stealthy," Monster promised. "Like an opossum."

She wasn't sure if opossums were all that stealthy. Before she could object again, Dad said, "It's true. You won't even know he's there."

Mom nodded. "Just go about your normal day,

84

and when you come home, we'll have dinner together and laugh about how silly we all were to worry."

Sophie looked from her mother to her father and back again. She saw fear in their eyes—fear they were trying very hard to hide. "I don't have a choice about this?"

"You could go to Aunt Abril's farm," Dad suggested. "Befriend a brood of chickens."

She deflated into her seat. There were a million ways this could go wrong. But she knew when she'd lost. At least since Monster had apparently been at her school before, she could hope it wouldn't be a disaster. "Fine. Monster comes to school."

Reaching up with one tentacle, Monster patted her on her cheek. "Don't worry, Sophie. Everything will be fine. Just please . . . pack extra snacks."

MONSTER DIDN'T FIT IN HER BACKPACK. SQUEEZING his rump into the bottom, he tried to curl all six tentacles around him. Sophie knelt beside him in the middle of the kitchen and shoved in tentacles. Every time she pushed one in, another popped out. "Can you put them under you?"

His fur ruffled as he shifted. He pulled in a tentacle, and another unfurled and flung her juice box against the kitchen wall. The box smacked into a cabinet and burst. "Oops." He popped his head out of the backpack. His wide eyes looked innocent and guilty at the same time.

Sighing, Sophie fetched a wad of paper towels and sopped up the mess. "For the record, I don't care if you've done this a dozen times before; I think it's a terrible idea."

He widened his lemur-like eyes even further. "Don't you trust me?"

"You just annihilated my apple juice."

"It was an accident."

"I don't want any accidents at school." Pausing, she studied him. His eyes seemed extra bright, and his back crinkled as if he were purring. "You're excited about this, aren't you?" she said accusingly.

He smiled, and his many teeth gleamed. "Oh, yes. Fun, fun, fun! Sneaking in on my own is okay, but this time, we're sharing the adventure!"

Sophie got herself a new juice box, and then, surveying all his tentacles, decided she didn't need it today. Or her lunch. Or her library books, music books, or history textbook. After Sophie removed those books, Monster tried again. This time, he fit all but one tentacle. She thought of how, when she was little, she had dressed Monster in doll clothes and tried to convince her parents to let them take him to the playground. "How about we put a dress on you and tell everyone you're a very furry kindergartner and not to make fun of your appearance?" Sophie suggested.

"Not funny."

"It's the perfect plan."

Monster narrowed his eyes to slits and humphed.

Squeezing in, he wiggled more. "Your pencils are jabbing me." Coming out again, he waited while she combed through her backpack and extracted the rest of her textbooks, all but one pencil, and a protractor. She left them on the kitchen table while Monster curled himself fully inside the backpack, along with her homework. She zipped it shut.

He unzipped it.

"Someone will see you." She zipped it shut again.

He unzipped it an inch. "I need a view."

"You don't need a view. It's a school bus. Only thing there is to see is old gum and unidentifiable sticky stuff on the floor." She waved her hands at the floor.

"What's sticky on the floor?" Mom asked as she walked into the kitchen. She halted next to the sink. "Oh, Sophie, is that apple juice on the cabinets?"

"He didn't fit." Sophie pointed at him.

Monster waved a tentacle from the backpack and then pulled it in.

Kneeling, Mom did a more thorough job of mopping up the spilled juice. It had dripped down the face of the cabinets. She tossed the paper towels away and, hands on her hips, examined the books and pencils that Sophie had discarded. She didn't criticize, though. "Did you pack extra snacks?"

Muffled, Monster demanded, "Extra snacks!"

Unzipping the backpack, Mom dropped in a cupcake from the stash of day-olds on top of the refrigerator. It landed directly in Monster's mouth, and he inhaled it. "That was for later," Mom said.

"This *is* later. Breakfast was an hour ago." Crumbs sprayed out of the backpack as he spoke. It looked as if the backpack itself were eating the cupcake. "Mmm, bacon."

"He's getting crumbs in my backpack," Sophie complained.

"He'll keep you safe," Mom said. "He's more responsible than he seems. He truly does have your best interests at heart."

"I know that, but he's still a monster." To Monster, she said, "No offense meant."

"None taken," he said, spitting more crumbs.

Mom zipped the backpack and patted it. "Just let him out in the bathroom when no one's around and try not to think about him during the day."

"Right," Sophie said. "Pass my math test. Ignore the six-tentacled monster. Got it."

Mom kissed her forehead. "Now hurry, or you'll miss your bus."

Scooping up the backpack with Monster in it, Sophie sprinted down the stairs. Dad was at the cash register. She waved to him.

"Love you, Pumpkin!" he called.

"Love you, Zucchini!" she called back.

Coming down the stairs, Mom waved. "Love you, Squash!"

From the backpack, Monster added, "Love you, Tomato! Love you, Carrot!" She thumped the backpack, and he quieted. The bells tinkled as she opened the front door and headed out. Monster bounced on her back. As she reached the end of the walkway, she glanced over her shoulder and saw her parents together, framed by the door of the bookshop. Side by side, arms around each other's waist, they looked like a photograph.

Sophie had the sudden, terrible, and irrational thought that she wasn't going to see them again. She wanted to run back inside and never leave. But the yellow bus was already rounding the corner onto their street, and all the other kids were at the bus stop. She jogged toward the corner of the street.

On the sidewalk, two girls were playing cat's cradle with a loop of string, and three boys were pretending to push one another off the curb. Flailing their arms, they fake-screamed as if they were plummeting from a cliff. One of their overprotective mothers hovered near them. She had a tight grip on the toddler brother of one of the three boys—Sophie had never bothered to figure out which one. The toddler had a stream of snot plastered to his cheek. He wiped it away with his sleeve, leaving a streak of slime, as if a slug had crawled up his arm. Sophie was glad to be the last one to the bus stop.

The mother beamed at Sophie. "Good morning, Sophie! Looks like a great day today!" She always tried to involve Sophie in conversation, as if talking about the weather with a parent would magically ease Sophie into playing with the other kids.

Other kids always seemed to play with one another so easily. See a kid; play. But not Sophie. Walking up to another kid felt like walking up to a stray dog. She worried they'd slobber on her. Or bite her. Or discover her secrets, tell the world, and draw the attention of the Night Watchmen . . .

The toddler clung to his mother's hand. "Mom,

Mom, Mom, *Mom,* can we go to Chuck E. Cheese's? Please, pretty please, with sugar on top! Can we? I promise I'll be good."

The mother sighed. "Remember last time?"

"Yeah, but I was *little* then."

"It was last week."

The bus turned on its blinkers as it stopped. All traffic ground to a halt behind it. The other kids jostled to line up, and the three boys continued to shove one another. One of them pushed extra hard and bumped into Sophie.

From the backpack, Monster yelped.

"Mom, Mom, *Mom,* there's something in her backpack!" the toddler cried.

"Of course there is," the mother said, pulling the toddler back from the curb. "She's going to school."

Hurrying, Sophie piled onto the bus with the others. Heading for the empty middle of the bus, she found a seat to herself and hefted the backpack with Monster onto her lap. She leaned her head against the window and hoped no one sat with her.

Monster poked at her from within the backpack. "I want a view," he whispered through the nylon.

"No," she whispered back.

He was silent for a moment. Then: "I'll eat your homework."

"No."

"Your book report looks tasty. Just needs ketchup."

"No."

"Munch, munch . . ."

Sophie unzipped the backpack one inch so that Monster could press his eyeball against the window. With all the streaks of dirt on the window, she didn't think anyone outside could see the odd eye looking out of her backpack.

"Ah, lovely," Monster said as they passed a post office. It had a flag by the front door and a golden eagle on its peak. "Tell me what that building is."

"We can't have a conversation."

"I'm being quiet."

"Yeah, but I'm sitting alone. This looks weird."

"Then don't talk. I'll do a monologue." He shifted within the backpack. "'But soft, what light through yonder window breaks—'"

"Shh." Sophie zipped the backpack closed.

He poked a tentacle tip through and wiggled the zipper open an inch.

Madison leaned over the seat behind her. "Hey, talking to yourself again?" She was chewing gum, smacking her teeth together. Her nails were painted sparkly pink, and she was wearing a T-shirt with a picture of a pooping unicorn.

"Yes. Just talking to myself." She zipped the backpack shut, and this time Monster didn't try to open it. He lay still inside, as inert as textbooks.

"Okay then," Madison said. "So long as you aren't talking to me."

"You're the one who started this conversation," Sophie said, and then wished she hadn't said anything. She did not want to draw attention to herself by arguing with Madison. She didn't know why Madison didn't just leave her alone. If she wanted to pretend that she and Sophie had no connection, simply ignoring her would work. The bus around them grew quiet.

"I don't talk to crazy people," Madison announced.

"Then you talking to me proves I'm not crazy."

"I'm telling you *not* to talk to me because you *are* crazy."

From the backpack, Monster murmured, "She's not very bright, is she?"

Madison's eyes narrowed. "What was that, Crazy Sophie?"

"What was what?" Sophie tried to mimic Monster's innocent look. "I didn't say anything. Are you hearing voices? Bad sign if you're hearing voices."

Other kids snickered—this time at Madison, not at Sophie. Before Madison could pick a new insult, the bus wheels squealed, and they turned into the school parking lot. Sophie bolted off the bus.

All the kids poured into the school, squeezing together in the doorway and then breaking apart on the other side. Monster chirped as kids pushed and jostled. As soon as she could, Sophie ducked into the girls' bathroom.

In a stall, she unzipped the backpack. Monster flopped his tentacles out and then immediately recoiled. "Ew, bathroom floor."

"We'll meet here after school, okay?"

Monster nodded. Before Sophie could warn him again to be careful, he hooked one tentacle up on top of the stall and used another to pop open one of the ceiling tiles. He climbed into the ceiling and replaced the tile.

"Clever," Sophie said.

"Yes, I am." Monster's voice drifted down. "Have fun at school."

Her backpack much lighter, Sophie left the bathroom. She crashed into three people on her way to her locker because she couldn't stop looking at the ceiling.

★★★

Sophie stared at her locker door and imagined all the things that could be inside: another card with a picture of a cat; an actual cat; a dead cat; spiders; snakes. Her hand was shaking as she twisted the dial on her combination lock. It snapped open. She took a deep breath before she opened the door.

Nothing jumped out.

She peered in and didn't see anything unusual. She exhaled, took out her notebooks, and shut it again. Maybe Mr. Nightmare was done with her. He'd gotten her parents' attention. They would give him what he wanted, and he'd go away.

Hurrying to class, Sophie slunk into her seat and tried not to make eye contact with anyone. *Don't look up,* she told herself. *Just act normal.*

As the teacher started class, Sophie listened for the sound of paws on the ceiling tile. She'd never been so distracted in her life. She was glad she hadn't known Monster was here the other times. Every time someone's chair squeaked, she jumped. Every time the wind blew the branches on the tree outside, she snapped her head to look. When a shadow passed overhead, she looked up—and saw the shape of Monster as he crossed above one of the fluorescent lights.

She spent the rest of the class worrying that he was going to fall through the ceiling, and then she spent the next few classes watching the ceiling while trying to simultaneously not watch the ceiling. But he didn't fall. And before she knew it, it was lunchtime.

She joined the stream of students pouring into the cafeteria.

Sophie hated the cafeteria. For one thing, it was orange—and not a nice shade of orange but the kind of orange that looked as if a pumpkin had gotten sick on all the walls. For another, it smelled like old eggs mixed with peanut butter. She did like that the cooks tried to make the food look interesting by doing things like carving chicken patties into cute shapes or spelling out words with limp carrots, but that wasn't enough to compensate for the stench or the noise. Today, the display read *Have a smiley day!* in slightly slimy asparagus.

She selected a tray and got in line. The line in front of her grew longer as everyone cut, but she didn't care. She wasn't trying to sit at a particular table with a particular group. In fact, she preferred to sit with no one.

Everyone else seemed to have a group, though there wasn't a popular kids group, or a nerd group, or jock group, like in a sitcom or cheesy teen movie. There were kids who sat together who knew each other through sports, band, ballet, or some kind of other after-school thing that Sophie didn't do. There were other kids who were in all the same classes together—all the honors students clumped together, and so did the kids in the remedial classes—but that was because they spent all day together and could complain about the same teachers. Of course, there was tension between a few groups. Some kids were mean to other kids, but it wasn't always easy to spot the bullies versus the bullied. Sometimes the bullies were bullied. When Sophie looked out over the cafeteria, she was sure of only one thing: she wasn't like any of them. It was better if she sat alone.

"Hey, can I cut?" a boy's voice asked.

Ethan stood beside her, holding an empty tray.

She glanced behind her to see who he was talking to and then realized he was talking to her. "Uh, sure?"

He hopped into line.

"Hey, no cutting!" someone called, despite the dozen people who had already cut in front of other people. Ethan waved at the complainer, and the boy said, "Oh. Ethan! Cool, man. Nice three-pointer." He gave Ethan a thumbs-up.

"I didn't know basketball points came with line-cutting privileges," Sophie said.

He shrugged. "It's a perk." He said it with such casual ease that Sophie could only stare at him for several seconds. She could never talk to people like that, words just rolling out of the mouth without any effort.

Reaching the front, Ethan took an apple from a pyramid of fruit. Sophie eyed a container of yogurt in a sea of half-melted ice. The cafeteria never had any normal flavors like strawberry or blueberry. It was always peach-pineapple or whipped lemon or rhubarb soufflé. She picked out one with mango—and saw a shadow swipe across the stack of chocolate milk by the cashier.

As she stared at the chocolate milk, Ethan nudged

her. In a soft voice, he said, "Hey, I wanted to thank you. That dream thing helped. I still had a nightmare, but it was . . . I don't know, more distant. Can't remember it as well. For the first time in weeks, I woke up to an alarm."

"Glad to hear it." There! Another shadow. And a carton was gone.

"So how does it work?"

Another chocolate milk carton disappeared, and this time, Sophie saw a furry tentacle snag it. *Oh no,* she thought. Glancing up and down the line, she hoped no one else saw.

Ethan was still talking, though she'd missed part of what he said. "Does it distract you, like meditation? 'Cause I tried that, and it didn't work. But this did."

She scooted over to the chocolate milk. As Monster reached up again, Sophie smacked the tentacle. She heard a muffled "Ow!" from underneath the counter.

Ethan looked at her, then the chocolate milk, then at her again. "Just out of curiosity, why are you hitting the milk?"

"Uh, no reason." Sophie scooted past the milk

and told the cashier her lunch number. The cashier rang her up. Continuing to glance back at the chocolate milk, Sophie went to the utensils bar to get a spoon for her yogurt and a fork for . . . shepherd's pie? She hadn't meant to take that. She grimaced at the congealed peas that poked out of the hardened mashed potatoes, like puke-green stones floating in a frothy sea. She wished she could have brought lunch today.

Leaving the utensils bar, she surveyed the cafeteria. You had to view it all like a chessboard, making your move carefully if you didn't want the entire lunch to be awkward, accidentally positioning yourself in the middle of a group that had to talk around you—or, worse, tried to include you. There were a few choices at the ends of tables . . .

"Come on," Ethan said, passing her. "I see some open seats."

She froze in her shoes.

He wasn't actually suggesting they sit together?

He was.

He looked back at her, as if expecting her to follow. Now several kids were looking at them, most likely wondering why she'd frozen in place and why the school's new star basketball player was talking to her. Ethan plopped his tray down at a table with only two seats open.

Feeling as if her face was bright red, Sophie navigated between the tables to Ethan. For a very brief second, she contemplated dumping her tray on his head and fleeing during the distraction.

He pointed to the chair. "Tell me about the dreamcatchers. They're from your parents' store, right? The Dreamcatcher Bookshop? My neighbor says it's the best bookstore in town."

"It's the only bookstore in town," Sophie said, sinking into the seat.

"You like to read?"

Sophie wasn't sure where this conversation was going, or why it was even happening. No one ever wanted to chat with her, and vice versa. She didn't have anything in common with any of them. The only person in school she talked to regularly—Madison—even went so far as to treat her like an enemy so that no one suspected Madison had any flaw, other than a dismal personality. "Yeah. Kind of a family requirement."

"I'm dyslexic. Took me forever to learn how to read."

Sophie blinked. He said it so casually, as if they

were already friends who shared things about their lives. "What's that like?" She wondered if that was an okay question to ask.

"I don't see the letters right. They squirm around. Flip all over the place. You have to force them to behave." He mimed cracking a whip on the table. "I do fine if I'm not distracted. Like now. You changed the subject."

"No, I didn't. You asked me if I like to read." Sophie felt as if she were two cues behind in the script for this conversation. She glanced around and hoped life wasn't like those sitcoms where a popular kid talks with an outcast and then suddenly everyone wants to befriend the outcast. She'd about hit her conversation quota for the week.

Ethan leaned forward and whispered, "Do you have them too? Nightmares? Is that how you know about the dreamcatchers?" When he moved, his blond hair flopped across his forehead. He had pop-star hair.

Sophie swallowed. She hated lying. It made her feel like she was a four-year-old who had eaten all the Halloween candy before Halloween. "I haven't had a single nightmare since I started using the dreamcatchers." There, that wasn't really a lie.

"Sweet." His face broke into a smile. He had a nice smile, like a puppy dog who just discovered how fun it is to stick his face out the car window. Between the smile and the hair and the basketball, it was no wonder half the girls in their grade had a crush on him. It *was* a wonder that he was sitting with her. A very irritating wonder that Sophie could have done without.

Sophie shot a glance at the other tables, checking to see if anyone was looking at them oddly. His friends must have noticed he was sitting with a girl. She imagined them whispering about her. She wondered if any of them knew her name. Ethan clearly did. This was *not* good. "Are you going to tell them I'm helping you with homework?"

"Tell who?"

"Your friends."

"Uh, no."

"But they'll ask why you're sitting with me."

"Then I'll tell them I'm sitting with you because I want to talk to you."

"No one wants to talk to me." She didn't say it to make him feel sorry for her. It was just a fact. And she was fine with it! This, she wasn't fine with. He asked too many questions, and she was already nervous enough with Monster—

Crash.

Trays full of dirty dishes clattered to the floor. Other trays backed up on the conveyer belt and spilled backward. Plates of half-eaten shepherd's pie splattered with a wet smack, and peas rolled underneath tables. A few glasses shattered.

Behind the wall, a man was yelling at someone to hit the emergency stop. The belt ground to a halt. The cafeteria was silent, and everyone stared. And Sophie knew, without any proof, that Monster was responsible.

Silence spread.

And then everyone started talking all at once, laughing and reenacting the crash with swinging arms and loud sound effects. Milk and juice spread over the floor, seeping into each other and forming white-orange pools. A half-eaten apple rolled and lodged itself under the utensils bar.

Sophie left her tray (and Ethan) and hurried across the cafeteria to where the lunch monitors were trying to clean up the carnage. Reaching them, she halted. If Monster had been found, she shouldn't claim him as hers. If he hadn't, she shouldn't draw them to him. But she also couldn't leave and pretend nothing had happened. He could be in trouble!

One of the lunch monitors noticed her. "Do you need something?"

"Just . . . wanted to help." She wished she could turn invisible.

The lunch monitor beamed at her. "Oh, that's a sweetie. Thanks, love, but we've got it. You can go back to your lunch."

Sophie backed away. A janitor's cart was wheeled out from the kitchen, and the trash from the spill was dumped into the garbage can. The cart had a curtain around the bottom to hide all the cleaning supplies from view.

As she watched, she thought she saw the curtain twitch.

When the cleanup was done, the cart was wheeled away and the bell rang. Everyone swarmed toward the dish return area, sidestepping the bits of shepherd's pie that still dotted the floor. She saw Ethan holding his tray and hers. He was trying to catch her eye, but she scooted through the crowd, hiding behind the taller kids, until she squeezed out the door. She hurried through the corridors. Rounding a corner, she saw the janitor's cart.

As the janitor hefted up a trash can, Sophie ducked beside the cart. She flipped open the curtain.

Monster was sitting inside. He had a circle of empty chocolate milk cartons around him. His full belly was sticking up. Mashed potatoes clung to the fur around his mouth.

She looked at him.

He looked at her.

He reached out one tentacle and flipped the curtain closed.

8

Sophie didn't see Monster the rest of the day. When the final bell rang, she sprinted to her locker, shoveled in her notebooks, grabbed her backpack, and ran to the bathroom. Hearing a flush, she ducked into a stall and locked the door. She waited while the other girl washed her hands for a ridiculously long time. Sophie wished she could yell at her to hurry up.

Eventually, the other girl left.

"Monster?" Sophie called softly. "Are you ready to go home?" She listened for the sound of his paws above and watched the ceiling tiles, expecting to see one shift. She planned to catch him so he wouldn't land on the slightly sticky floor. But he didn't appear.

Someone else came into the bathroom. She waited while the new person used the toilet, flushed, and washed her hands. After she left, Sophie called again, "Monster? I'm here. It's time to go home. Come on, the bus will be leaving soon!"

Still no answer.

What if he'd been seen? What if he'd been caught? What if the school thought he was a rodent of unusual size and called an exterminator? What if they *didn't* think he was a rodent and called some mad scientists who wanted to dissect him? Or the news, who'd want to put him on TV? He'd probably like being on TV, having stylists primp his fur, greeting his adoring fans . . . until the terrified mob showed up.

"Sophie! Stay—"

Monster's voice! It came from the hall, and it was cut off by the sound of claws scraping on tile, Monster's growls, and the slam of a door.

She burst out of the stall, out of the bathroom, and into the hallway in time to see Monster bound into a music room. Empty backpack slapping her back, she chased him across the hall.

Inside, a boy was huddled next to a piano. He was covering his head with his arms. Monster was in front of him, tentacles waving in the air, fur standing on end. He was baring his teeth and growling at a lanky, translucent-gray creature that looked like a cross between a giraffe and a man—if a giraffe had razor-like claws instead of hooves.

The creature dodged to the right. As Monster scampered to block him, the creature lunged left. His legs stretched like rubber bands, and his entire body swayed as if he were a balloon. His neck wobbled back and forth.

"Leave him alone!" Sophie picked up one of the chairs and raised it over her head. Ready to swing, she ran toward the gray giraffe-man.

Silently, the gray creature turned toward Sophie. He had no face, just an oval where his face should be. Staring, Sophie slowed.

From behind, Monster leaped at him and sank his teeth into the creature's ankle. Sophie bashed the chair into its chest. The creature didn't let out a sound, but its entire body shuddered.

Shaking off Monster, it loped toward the window, using its knuckles like extra feet. As it jumped onto the windowsill, its body shrank and thinned so it looked like a gray shadow. It slid out a gap in the partially open window.

Sophie and Monster ran to the window and watched the creature slither away, flat on the sidewalk. Gray, it blended in with the concrete.

"What was that?" Sophie asked.

"Vicious," Monster said. "Bad. Slimy. Faceless. I have lots of adjectives but no nouns. Told you to not come out of the bathroom."

"But what—" Behind her, she heard a whimper. The boy! She'd forgotten about him. She rushed to his side, and he raised his head. Sophie realized she knew him. "Ethan? Are you okay?"

"Uh, hi, Sophie. Is it gone?" Shaking and pale, he used the piano to pull himself onto his feet. "Did you just save my life? You and your—"

"Cat," Monster supplied. "I'm a friendly house-cat."

"Right." Ethan's voice was shrill, as if he wanted to scream but his vocal cords wouldn't let him. "You and your friendly talking housecat with six arms."

She guessed it was too late to tell Monster to hide. "Can I convince you you're dreaming?"

"Sure, it would be nice to be dreaming." He was clutching the side of the piano with white knuckles, and his eyes flickered around the room as if he was expecting another attack.

Wiggling her fingers, Sophie waved her hands in front of his face. "This is all a very bad dream. None of this happened."

"But I'm awake."

"You only *think* you're awake. If you were asleep in your dream, it would be a boring dream." Sophie had seen boring dreams before. She'd also seen dreams in which the dreamer seemed to wake several times, each time believing he was awake for real, until something impossible happened, like a chicken dancing the hokey pokey.

In a low voice, Monster sang, "Do-do, do-do, do-do. Ripple, ripple, ripple . . ."

Both Sophie and Ethan looked at him.

"What are you doing?" Sophie asked.

"Making that dream-sequence sound they do on TV." He swayed back and forth, repeating the same two notes. "Do-do, do-do, do-do . . ."

"Please, stop," Sophie said.

"Sorry." He stopped. "I thought it would help."

"It doesn't," she said, then looked at Ethan hopefully. "Does it?"

"Not so much."

The bell rang. Last bell before the buses left. Sophie made a quick decision. "You'd better come home with us." Her parents could decide what to do.

Maybe they'd know what that gray creature was. Was it from a nightmare? Where else could something like that have come from? Did someone dream it to life? Sophie felt a strange flip-flop inside her, as if her heart had done a somersault. Could there be someone else like her out there? She'd thought she was the only one and that Monster was the only monster.

Ethan didn't move. "Shouldn't we tell a teacher? Or call the police?"

"You can't!" She squashed down the instant panic—if he told anyone, they'd find out about Monster. They'd ask questions, and who knew where that would lead? Kneeling, she opened her backpack. Monster crammed himself inside, and she zippered it shut. "Besides, what will you tell them? You were attacked by a gray giraffe that shrank to squeeze out the window and then disappeared down the sidewalk? No one will believe you." She hoped. Last thing she needed was for more people to find out about Monster. Standing, Sophie picked up the backpack. "Come on."

"With you? And . . . your cat?"

"Unless you'd rather be on your own when the creature comes back?"

"Let's go," Ethan said.

Checking the hallway first, she exited with Ethan behind her. It was impressive—and spooky—how quickly the school emptied out as soon as the bell rang. Crumpled papers, candy wrappers, and other trash lay against the walls like tumbleweeds. Classroom windows were dark. Inside, desks and chairs created ominous shadows. She and Ethan hurried toward the front doors.

Outside, some of the buses were already pulling out of the parking lot. *Oh no,* Sophie thought. They were late! "Which one is yours?" Ethan asked.

"Fourteen." She pointed. Its doors were shut, and it was third in line to leave the parking lot. Ethan waved his arms over his head, and they both shouted, "Wait for us!" Ethan put on a burst of speed, sprinting toward it.

As he reached it, the doors opened. He waited for her to catch up. Panting, she reached him, and they clambered on. "Thank you," Ethan said to the bus driver.

The driver grunted.

Most of the seats were already full. Kids watched them as they came on. Sophie expected Madison to comment on how out of breath she was or how red her face was, but the queen bee wasn't on the bus. She must have had an after-school activity, like tormenting someone with less-than-perfect hair.

Several boys waved at Ethan. One high-fived him and said, "Nice shot last night."

"Thanks, man," Ethan said, as if he hadn't just been whimpering in a corner after being chased by a horrifying creature that shouldn't exist.

Sophie slid into an empty seat and put the backpack with Monster on her lap.

Ethan sat down next to her. Across the aisle, two girls whispered and then giggled, looking directly at them. It was as subtle as if they'd waved a sign that read *We're talking about you*. Sophie reminded herself she didn't care, so long as they weren't talking about Monster.

"So . . . what was that thing?" Ethan asked conversationally. He was, she thought, very good at bottling up his fear. Maybe this was why no one but her had suspected all his visits to the counselor's office.

She shushed him. "We'll talk at my house."

"No one's paying attention."

"Are you kidding? Everyone watched us run for the bus, together."

"Yeah, but no one cares."

"Everyone cares. It's middle school. Gossip is practically a gradable subject."

He fell silent. Both of them looked out the window.

Monster huddled motionless and silent within the backpack. This trip, he didn't ask for a view. The bus passed the post office, as well as a park with a baseball diamond and a convenience store that advertised 50 percent off windshield-wiper fluid and freshly fried corn dogs. Sophie suddenly realized that in the chaos of fighting the gray creature and running for the bus, she'd forgotten entirely about Mr. Nightmare meeting with her parents. It should be all over by now, right? Maybe she shouldn't have insisted that Ethan come with her. She wanted to ask them what happened.

"What did it want with me?" Ethan asked, breaking the silence.

Sophie glanced around them, but no one was paying attention to her and Ethan anymore. The chatter was loud enough to drown out his voice. "I don't know. Lunch?" She wished she'd let him go home. Her parents didn't need a second crisis. But he'd seen Monster. And there was that gray creature, who might or might not have been from a nightmare . . . She couldn't just let him waltz off and tell his parents all about the crazy day he had. Her parents would convince him to keep their secret. Softly, she asked Monster through the zipper, "Why was that thing attacking Ethan?"

"No idea," Monster said, muffled. "It's not like there's a monster bulletin board where we send messages to each other. I was on my way to meet you, and the boy was waiting for you outside the bathroom when the freaky giraffe attacked. By the way, did you notice he had no face? I'm voting that he breathes through his skin. Like bullfrogs and earthworms."

Ethan looked pale. Sophie wondered if he was about to faint. She hoped not. She didn't know what she'd do if he fainted. "There are *more* monsters?" he squeaked. He cleared his throat and said in a more normal voice, "I mean, that's cool, if there are more. You know, if they're friendly or whatever. No offense meant."

Monster was silent for a moment. "Actually, I thought I was the only one."

"Guess you aren't," Ethan said.

"Indeed," Monster agreed. "Fascinating."

"Not the word I'd use," Ethan said, and Sophie had to agree with that. "Do you really think it wanted to eat me for lunch?" His voice cracked on the last word.

"It didn't look friendly," Sophie said.

"Lots of things don't look friendly but don't want to eat me. Take your bus driver, for example." Ethan gestured at him. Stopping at the next bus stop, the driver scowled at the kids as if he was offended they wanted to leave.

"Maybe the driver wants to eat you but is disappointed he can't?" Monster suggested.

"Not helping," Sophie told him. She asked Ethan, "Why were you waiting for me?"

"I wanted to talk to you."

She blinked at him. "But we talked at lunch."

"I wanted to talk to you more. You're the only one who's ever noticed . . . Only a few people have ever guessed about the nightmares, and those people are mostly relatives who have heard me wake up screaming." He spoke so softly that she had to lean toward him to hear. "And all they did was send me to counseling. They never helped, not really. Not the way you did in less than twenty-four hours."

The bus squealed to a halt at her stop, saving her from having to think of a response. She jumped to her feet with the backpack in her arms. "This is us."

The kid who had high-fived Ethan called out, "Hey, man, where you going?"

"Sophie's," Ethan answered.

"Dude, why?" he asked, and Sophie thought, *See?*

I'm not the only one who thinks this is weird. The school's new basketball star did not go home after school with the resident weird girl. No one ever went home with Sophie. She'd perfected the art of being friendless.

"I'm helping him with homework," Sophie said at the same time as Ethan said, "Because she's cool."

Feeling her face turn bright red again, Sophie yanked his sleeve toward the front of the bus. The driver glared at them as they got off, and then the doors closed and the bus pulled away. The other kids scattered toward their houses.

"Why did you say that?" Sophie asked.

"Why did you lie?" Ethan countered.

"I wasn't going to say I was taking you to my parents so we can talk about monsters," Sophie said. "Why did *you* lie?"

"I didn't," he said. "You *are* cool. You stopped the nightmares, and you saved me from the whatever-it-was. By the way, did I say thank you for that? Because, thank you. You were amazing. Weren't you scared?"

She wasn't used to so many compliments. "Uh, sure. I'm not an idiot."

Low, so only she could hear him, he confessed, "I was terrified. Not sure I've ever been that scared and been awake."

"That just means you're not an idiot, either."

He smiled sunnily. Sophie thought he was the kind of person that the phrase "his smile brightened the room" was invented for. Even though the sun was out, it felt extra sunny when he smiled. If she practiced for hours, she'd never be able to achieve that effect. "That's the nicest thing anyone's said to me all day," he said. "Knew you weren't as prickly as everyone says."

"Yes, I am."

Sophie walked quickly toward the bookshop. Wind whistled down the sidewalk, stirring bits of trash. A few people were around—a woman carrying both a baby and dry cleaning to her car, an elderly man walking a shriveled, fuzzy dog, and the kids from the bus, heading for their own houses. On this street, homes were mixed with shops. She usually liked that, because it meant there were lots of people to watch. She liked to stroll home and imagine what people's lives were like—and their dreams. But today, she only had eyes for the bookshop.

Ethan hurried to keep up with her. "Do you think it followed us?"

"Hope not."

"That's not exactly reassuring."

She didn't have anything reassuring to say. Maybe her parents would. The sooner she could reach them, the better. They could talk to Ethan, send him home, and this would be over. She could stop feeling like her stomach was a shaken snow globe.

He caught up with her, walking fast beside her. "Why do I get the feeling that there's a lot you're not telling me?"

"Because there is."

Up ahead was her parents' bookshop. The lights were on, a warm glow through the windows, and the sign said *Open*. Mom and Dad would know what to say and what to do. She hoped.

SOPHIE PUSHED THROUGH THE DOOR TO THE bookshop. Overhead, the bell rang cheerfully, as if welcoming her home. She lowered her backpack to the floor and closed the door behind Ethan. She felt as if she was shutting out the world. "We're safe now."

"Are you sure?" Ethan peeked through the bookstore, checking the aisles.

"Absolutely. Mom and Dad wouldn't allow anything dangerous here after school. Except Monster. But he's the friendly kind of dangerous." Raising her voice, she called, "Mom? Dad? I'm home! I brought . . ." She hesitated over what to call Ethan. A friend? A classmate? ". . . someone," she finished. She'd never brought anyone home from school before. She hoped they didn't make too much of a fuss.

"Are they here?" Ethan asked.

"Of course," Sophie said. "It's business hours."

Muffled by the backpack, Monster asked, "Any customers?"

She peered down each aisle. No customers. And no parents, either. "Nope. All clear. You can come out. But hide yourself, just in case."

Monster unzipped the backpack with a tentacle, wiggled out, and then scampered up one of the bookshelves to his usual perch. He blended in with the shadows at the top of the shelves. From here, if anyone bothered to look up, he looked like an ordinary housecat.

Ethan shrugged off his backpack and left it next to hers, near the checkout desk. His backpack was covered in sports key chains. It made Sophie's look drab in comparison. "So are you going to explain how you have a pet monster? Also, what was that thing that attacked me? Is it going to come back? What does it want? Where did it come from? Are there more like it? Why aren't you more freaked out about all of this?"

"My parents will explain." She called again, "Mom? Dad? Hello?" It was strange that they weren't here. One of them should have been in the shop in case someone came in.

Ethan exhaled heavily, as if breathing out all his additional questions. They waited in awkward silence. She listened, expecting to hear her parents' footsteps upstairs or the flush of the toilet or the beep of the microwave—something to explain why they weren't in the shop. Her parents hadn't even left any music on. Usually they piped in piano or harp music, but the only noise was the whoosh of cars passing on the street outside.

Eventually, Ethan spoke again. Another question. "Is there bacon on that cupcake?"

Not the question she'd expected. "It's our neighbor's new experiment. Don't judge."

"I wasn't judging; I was drooling."

"You're really thinking about food right now?"

He lifted the glass dome to peer at the bacon cupcakes. "You know what I do after a nightmare? Eat a sleeve of Oreos. That's one reason my parents agreed to let me go out for sports."

She hadn't thought about *his* parents. "Will they panic if you don't get off your own bus? You should call them. Let them know where you are."

Ethan shrugged. "They're working. They won't notice."

"Really?" If Sophie failed to come straight home after school, her parents would freak . . . which was part of why it was so weird that they weren't coming out to greet her, especially since they had to know she'd been worried about Mr. Nightmare.

"I usually have practice or a game after school. Or I go to a friend's house. Then I grab whatever's in the fridge and do homework. I don't see them much, weekdays." He peered down the aisles, checking the place out.

"You don't eat dinner together?"

"Dad labels meals in the fridge—Monday, Tuesday, Wednesday, you know. Then I just heat it up in the microwave or toaster oven or whatever. Hey, it's not a big deal. It's not like I starve. Dad's a good cook. You don't have to look like I said my cat died."

She didn't know what expression was on her face, but she felt herself blush. "Sorry. I didn't mean—"

"It's fine." He cut her off. "So, where are your parents?"

Monster poked his head over the bookshelf. "Maybe upstairs?"

They should have come down by now. Maybe they were having a snack, or were reading some really good books and lost track of time. It could happen. Or they could be watching TV and it drowned out the sound of the bell over the shop door, except that they never watched TV, not when there were dreams to view.

"Come on, there are extra cupcakes in the kitchen. You can leave your backpack here." Sophie checked the bathroom on the way to the stairs. Empty. She tried the basement door. Locked and not from the inside. She headed up the stairs.

Bounding up the steps, Monster scooted between her feet. At the top, he halted.

Sophie was close behind him. Bumping into him, she stopped too and gasped.

All the books—the towers of books that had been laid out like a labyrinth, the stacks that had crowded the top of the coffee table, the books that blocked the TV and filled the dining room table— had fallen like dominoes. Books were scattered everywhere. Some were spine-down, the pages flopped to the side. Others were crushed against the walls or on the couch. If books could bleed, the room would be red.

Seeing the mess, Sophie felt as if something were

squeezing her heart. *Something's wrong,* she thought. *Something's very, very wrong.*

She felt Ethan stop behind her, one step down. "Um, is it supposed to look like this?"

"What happened?" Sophie asked Monster.

"Stay here, and be quiet," Monster instructed. Leaping off the stairs, he hopped over the fallen books, checked each room, and then ran upstairs to the bedrooms on the third floor. Sophie's heart thumped hard in her chest. *Don't panic,* she ordered herself. Everything could still be fine. Just messy.

"What's going on—" Ethan began.

"Shh." Sophie wanted to run through the house shouting for her parents. Instead, she waited at the top of the stairs. *Please be here!* she thought. *Please be okay!* Mom said she didn't have to worry. Mom wouldn't lie to her.

But her parents would never, ever leave books just strewn like this. Pages were bent. Spines were cracked. Covers torn. All her life, Sophie had been taught that books are precious. Each one holds people and worlds. Each one is a piece of someone's heart and mind that they chose to share. They were shared dreams.

Monster clattered down the stairs, spilling more

books in his rush. He ran across the top of the books to Sophie. "No one upstairs." His voice was hushed.

"Downstairs?"

"I'll check. You try to call them." Silently, on the pads of his feet, Monster darted down the stairs. He knew how to unlock the basement door with his tentacles. He'd claimed he learned it from a book on lock picking.

Passing Ethan, Sophie raced back down to the bookshop and ran for the phone by the cash register. She dialed her father's number. It rang. And rang. Soon, it switched to voicemail. "Dad, it's Sophie. Where are you? I'm at the shop. Please come home." *Stay calm,* she told herself. They could have ducked out to run an errand. Quick trip to the supermarket or post office . . . Hanging up, she tried her mother's number.

A phone rang at her feet.

She looked down—her mother's purse was tucked into a shelf. The phone was inside it. Sophie hung up and tried even harder not to panic. Mom never went anywhere without her purse.

Monster's voice drifted up from the basement. "Sophie! Down here!"

Sophie hurried across the bookshop. Her stomach was flip-flopping, and her heart was pattering extra fast. "Monster? Are you okay?" She ran down the stairs, taking two at a time. "Are Mom and Dad there?"

"No," Monster said. "But you need to see this. Oh, this isn't good."

Downstairs, the dusty yellow glow of the lights filled the room. Bottles glistened from the shelves. The somnium sat quietly under the stairs. But the distiller—all the glass tubes and levers that used to overflow a table . . . It was gone.

Sophie gawked at the empty table. Dust outlined where the distiller used to sit. The wood was faded and stained in places that she'd never seen before. "I don't . . . Where . . . How?" They'd never moved the distiller. There was no reason to move it.

Monster hopped onto the distiller table and prowled over the empty surface, sniffing at the wood. Droplets of old spilled dreams shimmered in the cracks in the wood.

First the books, now the distiller. And her parents weren't here.

Sophie felt sick. Her heart pounded, her ears

roared, and her palms were slick with sweat. The walls seemed closer. The air felt hotter. In short, she felt, for the first time, like all those dreamers must have felt in the middle of a chased-by-something-horrible nightmare.

Behind her, Ethan said, "Whoa, what is this place?"

Oh no, she'd forgotten about him, and he'd followed her! "Go back up," Sophie ordered. "Forget you saw any of this. Please!"

"Let him stay," Monster said. "He's already involved, thanks to the gray giraffe. Besides, we have worse problems." He paced back and forth on top of the distiller table. His tentacles waved at the shelves. "Look!"

She looked at the shelves. Several were empty. There had to be two dozen, three dozen . . . maybe fifty missing bottles, all from the same set of shelves. "I don't understand," Sophie said. Or more accurately: she didn't want to understand.

Ethan raised his hand. "And I seriously don't understand."

Ignoring him, Sophie touched the empty shelves. "Which dreams were these?"

"Nightmares," Monster said grimly. "Specifically, monster dreams."

"But why . . ." She sucked in air. She felt as if her throat wanted to close. Her eyes felt hot. This was too much. First the gray giraffe, and now her parents . . . "Do you think . . . Something must have happened when they met with Mr. Nightmare."

Ethan held out both hands. "Wait. Slow down. Monster dreams? Mr. Nightmare? Sophie, what's going on?"

"You need to explain," Monster said, "before he overreacts."

She looked at Ethan, whose eyes were nearly as wide as Monster's. Trying to sound calm, she said, "You asked how dreamcatchers work. They catch the dreams in their strings." She pointed to a pile of unfinished dreamcatchers that sat on one of the counters. All they needed were beads and feathers, and they'd be ready for display in the bookstore. "My parents distill the dreams into liquid, with a device that used to sit here." She next pointed at the empty table. Her hand was shaking. She lowered it before he saw. "And we watch them there, so we can sort them." She turned to point last at the somnium. "And then we

131

label the bottles and put them on the shelves to be sold."

Ethan turned in a slow circle. "Dude, are you serious?"

"Those bottles have happy dreams." She waved at one shelf of bottles, then another. "Here, the falling dreams, and next to them, the embarrassment dreams. Over here are the food dreams. There are lots of those, split between happy food dreams and bad food dreams."

"Bad food dreams?" Ethan repeated, dazed.

"You know, pizza with live fish. Peanut butter and ketchup smoothies. Spaghetti that transforms into worms—you'd be surprised how common that one is." She was amazed at how calm and ordinary her voice sounded, when inside she was shrieking.

"And you sell these?"

"My parents do. Food dreams sell really well to buyers on diets—some want happy food dreams so they can eat without eating, and others want bad food dreams so they can train themselves to want less food. It helps people. All our dreams help people." Sophie took a deep breath. She was *not* going to panic. Panicking wouldn't help with anything. She was going to stay calm, think about this rationally, and find answers. "Mr. Nightmare is a buyer. He bought a dream from my parents yesterday but didn't like their prices, I guess. He left a note in my locker. My parents planned to meet with him today to sort it all out. And now they're missing—and so is the distiller and the bottled nightmares with monsters in them."

And then Sophie burst into tears.

SOPHIE GULPED SOBS — BIG, UGLY GASPS LIKE A
fish on shore—while tears poured out of her eyes.
She wiped them furiously with the back of her hand.
Leaping from the table, Monster wrapped himself
around her ankles. She sucked in air, telling herself to
stop, stop, *stop!*

Ethan patted her back awkwardly. "It's okay.
You're okay. Everything's okay."

"It's not okay! Don't say that!" She got herself
under control and yanked away from Ethan. Spinning
to face the shelves, she clenched her fists and forced
herself to take deep, hiccupping breaths until her eyes
and nose quit leaking like a broken faucet.

"We'll find them," Ethan said. "Your parents, I
mean."

Sophie wiped her face with her sleeve. "How? Where?" She took another deep breath. There. She had control again. She felt as if her face was lobster-red, and wished Ethan hadn't seen her freak out.

"I don't know. But don't . . . cry, okay?"

"Okay."

He was silent. Tentatively, he asked, "Are you okay?"

"Fine . . . I just . . . I didn't expect this." She waved her hand at the empty distiller table, the shelves, and upstairs. She felt as if she was going to fly apart again, and she scooped up Monster and hugged him tightly. He wrapped all six tentacles around her middle.

"Yeah, know the feeling."

They stood in awkward silence again. Sophie tried to think of a not-terrifying explanation for the missing distiller and dream bottles. Maybe her parents had sold them all. Maybe they were out celebrating their new wealth. Maybe they were buying her a pony.

"So . . ." Ethan said conversationally, as if she hadn't just lost it. His voice was falsely cheerful. "I'm supposed to believe each of these bottles is a dream?"

"Believe whatever you want. It's true."

"But why would anyone buy bad dreams?" Hands

clasped behind his back, he examined the shelves with bottles. The liquid swirled inside, sparkling like glitter paint. She didn't believe for a second that was the question he most wanted to ask. He was just trying to keep her from crying again.

"Same reason some people love to ride roller coasters. Or read horror novels. Or see scary movies. Except dreams are even more immersive. Mom says it's therapeutic for people. Dad says it's also fun." If Mr. Nightmare had bought all those dreams, why? She'd never heard of anyone buying so many. And she didn't know why her parents would sell him the distiller. *They wouldn't,* she thought, and she swallowed a lump in her throat. "That buyer—he calls himself Mr. Nightmare. Guess he really likes nightmares."

"You think he stole them?" Looking at a pile of unfinished dreamcatchers, Ethan picked one up and then put it down quickly, as if it had stung him. He put his hands behind his back again.

Monster leaped onto the empty shelves. "Stole them and kidnapped her parents. They'd never sell the distiller. And they're always here when Sophie comes home from school. It's the only logical explanation."

Sophie clenched her hands into fists to keep

herself from bursting into tears again. It was no different from what she'd been thinking, but hearing it said out loud . . .

"Then we should call the police," Ethan said.

Pivoting on his hind paws, Monster drew himself upright and fluffed his fur. He spread his tentacles wide, waving them in the air. "You cannot!"

At the same time, Sophie cried, "You can't!"

Ethan shrank back. His eyes shifted from side to side, as if checking for the nearest exit. "Why not? If they're missing—"

Sophie tried to sound calm and logical. She didn't want him to bolt, babbling her secrets to whoever would listen. "What do we tell them? A man called Mr. Nightmare wanted to buy some dreams and now my parents and the machine that liquefies dreams are gone? They'll never believe us." Or worse, the police *would* believe them and tell the world . . . and then the Watchmen would hear and come. She couldn't risk that.

"But if they're—"

"No police." If the Watchmen came, they'd destroy the shop. And when they found out about Sophie, they'd take her away, or worse. If that happened, she might never see her parents again. At least now there was a chance she was wrong and her parents were at the supermarket and everything was fine, and they'd be together, laughing about how silly she'd been to overreact. "They can't find out about all of this—the Dream Shop, my family . . . It's a secret, okay? It has to stay a secret, or everything's over."

"Then what do we do?"

"*We* don't do anything. *You* go home." She'd been stupid to tell him. He wasn't family. She couldn't trust him. "And you don't tell anyone anything. Please!"

He shook his head, though he continued to retreat. "I'm not leaving you with your parents missing. Plus what about the gray creature? It's still out there, somewhere."

She had forgotten about the giraffe-man. Pressing her hands over her face, she wished she *did* have nightmares and this was one and she could wake up.

"Listen, what if we call the police and tell them your parents are missing"—he held up a hand to stop her from interrupting—"but not mention any of the dream stuff. There's still the mess upstairs, right? That's evidence."

Monster snorted. "Yeah, they'll be very impressed

to hear a few books fell over. Her parents haven't been gone long. They'll pat Sophie on the head and tell her to be patient. Or worse, they'll take her into the station, call Child Protective Services, and keep her there. Then we'll lose our chance to look for them."

Lowering her hands from her face, Sophie looked at Monster. "You think we can find them?"

"Of course."

Ethan shook his head. "Where? How? Do you know where this Mr. Nightmare lives? Do you even know his name? 'Mr. Nightmare' can't be his real name."

"Check the ledger," Monster suggested.

Yes, she thought, *the ledger!* "Monster, you're brilliant." Mr. Nightmare might have stolen dreams today, but he'd bought one yesterday.

"Obviously, but don't feel too bad. As Eleanor Roosevelt said, 'No one can make you feel inferior without your consent,' which is a little victim-blaming, if you think about it."

She brushed past Ethan to the counter by the dream shelves. Monster jumped up onto the counter beside her and stuck his tentacles into the lock on the drawer that held the ledger. Twisting his tentacles, he unlocked it with a loud *click*. Hands shaking, Sophie pulled open the drawer and took out the ledger. She set it on the counter with a thud.

"What's that?" Ethan asked.

"It's a book," Monster said.

"I *know* it's a book. I meant, how's it supposed to help?"

"Most answers can be found in books," Monster said solemnly. "As a wise man who wasn't Eleanor Roosevelt once said, 'Outside of a dog, a book is a man's best friend. Inside a dog, it's too dark to read.'"

Sophie shot him a look. "This is serious, Monster."

"Just lightening the mood."

"Yeah, don't."

The ledger was bound in brown leather. A thick red ribbon marked the middle, and several pages were dog-eared, stained, and torn. It was at least a thousand pages, with more than half of them filled. She opened it.

Here was every dream, every sale, every purchase. She flipped through pages, seeing her mother's neat handwriting contrast with her father's scrawl. They recorded everything here. "My parents make every buyer and supplier leave their name and address . . ."

Ethan peered over her shoulder. "Why?"

"It's a safety thing," Sophie said. "This is a reputable dream shop, and my parents want to be sure they aren't dealing with criminals."

"How would they know that?"

Sophie paused. She hadn't thought about that before. "I don't know. It's just what they do. If you want to buy or sell us a dream, you have to say who you are."

"Clearly didn't work, since they got robbed."

Swallowing a lump in her throat, Sophie flipped faster.

"What's to stop a criminal from lying?" Ethan asked. "I mean, 'Mr. Nightmare' doesn't exactly sound like a real name. Plus, if I were a thief or whatever, I wouldn't give out my real home address."

Sophie stopped at yesterday's date.

And there it was, in her mother's clear handwriting, in blue ink: *Eugene Federle, 263 Windsor Street, Eastfield.* They'd made only one sale yesterday, a nightmare filled with mythology. This was it. Sophie stepped back from the book. Her heart thumped wildly.

Ethan scooted past her to read. He put his fingers

on the words, and his mouth moved silently before he spoke. "*That's* your Mr. Nightmare? Eugene Federle? That doesn't sound nightmarish."

"Where's Windsor Street?" Sophie asked.

Ethan pulled a phone out of his pocket, typed in the address, and then showed it to Sophie and Monster, who inched closer. "Across town, other side of the baseball fields, I think. Look, how's this for a deal: we go there, look around, try to figure out if it's really his house and if he left any clues, and if we see anything suspicious, then we call the police."

It was . . . not a terrible plan.

She found herself nodding, then stopped. "Wait. 'We'? Why are you being so nice to me? Why come with me?"

"As Monster said before, I'm involved."

"Yeah, not really. We don't know that the gray giraffe is after you. It could be a random coincidence. It might not have anything to do with Mr. Nightmare or my parents. And I could be wrong about Mr. Nightmare and my parents anyway. Why not go home, play basketball, and live your normal life as if none of this had ever happened?"

Ethan opened his mouth, then shut it as if he was

considering what to answer. Finally, he said, "Because you need help. And I can help you. Or at least try."

★★★

Sophie flipped the sign in the bookshop window from *Open* to *Closed,* turned off the lights, and locked the door while Monster squeezed himself into her backpack again. Scooping him up, she headed through the stacks to the back door. Ethan followed her.

The bikes were in the shed behind the house. She didn't ride much, so hers had cobwebs. Dusting it off, she wheeled the bike outside and hoped she didn't break an arm on top of everything else. Ethan picked her dad's bike and found helmets on a shelf next to a garden hose. He handed her one, and she strapped it on. It was pink with butterflies on it, and it barely fit. His was rust-colored and looked a decade old. It occurred to her that she'd never been on a bike ride with a friend, and that's exactly what this would look like to anyone who saw them. She hoped no one saw them. "You have that map ready?" Sophie asked.

"Consider me navigation guy," he said.

"Good." She pictured her parents waiting for her,

trapped in a stranger's house. Her heart was thumping hard. She wondered if this was what it felt like to be stuck in a nightmare. "What did you dream about last night?"

He jammed his helmet on his head and didn't meet her eyes. "Nothing."

"Nothing as in no dream, or nothing as in the Nothingness that destroys Everything?"

Foot on the bike pedal, he froze. "How did you know that?"

Sophie shrugged. She'd seen it plenty of times before. It was always creepy. Dad filed those dreams under "existential dread." They didn't sell well, unless the terror was acute enough. Given Ethan's reaction, she guessed his was acute. She wondered why.

He pushed off the ground and rode forward. Backpack balanced on her back, she pedaled after him. They skirted the side of the house. She caught up with him as they rode out onto the sidewalk. "I've had that dream before," he admitted. "And worse. Sometimes I dream I can't scream, no matter how much I want to. Or that I can scream, but no one hears me. Or I dream that I'm alone in the middle of the ocean."

"Sharks?" She veered around a parking meter. Concentrating, she tried to keep her balance. Last time she rode her bike, she'd crashed into a mailbox. She wouldn't be able to help her parents if she hurt herself.

"No sharks. No birds. No raft. No nothing. And the ocean goes down for miles underneath me. The dreamcatcher last night . . . That was the first time in days that I didn't wake up terrified. And I'm only saying the word *terrified* because I'm trusting you not to tell my team. But seriously, the dreamcatcher helped. I still remember the dream, but it's more like the way I remember something I watched on TV or read. It's not as intense. It doesn't feel like I lived it."

"You're welcome." She wanted to ask why someone with so many friends would have such classic loneliness dreams. But before she could figure out how to ask, Ethan sped up and crossed the street at a break in the traffic.

Sophie braked as a truck rattled past. Two more cars zoomed by in its wake. She looked up and down the street, then up and down again. *Don't be a chicken,* she told herself. *Mom and Dad need you.* Her head down, she pushed off the curb and biked across the street. Ahead, Ethan was turning onto one of the side streets. Speeding up, she followed him.

Monster bounced on her back. "Ow, ow, ow."

"Sorry!" She tried to steer around the potholes, but she couldn't help hitting patches of dirt and cracks in the road. On the side street, the houses looked as if they were waking up—people were out walking their dogs, coming home from work, kids were playing in the driveways. She'd been down these streets before, but they looked different from a bike than they did on a bus. She noticed every tiny incline.

As they rode farther from the center of town, the houses were more spaced out, and the sidewalks disappeared. When they were side by side again, Ethan asked, "Would you really have sold my dream?"

She was panting, but he looked as if he'd just hopped on the bike. She reminded herself this was her idea. It wasn't her fault she was out of shape. Well, technically, it was. "Weren't you happy it was dulled?" she puffed.

"Yeah."

"Then why does it matter what happens to it afterward?"

"Because it's *mine*."

"But you didn't want it," Sophie pointed out. "We're just recycling your trash. Really, it's not so different from the people who ride around in pickup trucks on trash day and rescue things from people's trash to sell at scrap yards or at flea markets."

"But people don't know dreams *can* be sold."

And so long as the Watchmen are out there, they never will, Sophie thought. It was sad. There were so many wonderful dreams that could be shared. Her parents sold thrill rides and sweet moments and surreal journeys and experiences that you couldn't find in the awake world. They shouldn't have to do it in secrecy and fear. Her parents, the way they could distill a tangled dream . . . they were artists. It was beautiful, and she wished it didn't have to be hidden. But it did. They didn't dare stop hiding. If the Watchmen found out about the Dream Shop, they'd destroy it, down to the very last bottle. Her parents had heard of it happening before. Even the police hadn't been able to help—all they'd seen was a bunch of broken bottles and two scared people babbling about things that the police believed couldn't be true.

Pausing at a stop sign, Ethan checked the map. "This way." He pointed toward a street, and she winced. Of course it had to be uphill. "How long have your parents run a dream shop?"

"As long as I can remember," Sophie said, pedaling

again. "My grandparents—my mom's parents—used to have a shop too. They retired to Florida a few years ago. Not near Disney World, though."

"I don't know why anyone would live in Florida not near Disney."

She wondered if he was distracting her on purpose, keeping her talking so that she wouldn't panic. He didn't seem to be good with tears, which Sophie understood, since she hated crying. "There's supposed to be a dream shop inside Cinderella's castle, but that could be just a rumor." She puffed as she pedaled, and then they hit the top of a hill.

Side by side, they coasted down. Trees flickered past on either side of the street. There were fewer houses here. In fact, she realized, she hadn't seen a house in a while. It was mostly swampy woods. She'd never been out this way before.

Ethan led them down another street. They passed a field, a house, then another stretch of dense trees. "How many dream shops are there?"

"I don't know. We're rare. A few, I guess? My parents don't let me meet too many people in the dream business. Anyone, really. I wasn't supposed to meet Mr. Nightmare. It was an accident." Did that somehow lead to whatever happened with her parents? Was this all her fault? If she hadn't met Mr. Nightmare, he never would have left the birthday card. If she hadn't found that card, Mom and Dad wouldn't have met with him again. The bike wobbled under her, and she concentrated on keeping her balance.

"Just keep talking," he coached her. "If you think too much about bad stuff, you'll lose control and fall. Take it from a guy who's broken his arm twice. How do people know about your dream shop? I mean, it's not like you have a sign or anything."

She forced herself to focus on the question. "It's like people who are really into knitting. They know where all the yarn stores are and they tell each other. Dream collectors are the same way. Word of mouth. But more, you know, secret."

Ethan braked.

She squeezed the hand brakes and jolted forward as the bike jerked to a stop. Ahead, surrounded by marshy woods, was a house with a freshly shorn lawn, pink flowers along the walk, and a mailbox in the shape of a swan. It was all alone, the only house visible in either direction. It looked as if it was all dolled up for a party, just waiting for neighbors to join it. It didn't look like the house of a thief and kidnapper. "That's it?"

"263 Windsor Street. It's not very . . ."

"Ominous?"

"Yeah."

It wasn't. It was the kind of house where kids would set up a lemonade stand in the front yard while the adults barbecued hamburgers in the backyard. Stepping off her bike, Sophie walked closer. Parked in the driveway was a sleek blue car with a license plate that read: *MISTER N. Mr. N,* she thought. *Mr. Nightmare.* At least this was really his house, so that was one question answered. He hadn't lied in the ledger. Of course, that didn't prove he had anything to do with her parents' disappearance . . .

Steering her bike off the road, she knocked the kickstand down and removed her helmet. Ethan parked Dad's bike next to hers. Kneeling, she took off her backpack, lowered it to the ground, and opened it. Monster was curled into a tight ball. "Are you okay?" she asked.

"Seasick." He slunk out of the backpack. Groaning, he flopped on his side under the bushes. "Never, ever want to do that again."

She winced. "Sorry."

He waved a tentacle weakly, which could have meant either "I forgive you" or "I surrender."

"You stay here," she told him. "We'll check it out."

Launching himself to his feet, he said, "Oh no, I have to protect you." His knees wobbled and his eyes widened. His cheeks bulged as if he was trying to keep from being sick.

"We're just going to peek in the windows, right?" Ethan said. "Nothing dangerous."

Sophie nodded. "We'll be as sneaky as opossums."

"Are opossums really sneaky?" Ethan asked.

"No idea," Sophie said.

Monster shook his head. "Coming with you . . ." And then he clapped tentacles over his mouth and sank into the pine needles.

"Stay. I'll scream if I need you."

"I'm fine. But I'll . . . keep to the bushes." Slinking underneath the bushes, Monster headed for the house. Sophie and Ethan followed, tromping between the trees.

The mossy ground squished under her feet. Birds chirped from the branches overhead. She spotted squirrels scurrying through the trees. It felt like they were on a nature walk, not a spying mission. Everything about this felt wrong.

The forest ended abruptly at the lawn, as if both

the grass and the trees were respecting the border. No weeds sneaked onto the lawn, and no grass ventured into the woods. Sophie squatted in the underbrush and stared at the house.

"You sure you want to do this?" Ethan asked.

"We came all the way here," Sophie said. "Besides, maybe this is a disguise. Maybe we're supposed to think he's innocent." Evil people could still mow their lawns.

There were neatly pruned bushes all around the house, framing it in a ring of green. If they could hide in those bushes, they'd be fine. Sophie, Ethan, and Monster darted across the lawn and dived into the bushes.

Keeping low, Sophie crept along the side of the house. Her sneakers sank into the mulch. It smelled fresh and a little bit like manure. Clearly, Mr. Nightmare liked to garden. It didn't match her image of him.

Under the first window, she held a finger to her lips. Standing slowly, she peered through the window: living room. She saw a couch, a TV, a fireplace with a mantel that had a model of an old airplane and a few framed photographs. The table in front of the couch had a couple of books, a remote control, and a half-empty bowl of tortilla chips. It looked very ordinary.

She crouched back down. Ethan looked too. Together, they crept to the next window. "I feel like there should be a spy theme playing," he whispered.

Rising up, she looked into a dining room. Stacks of mail were piled on one end of the table, and a vase with dried flowers sat in the center. Again, ordinary.

The next room was a kitchen. There were dishes in the sink, ready to be washed, and a box of cookies on the table. A kid's pink and purple backpack sat on the table, next to the cookies. Sophie ducked down. "He's a dad," she whispered. She tasted disappointment, hot and thick in the back of her throat.

"He could be an evil dad," Ethan whispered.

"I don't know. It all looks so . . . normal. Maybe I'm wrong."

Ethan patted her on the shoulder, again awkwardly, as if he didn't have much practice being comforting. She didn't have much practice being comforted, at least not by anyone who wasn't Monster. They stared at each other for a second. "Let's keep looking," Ethan suggested. "How do we see what's upstairs?"

"I can do it," Monster whispered.

"Are you sure you feel up to it?" Sophie asked.

"Of course. I'm very heroic," Monster said. "And I have no moral qualms about vomiting on bad guys."

"We don't know he's a bad guy," Sophie said.

"He has a supervillain name," Ethan said. "But this isn't much of a lair."

Monster scampered up a drain pipe, using his tentacles to grip as he climbed. Below him, Sophie and Ethan continued to creep around the house. What if she didn't see any clues? What if Mr. Nightmare really hadn't kidnapped her parents? It felt strange and wrong to be hoping for him to have done so, but if he wasn't responsible, then who was?

Sophie peeked around the corner into the backyard and saw an aboveground pool (empty), a fancy barbecue grill (unused), and a garden hose (neatly coiled) next to blue cellar doors. There was no sign of her parents or anything remotely unusual.

This was the home of a nice, normal family, who watched sports together as they ate dinner and their kid did her homework and their dog begged for extra treats or whatever. She thought of the bowl of chips in the living room, the backpack and cookies in the kitchen, the stacks of mail in the dining room. The backpack even looked familiar. She probably knew the kid it belonged to. She—it was a pink and purple backpack, so Sophie was guessing it was a girl—was probably in their school.

Monster dropped next to them. "Just some bedrooms and a bathroom."

"My parents?"

He shook his head.

"The distiller?"

"I'm sorry, Sophie." He curled his tentacles around her.

"But . . ." If this wasn't the place and Mr. Nightmare wasn't responsible . . . then she had no idea where her parents were or what could have happened to them. There had to be some kind of clue here. He had to be responsible!

"Maybe they're fine and waiting for you at home," Ethan said.

She shook her head. "The distiller's gone. And they weren't home when the bus came. They always are. And what about the books upstairs?"

Ethan rose up and peeked through the window. "Well, whatever happened, this guy looks innocent."

"Let's just look a little more," she begged.

They circled the house twice, three times, until Sophie had to admit this was pointless. There wasn't anything here to even hint that Mr. Nightmare had anything to do with her parents' disappearance. All this was a waste of time.

Together, they trudged back to their bikes. Sophie and Ethan put on their helmets. Groaning, Monster squeezed into the backpack. After zippering it, Sophie picked him up and steadied the backpack on her back before swinging her leg over her bike.

She heard a man's voice call: "Betty?"

11

It was Mr. Nightmare.

Sophie put one foot on a pedal, ready to push off, and glanced back over her shoulder at him. He was in his front yard, and he looked . . . the word that popped into her head was "silly." He'd traded his ominous trench coat for baggy sweatpants and a faded T-shirt from some unrecognizable university. His stomach stuck out from under the bottom of it. Without his hat, his hair was a mix of gray and brown that stuck out at odd angles, as if he'd combed it with a broom, and his eyes looked merely old, not bloodshot and sunken. He was carrying two trash bags out of the detached garage. He dumped them into trash cans at the end of the driveway. "Nice to see you, Betty! Did you have a good birthday?"

"Uh, yeah, um, sure."

He smiled broadly. "Splendid! Did you get my card? Bet you were surprised!"

Sophie stared at him. "Very surprised."

"Thought you'd like it." He sounded smug. "Kids love surprises."

She felt Ethan looking back and forth between her and Mr. Nightmare. She knew what he was seeing: a dumpy man who didn't look anything like the creepy, shadowy man she'd described. "How did you get the card in her locker?" Ethan asked.

A key question, she thought. She waited for his answer.

"Easy-peasy," he said. "After I visited with your parents, Sophie, I stopped for a cup of coffee. I saw you get on your bus. Later, I went to your elementary school and talked to your principal about leaving the card for you. He inspected it, of course—cautious one you have there. Anyway, clever of me, huh?"

"You just wanted to give me a birthday card?" Sophie couldn't quite believe what she was hearing. She'd been so afraid . . . and so sure he was the one behind her parents' disappearance. Even after seeing his house, it was hard to let go of that belief.

"I believe in random acts of kindness. Besides, I

wanted your parents to know I appreciated their shop. Independent bookstores are rare these days." He gave a broad wink, to make it clear he wasn't talking about the bookstore, and then he put the lids on his trash cans.

"Uh-huh, so . . . my parents." She continued to stare at him as he puttered through his yard, bending to yank out a few stray weeds. "You met with them this morning. How did that go?"

He smiled again, and his face stretched like putty around his lips. "They sold me three more 'books.' Great people, your parents. Family-run stores like theirs make me glad I moved here. You don't find places like that in the city."

He'd only bought three? But dozens of bottles were missing. And the distiller. "Oh? You moved recently?"

He wiped his dirt-streaked hands on his sweatpants. A few leaves were stuck in his hair. It made him look as if he'd rolled out of bed and into the garden. "We were supposed to move sooner, but the house had to be remodeled. It was quite the fixer-upper." Hands on his hips, he regarded it proudly. She had the feeling if she asked, he'd pull out before-and-after photos to show off his renovation. This was not the conversation she'd expected to have. This was pointless. She shouldn't have come.

"So you just bought three dreams? Not the distiller?"

He blinked. "What would I do with a distiller? It requires expertise and experience . . ." Trailing off, he waved a hand at Ethan. "Oh, does your friend know about you-know-what?"

"She told me about the Dream Shop," Ethan confirmed.

"Wonderful!" Mr. Nightmare clapped his hands together, as if he was truly delighted. "Good to have friends you can share things with. So many children of dream sellers grow up lonely. Secrets can be hard to bear. Guess you didn't need my silly card to cheer you up. I thought . . . well, never mind what I thought. I hope you liked it anyway." He smiled again, and Sophie wondered why she ever thought he was sinister. It must have been bad lighting. And the hat. And her imagination, convincing her that one small mistake was actually a disaster.

"It was very nice," Sophie said distantly. It was hard not to feel deflated. She'd been so certain he was responsible and that she'd see a clue ... But he was just a middle-aged man cleaning his garage. And he happened to like nightmares. On her back, she felt Monster shift. "Thank you. Have you talked to my parents since this morning?"

He crinkled his face in concern. "No, why? Is anything wrong?"

For an instant, she was tempted to tell him the truth: that her parents were missing, that she'd suspected him. But even though she knew he was innocent, she still couldn't bring herself to trust him. "Just curious," Sophie said.

"Why do you buy nightmares?" Ethan asked.

"For the fun of it," Mr. Nightmare said with a shrug. "Some people like horror movies on the silver screen; I like them in my mind. It's relaxing, you know?" He sounded so very ordinary. Just like his house. She felt like she should apologize for ever suspecting him. At least he didn't know why they were really here.

Sophie swallowed a lump in her throat. She had even been willing to let Ethan call the police, if they'd seen anything at all suspicious. That would have been a horrible mistake. The police would have found nothing here and then come back to the shop and begun asking questions that Sophie didn't want to answer. "Hope you enjoy them."

"Thanks, Betty! Back to cleaning the garage. Fun times. But maybe I'll watch one of those nightmares tonight." Whistling, he headed back into his garage.

Ethan turned to her. "I'm sorry, Sophie."

She nodded. Her eyes felt hot, but she didn't let herself cry. There wasn't much to say. She'd been wrong, and now she had no idea what to do. "Guess we go home."

They got on their bikes and rode away.

★★★

Her eyes fixed on the street, Sophie pedaled as hard as she could, keeping ahead of Ethan so she wouldn't have to talk. She'd been wrong about Mr. Nightmare. He didn't have anything to do with her parents' disappearance. He was a "red herring," as her English teacher would have said. And she was out of ideas. She was stuck with hoping that they'd be home when she arrived. Maybe they'd have some ridiculous explanation, like the distiller broke and they took it to the distiller fix-it shop, if there was such a thing, and they'd be mad at her for taking off without leaving a note. She'd be fine with being punished—no somnium for a week, or even no books—so long as they were there. *Please, please, be there!* If they weren't, she didn't know what she was going to do.

Within the backpack, Monster moaned. She hoped he was okay. He'd suffered through this for nothing. The entire trip, a waste. She wished she dared let him stick his head out. "Almost there," she told him. Only a few more streets . . .

Behind them, she heard a siren. She steered onto the sidewalk as the siren grew louder. Oddly, it didn't pass. Instead, the siren wailed, close and loud, directly behind Sophie and Ethan, as if the police car was following them.

Braking, Sophie twisted in her seat. Beside her, Ethan braked too, and the police car stopped. Its lights flashed red and blue, and the headlights made her eyes water. A policeman stepped out. Frowning at them, he looked serious, as if he'd walked out of a crime show.

Oh no, my parents! She knew it! Something terrible had happened and—

But the policeman smiled and held up his hands as if to calm them. "Don't worry. You aren't in trouble.

But I do need you to get on home. You probably noticed there aren't many people out. There's a town curfew tonight. A couple kids have gone missing, and we're asking everyone to stay in tonight until the matter is resolved."

Sophie felt her rib cage loosen as relief washed over her. Not her parents. *Of course it's not,* she scolded herself. He didn't know who she was or who her parents were. She was just a kid on a bike. She'd been so wrapped up in her own thoughts that she hadn't noticed fewer people were out. She looked right and left—there weren't any cars moving, and this was usually a busy street. It was weirdly quiet.

"We were just heading home, sir," Ethan said.

"Good," the policeman said. "Where's home?"

"Dreamcatcher Bookshop," Sophie answered. "I live above it."

He nodded approvingly. "Great store. My wife shops there all time. Constantly hanging those dreamcatcher things all over the house. Your parents own it?" He was chatty now, all smiles.

"Yes." Her throat felt clogged. She wanted to make herself say more. This was her chance. She could tell this smiling policeman that her parents were missing, explain about the theft, and ask him to help

. . . but what if they weren't missing? And what if the policeman wanted to search their house? What if he saw the dream bottles and the somnium? How would she explain that? The Dream Shop could be exposed, all because she was worried. Really, she didn't actually know her parents were missing at all. They could simply be at the neighbor's, trying out more of Ms. Lee's cupcakes.

"And you?" the policeman asked Ethan.

"I'm going to her house." Ethan jabbed his thumb toward Sophie. "We're doing a school project together."

The policeman nodded. "Make sure you get a ride home. We aren't allowing kids out without adult supervision tonight. Just a precaution. No need to be alarmed." He headed back to his car. "I'll follow you to the shop. Make sure you're home safely. After that, stay put—we'll make an announcement on local news when it's all resolved."

"Uh, thanks." Sophie got back on her bike. So did Ethan. The police car drove slowly behind them the last half mile to the bookshop. Now that she was paying attention, it was eerie—the town felt too still and quiet, as if everyone were inside peering out through closed curtains. She wobbled at the traffic light, checked in both directions twice, even though there were no cars, and crossed. Beside her, Ethan was just as cautious. He kept pace with her and didn't zoom ahead. Every few feet, he glanced over his shoulder at the cruiser creeping along behind them. Sophie was very, very conscious of Monster in her backpack. She hoped he'd stay still and silent.

At the Dreamcatcher Bookshop, the policeman waved to them as they dismounted. Robot-like, they waved back. Speeding up, he drove away. "That was the most nerve-racking ride ever," Ethan said. "I kept worrying I was going to accidentally ride through a stop sign or mow down a little old lady. Not that I saw any. Or anyone."

"I kept worrying he'd see Monster."

"Ughhhhh," Monster moaned from the backpack. Glancing down the street, Sophie saw the policeman turn left at the next light. No other cars moved.

"Let's get inside," Ethan suggested. "It's too quiet out here. Kind of freaking me out."

"Murrrrrrrrrrrr-ugh," Monster said. Sophie took that to mean he agreed. Leading the way, she steered her bike onto the walk that led to the shop.

They stowed their bikes in the shed, and then Sophie unlocked the back door. Inside, the lights in the shop were off, and the aisles were filled with layers of shadows. It was silent. *They're not home,* she thought.

For an instant, she felt her eyes heat up. She wanted to curl into a ball and cry, or run out the door and scream until the policeman came back. But she didn't. When her parents got home, they were going to see she'd been brave, strong, and resourceful. They were going to see she could be trusted when things went wrong. They were going to be proud of her.

Lowering her backpack to the floor, Sophie unzipped it, and Monster lurched out. "Are you okay?" she asked.

"Just peachy." He flopped against a bookshelf. "Worst way to travel ever. Next time we go on a field trip, anything but bikes."

Sophie nodded, not entirely trusting herself to talk without bursting into tears. *Brave and strong,* she reminded herself. Like the heroes in her favorite books. She laid her hand on the spines of the nearest books, as if she could suck strength from them.

Ethan wandered between the shelves, peering down the aisles. "I take it your parents aren't back?" He peeked into the bathroom and tried the basement door—locked. "Why didn't you tell the policeman—"

His phone chirped from his pocket, and he pulled it out. "Huh. My parents." He sounded surprised. He began texting them back.

"What are you telling them?" Sophie tried to keep the worry out of her voice and was proud when it came out calm. She knew why she hadn't told the policeman; she wasn't sure why Ethan hadn't. He had the perfect opportunity to spill her family's secrets. If the Watchmen heard and came, he'd be fine.

He didn't look up from his phone. "Same thing I told the policeman: staying with a friend to do homework. It's weird, though—they never check on me."

"Maybe they heard about the missing kids?" She'd been so worried about her parents that she hadn't spared more than a second to wonder who the kids were or what happened to them.

"Wonder if it's anyone we know." Ethan typed more.

The odds that it was anyone she knew were low. It was more likely that Ethan knew them. He knew a lot of kids. Or, more accurately, they knew who he was. Checking Monster, she stroked between his eyes. He was taking deep breaths as if to settle his stomach. He flopped his tentacles over his face. "I have no appetite," Monster said.

"You'll feel better soon," she told him.

"It's unnatural," he said. "I'm *always* hungry. Maybe I should eat a cupcake, just to see." He placed a tentacle tip on Sophie's cheek. "Sophie, please don't worry. We'll figure this out. We'll find your parents."

Before she could reply, Ethan's phone chirped again. "Girl in seventh grade, they say," he said. His eyes widened. "Hey, I know her. Madison Moore."

Sophie gasped.

"You know her too?" Ethan asked. "She's the one with black hair and a shrill voice, right? You can hear her all the way down the hall."

Nodding, Sophie thought of how she'd been glad Madison wasn't on the bus. She hadn't wanted something bad to happen to her, though. She'd just been relieved to not be teased. "Madison's memorable."

"She has a little sister who's sick. Born sick. The family spends most of their time in the hospital with her. That's why Madison acts the way she does, like she's afraid she'll disappear if everyone doesn't notice her every second of the day."

Sophie blinked. "How do you know that?"

"My mom's her sister's doctor." The phone chirped again. "Oh, the other one I don't know. First-grader, named Lucy Snyder. The police don't know any connection between them, which is why everyone's so freaked out."

The name hit Sophie like a punch.

"Sophie?" Ethan touched her arm, but Sophie barely felt it. She knew both of them. She'd talked to them yesterday, taken their old dreamcatchers and given them new ones.

She sank to the floor next to Monster and told herself it was all a coincidence: her missing parents, the missing dreamers, the missing dreamcatchers, the missing dreams and the distiller . . . Just a coincidence.

"Sophie?" Monster echoed Ethan.

She felt as if her thoughts were swirling, bashing into one another. "I'm the connection."

"What do you mean?" Ethan asked.

"They're both dreamers. Nightmares. Bad ones. Like you. Madison dreams about fire and bugs. Lucy dreams about alligator people, ninjas that vanish into smoke, pit bulls that can fly . . ."

"Lots of people have dreams. Me, for instance." His phone beeped again. "Dad wants to know if I can stay here for dinner. Mom has to work late tonight, and he has meetings." Ethan gave a humorless laugh. "And there ends the extent of their concern." After texting back once more, he shoved the phone into his pocket. "Guess you're stuck with me."

Sophie felt as if every vein in her body suddenly ran with ice water. She couldn't move. She felt the blood drain out of her face.

"Hey, I'm not that bad," Ethan said.

She shook her head. "I know where I've seen that backpack."

"What backpack?"

Sophie jumped to her feet. "The one on the kitchen table, in Mr. Nightmare's house. I have to go back." She spun and headed for the back door.

Ethan caught her arm. "Whoa, hold on. You can't. Curfew, remember? What do you mean you've seen that backpack?"

"It's Lucy's." She was sure of it. Mostly sure. Maybe sure. "Or at least it could be."

"But you aren't positive?" He didn't release her arm. Trotting to her, Monster weaved between her ankles, as if to calm her.

Sophie shook her head. Lots of kids could have a pink and purple backpack. But she thought she remembered Lucy carrying one . . . "I'm not posi- tive." She sagged against the shelves. It could be her imagination. She wanted so desperately to find clues and connect the dots. Rubbing her forehead, Sophie tried telling her shrieking brain to quit overreacting. She didn't know it was Lucy's. It was far more likely it belonged to whatever little girl lived there.

"Sophie, we looked in every window," Ethan said. "Monster even looked in the upstairs windows. Right, Monster?"

"There could be a basement," Monster said. "Also, closets. Take it from me: You can hide anyone in a closet." He was right. Plus she'd seen cellar doors on the back of the house.

Maybe they'd all missed something. Maybe they simply hadn't explored enough. Maybe she'd been right to suspect him, even though she hadn't known about Lucy and Madison.

"We all agreed it looked normal," Ethan said.

"If you wanted to hide that you were a thief and a kidnapper, you'd make your house look normal too," Monster pointed out. "Lull people into thinking you've nothing to hide."

Sophie nodded. "Mr. Nightmare could have pretended to be cleaning out his garage like a normal person. He could have lied to us so we'd think he was innocent and go away."

"No one's that good an actor," Ethan objected.

Monster rolled his lemur-wide eyes. "Tons of people are great actors. Haven't you ever seen a movie? All actors. TV shows, actors. Broadway. Community theater. Every commercial ever made."

Sophie began to pace between the shelves. Her footsteps were loud on the wooden floor, and she was conscious of how quiet the house was. Her parents were always playing music somewhere, or talking, or making some kind of noise. She felt as if she could hear the emptiness. "I should have looked harder. Found a way to get inside. They could have been there, and we just left and rode away!"

Monster trailed after her as she zigzagged. "We'll go back."

"How? There's the curfew . . ." Stopping, Sophie faced Ethan. "Can you text your parents again? Ask them to drive us?"

Ethan snorted. "When I was six years old, my parents sat down with me and explained that if I wanted to do extracurricular activities, I'd have to arrange my own rides. Said they were teaching me self-reliance. When I asked what *self-reliance* meant, they said to look it up myself. So, short answer: no, they won't drive us."

She couldn't imagine her parents giving her that

kind of speech. She'd had it drilled into her to never, ever get into a car with anyone but them.

Monster was studying Ethan. "So your alone-in-an-ocean dream is directly metaphorical. How disappointing."

Ethan shot him a look. "What's wrong with my dream?"

"Much more interesting if it's random," Monster said. "Like the little kid who dreams about robot Muppets that shoot M&M's out of their Gonzo noses. Or the fifty-year-old businessman who dreams about chickens that transform into pigs for no apparent reason. There isn't as much demand for classic lonely dreams."

"Sorry my dreams are too boring for you." Ethan turned back to Sophie. "Anyway, I think you're jumping to conclusions. Just because you know the missing kids, and just because you think the backpack looks familiar . . . And because Mr. Nightmare left you that birthday card and we never asked him about the missing dreamcatchers. And because he was supposed to meet with your parents, and you came home to a mess upstairs and stuff stolen downstairs . . . Okay, maybe you have a point. Maybe we missed something."

"Exactly. You see why I have to go back," Sophie

said. "And this time, I have to get inside." She turned to Monster. "Do you think you could open a window lock?"

"I know I could," Monster said, flexing his tentacles.

"Wait a minute. Calm down. Let's talk about this," Ethan said. "I admit, it's possible we were wrong. *Possible*. But you want to break into this guy's house? You know that's illegal, right?"

Sophie didn't want to calm down. She paced between the shelves again. Outside in the distance, a dog barked. She didn't hear any cars. She imagined people home, glued to their TVs, wondering what had happened to the two missing kids. "I know Mr. Nightmare loves nightmares. He admitted as much. And I also know that both people I talked to yesterday have nightmares and are now missing."

"So? You talked to me, too—"

"And you were attacked by a gray giraffe," Monster finished.

Ethan's jaw dropped open. "You think . . ."

"I think you were next." In the shadows, Monster's eyes glowed bright. Sophie couldn't see his soft fur. All that was visible were his eyes and teeth. "It's too much of a coincidence otherwise. Two people who talked to Sophie about dreams are missing, and the third—you—was attacked."

Ethan closed his mouth but didn't speak.

It made a horrible kind of sense, Sophie thought. That gray creature . . . It could have kidnapped the other two and been trying to kidnap Ethan when Monster spotted it. It could work for Mr. Nightmare.

"I don't believe in coincidences," Monster said. "Except when they happen, which they do—coincidences aren't statistically improbable. But I don't think this is a coincidence."

Ethan's eyes were wide, rivaling Monster's. "You think he's not innocent, and we just rode away."

"I think I have to go back and at least see," Sophie said. "If I don't and I'm right and they're there . . ." She trailed off. She knew it was a stretch. She didn't have any proof, and everything they'd seen said she was wrong. But if she was right and she *didn't* go back . . . she'd never forgive herself. Ever. "He said he likes nightmares. If he did kidnap them, then he has his own personal supply—dreamers and people who can distill their dreams. I know you don't believe me . . ."

He swallowed hard. "I'm beginning to."

She turned to him. "Really?" He looked pale, as if he wanted to scream, flee, or faint, and she realized he must be thinking about how close he'd come to being one of the missing kids. He must want to run. In his shoes, she'd be out of here and home so fast . . .

"I'm coming with you."

Sophie blinked at him. "You don't have to—"

"Yes, I do," he said.

Monster looked at him piercingly. "Of course you do. You're the boy with boring, lonely dreams. Your parents taught you no one would save you. So you have to save yourself. If we're correct and that gray giraffe was really coming for you, then you believe you have to be the one to stop it."

Ethan looked uncomfortable. Watching him, Sophie wondered if Monster was right. It was hard to imagine her school's star basketball player—the new kid that everyone instantly befriended—as lonely, but he did have the Nothing dream . . .

"Besides," Monster continued, "if you're a hero, maybe your parents will finally notice you."

Without responding, Ethan walked toward the front of the store. He stopped next to the cash register and looked out the window at the street. "So how do we get back to Mr. Nightmare's?"

Sophie joined him at the window. "I don't know."

Keeping to the shadows between the shelves,

Monster said hesitantly, "Sophie, I have an idea, but you aren't going to like it."

She'd like any idea that wasn't them standing here, worrying about whether she was right or wrong, worrying about whether her parents and Madison and Lucy were trapped in that house and she'd ridden away without knowing . . .

"We could fly," Monster said.

12

"YOU CAN *FLY?*" ETHAN ASKED.

"Not me. No wings." Monster flapped his tentacles. "But there are plenty of dreams about creatures who can fly . . ."

Sophie suddenly realized what he was suggesting, and she retreated so fast that she smacked into a bookshelf. Books wobbled as the shelf rocked. "No. No. And in case that's not clear: No! I promised!"

Monster ducked farther into the shadows. He drew his tentacles around him, making himself as small as possible. "Knew you wouldn't like it. Never mind. It's a terrible idea. We'll come up with another plan."

Ethan looked from Sophie to the shadows that held Monster and back again. "Wait, what's the idea? Fly how?"

"He wants . . ." She stopped. He wanted her to drink a flying dream, but she couldn't say that without revealing what happened when she dreamed. "Never mind. Maybe I'm wrong about this. Maybe it wasn't Lucy's backpack, and Mr. Nightmare has nothing to do with my parents or the gray creature."

"Or maybe you're right and we missed something," Ethan said. "He won't be expecting us to come back. If we can find a way to sneak in without him noticing . . . Maybe go in through the basement?"

"You changed your tune quick," Monster commented.

"You convinced me. Or, more accurately, the gray giraffe did."

Sophie stared out the window, wishing that she saw her parents walking up to the door as if nothing had happened. A dreamcatcher twisted as she brushed against it. It sparkled in the sunlight, casting a hundred shards of light on the floor. This late in the day, the sun was low in the sky, and it spilled straight through the window. Outside, all the shadows were rosy and long, blending as they melted together on the asphalt. Car windshields reflected the soon-to-set sun, and she heard a dog bark, wanting to be walked. But no one came outside. A police car drove by again, slowly. The street was empty. Yards and driveways were empty. No one was taking out the trash or taking in the mail or playing basketball or jumping rope or riding bikes or doing anything at all outside. It was even more noticeable than earlier— word must have spread. She thought of the policeman saying there would be an announcement on the local news and wondered if everyone was glued to their TV, waiting for the kids to be found. But the kids wouldn't be found if she was right, because no one knew about Mr. Nightmare or the gray giraffe-man. "Fine. I'll do it." She turned to Monster. "But we take a dream-catcher, and we turn the flying whatever back into a dream as soon as Mom and Dad and the others are safe."

Without waiting for Monster or Ethan to respond, Sophie spun around and marched to the basement stairs. She hoped she wouldn't regret this. For six years, she'd kept her promise. But for six years, her parents had been safe. If Mr. Nightmare really had them . . . If she'd been to his house and they'd been there, or if she'd missed a clue to where they were and she'd left without noticing . . . then she had to do this.

"Anyone want to fill me in?" Ethan asked, following.

"She's going to drink a dream," Monster said.

"Okay. And?"

"And then she'll dream."

Sophie hurried to the ledger and flipped through. She needed a flying dream, but not just a dreamer-flies-like-a-superhero kind of dream. All three of them needed to fly.

Not a plane. She wouldn't know how to fly that.

Magic carpet? Maybe. But not a runaway one.

Monster hopped onto the counter to look at the ledger with her. "I think whatever you bring out of the dream has to *want* to come out of the dream."

"What do you mean?" Sophie asked.

"I've given it a lot of thought over the years—why me? Why not the bed or the blanket or the toys? There was an entire room of things, yet only I came out of the dream. I think it's because I wanted to come. In the moment you said you wished I could be your pet, I chose to be with you."

Sophie looked at the ledger again. "So you think I have to convince a dream thing to come?"

"It's possible. Or maybe I came out because I'm furry and cute. Or it's the tentacles. Or it's random luck. I only have one data point."

Ethan held out his hands. "Wait. Back up here. You came out of Sophie's dream?"

Sophie took a deep breath and hoped her parents would understand. "I don't dream, not normally. When I do . . . things come to life. That's where Monster came from. So I'm going to drink a dream with something that can fly us across town."

Ethan's jaw dropped. He then shut it and nodded. "Yeah, that's not any crazier than anything that's happened so far. Okay, so what kind of flying thing?" He joined them at the ledger.

"Just like that?" Sophie asked. "You're not freaking out?"

He shrugged. "I'll freak out later. The school counselor calls it repression. Says it's an unhealthy coping mechanism. But at least I'm coping, right?" Looking over Sophie's shoulder, he pointed at a line. "What's that?"

Sophie tore her gaze from him and looked at the ledger. "Flying hippopotamus."

"Not stealthy enough," Monster said.

Sophie read on, skimming for relevant dreams. "Giant bat?"

"Possible." Monster scampered over to the shelves.

"No. Gone. It was filed under monsters, and it's missing with the others. Pity. That would have been fun."

She scanned down the list, picking out a few more flying creatures. Dragons—all of those had been sold. Gryphons—also sold. Fairies—too small. Phoenixes—too fiery. Gargoyles—filed under monsters, so they were gone. "Winged ponies?"

Monster wrinkled his nose.

"They're meant to carry people," Sophie said.

"But they're so sparkly," Monster complained.

"All the monsters are gone. Besides, this isn't about looking good."

"I always look good," Monster said automatically, then sighed. "Fine. I'll find the ponies." He climbed the shelves, sorted through a few bottles, and then selected one. Carrying it in his tentacle, he climbed down. "Check it first. It would be a shame to drink the dream and then discover the ponies are six inches tall."

Carefully, as if she were holding the most fragile egg in the world, Sophie carried the bottle across the basement to the somnium. *Please work,* she thought as she poured it in the top.

The clouds swirled in the base of the somnium.

"What are we looking for?" Ethan asked.

"You'll see the dream here." She pointed to the fattest part of the tube.

The blue sparkle touched the smoke, and Sophie leaned closer to the glass. Ethan squeezed next to her, and Monster put his front paws on the table and rose onto his hind legs to see. He tucked his tentacles underneath the somnium.

Images began to appear: the post office, the supermarket, the gas station, and then a house she didn't recognize. It was white with blue shutters. The windows were dark, as if smudged with soot, or as if nothing were outside. Dreams were often like that, with incomplete houses and hints of objects that implied full rooms. The dream was silent, of course — the somnium was always silent, another way watching a dream wasn't the same as experiencing one.

Sophie tried not to feel excited. She was doing this because she had to, because her parents were in danger (possibly), not because she was seizing the first excuse she'd had in years to drink a dream. She *had* said no.

The dreamer opened the door of the white house, stepped inside, and onto a cloud. Clouds were all around: a town shaped out of them. Houses were shaped out of clouds. Trees were puffy swirls of cloud.

Rainbows arched between them. And then the winged ponies appeared: a herd of them, flying between the clouds.

One of the ponies halted in front of the dreamer. She climbed on and they flew, swooping and soaring, joining the herd as more rainbows shot into the sky around them.

Below, there was an ocean. All the ponies plunged into it, and then they were gone, and the dreamer was in a classroom clutching a pencil . . . The dream shattered as the teacher turned around with a mouth that filled his entire face. He stretched his mouth in a silent roar, which widened and widened until it swallowed the classroom like a whale in the water.

The dream went dark.

"Weird," Ethan said.

"Actually that was reasonably coherent," Sophie said. "You should see some of them. Completely useless for resale. This one will be hard to sell because it's a mix of nice parts and not nice. Buyers prefer the dreams with more consistency." Or so her parents said. It felt strange trying to sound like an expert. "Guess I try to wake up before the part with the teacher."

"You don't need to be afraid. I'll be right here with you the whole time," Monster promised.

The dream dripped back into the bottle, and she picked it up, then turned to Ethan. "I need you to promise that you'll never tell anyone about this." She clutched the bottle to her chest. If she was wrong about what was going on, her parents were going to be furious. But if she was right . . . Either way, she couldn't sit here, hide, and hope everything was okay. It was already very much not okay. "Please."

He shrugged. "Still not clear what's going on."

"That wasn't a promise." Monster drew himself up taller on the counter. His tentacles writhed around him, making him look like an octopus with the ocean currents around him. "You will promise."

Ethan took a step backward toward the stairs. "Sophie, I think your 'housecat' is threatening me."

Not for the first time, Sophie wondered what Monster had been like in the original dream, before she'd interfered. The dreamer must have woken up terrified. "He won't hurt you."

"That is not an entirely correct assumption." Monster bared his three rows of teeth. "Promise, and I won't. Don't promise, and you won't like the consequences."

Sophie smacked Monster lightly. "Stop that."

"This isn't the time for your delicate human

sensibilities, Sophie. He needs to promise. Your safety depends on it." Before she could stop him, Monster launched himself off the counter and across the floor toward Ethan. Sophie hurried after him, but Monster was quicker. He wrapped his tentacles around Ethan's wrists, black bands like handcuffs. "My Sophie is very special to me. You *will* promise."

Trying to shake him off, Ethan shrank away. "Okay, okay, I promise."

Monster released him so fast that Ethan staggered backward and bumped into a shelf. Bottles rocked and clinked into one another. Kneeling, Sophie scratched Monster on the head. "Uh, he's normally very sweet." She'd been right never to bring friends home. She shot Monster a warning look and mouthed, *Behave.*

Sweetly, Monster wrapped his tentacles around her neck. "Don't worry, Sophie. I'll be right here with you." Tentacles around her shoulders, he led her to a beanbag chair in the corner. She sank into it.

Ethan hung back. "Now what happens?"

"Now, Sophie sleeps."

"But what—"

"Shh." Monster snuggled next to Sophie. She put her arm around him and stared at the bottle. The promise she'd made to her parents echoed in her head.

She thought again of the backpack she'd seen on the kitchen table. She wished she was sure whether it was Lucy's. It could all still be a coincidence, including the gray giraffe.

There was one way to be sure, if she dared.

Taking off the stopper, Sophie drank the dream.

13

SHE WAS ON THE STREET OUTSIDE THE POST OFFICE building.

Above the post office, the sky was smeared blue. On either side, the buildings were blurry, as if she were seeing them through cloudy glasses. All the windows were gray. She didn't know why she was here. Did she have to mail a letter? She opened the door to the post office . . .

Inside was a classroom. Back to the door, the teacher was writing on the chalkboard, and Sophie remembered in a rush: watching the dream in the somnium, sitting on the floor with Monster, drinking the bottle. But in the somnium, the teacher appeared at the end of the dream. She was messing up the order. She was supposed to find the winged ponies first.

Shutting the door, Sophie jogged away from the

post office. The houses were indistinct smudges on either side of her. She craned her neck, looking for the white house with blue shutters. The street was silent. No cars, no buses, no bikes.

Behind her, she heard footsteps.

Glancing over her shoulder, she saw the teacher. His face was only a mouth. No eyes. No nose. He spoke: "You cannot escape me."

His mouth began to open, wider and wider, and the post office was sucked into his mouth. A few buildings followed, like a painting ripped from a wall. This wasn't what was supposed to happen! She must have changed the dream.

Sophie ran.

Ahead was the white house with blue shutters. She heard a whooshing sound, like water going down a drain. *Don't look. Just run.*

She threw herself at the door. Yanking it open, she glanced back. The teacher's mouth had stretched impossibly wide, and the street was flowing into it like a river. She jumped through the door and shut it behind her.

The door promptly disappeared.

She was in the clouds. Sophie exhaled. She didn't think he could follow her if the door was gone. And the teacher hadn't been in this part of the dream. Only the winged ponies. She was safe. Maybe.

Harp music played, chords plucked at random, no clear melody. All around her, pink fluffy clouds drifted into the shapes of castles and trees and mountains. She was standing on one cloud, and a rainbow unfurled over her head as if it were a ribbon tossed through the air.

Monster would hate this, she thought.

Several winged ponies flew between the clouds, a rainbow of pastel colors: pinks, purples, baby blues, above the real rainbows.

"Hello?" she called to the ponies. "Can any of you help me? I need help!"

One of the ponies paused midflight. "Who calls for help?" His voice was as deep as a foghorn. Leaving the herd, he flew toward her. His hide shimmered as if he'd been painted with glitter, and he had a silver unicorn horn spiraling up from the center of his forehead. "Oh, my, it's a damsel in distress!"

"I need—" she began.

Flapping his wings, he rose higher. "Come with me," he commanded. "The others must hear your words."

"But I can't fly!"

"Use the rainbow." He pointed with his horn at a rainbow that kissed the nearest cloud.

He couldn't mean she should walk on the rainbow, could he? She'd fall! Except she wasn't falling through the cloud, and this *was* a dream . . . Crossing to the rainbow, Sophie tapped the yellow band with her foot, and her toes sank into the colorful mist. She tested putting weight on her foot—and it held. Taking a deep breath, she climbed onto the rainbow.

Ahead of her, the winged pony trumpeted, "Assemble, my friends! There is a damsel in distress!" He whinnied loudly and flicked his tail to catch the attention of the other ponies. "Attend to me!"

Several ponies circled closer, flying around the rainbow. A few of them had unicorn horns; a few didn't. One had flowers braided into her mane. "How can we aid you, Damsel?" the pony with flowers asked. She had a voice like a wind chime, light and tinkling.

Quickly, Sophie explained everything as best she could: about herself, about the Dream Shop, about her parents, about the missing kids, and about Mr. Nightmare.

When she finished, the ponies turned to each other, whickering and whinnying. She heard one say,

"I am *not* a dream. Such lies! Such nerve!" Others echoed her.

One by one, they took flight. Plucking at the top of a cloud tree, one pony swallowed a mouthful of pink cloud before flying away. Another dived inside a cloud castle, and the drawbridge (made of clouds) shut behind him with a poofing noise. The pony with flowers snorted at Sophie and then flew up toward the sun.

"Wait! Please! It *is* true, I swear!" Sophie called after them. "And after it's over, I promise I'll send you back into a dream." This *had* to work! She was risking so much . . . "Come back!"

At last only the glittery unicorn remained. Lowering himself onto the rainbow beside her, he sniffed her hair and puffed air in her face. "I have often wished for a quest of my own. Please, tell me more, Damsel. What would I have to do to complete this implausible task?"

She took a deep breath and told herself it wasn't over yet. She needed only one pony. "You have to come with me out of the dream, and then fly me and my friends to a particular house and then back safely, without being seen."

"And what will be my reward?"

She had no idea what a winged unicorn who lived in a world made of fluffy clouds would like. She'd never even ridden a regular horse. She'd read a few girl-with-horse books—one showed a girl giving an apple to a stallion on the cover. "An apple?"

He considered it. "Indeed, that would be most—"

Before he could finish, the rainbow beneath them evaporated. Sophie plummeted. Wind tore at her as she clawed at empty air. She felt as if her whole body was screaming.

"Dive, Damsel, dive! Down into the foam, down in the briny deep!" the iridescent unicorn cried. "Down to our destiny! Dive, my brave friends!" He flattened his wings to his sides, and dived straight down toward the sea. Other ponies dived around him.

No, no, no! She knew this part of the dream— below was the ocean, and once they splashed down, she'd be in the classroom with the teacher. The dream couldn't end yet! He hadn't said yes. "Come with me!" she called. She didn't know if he could hear her.

The ocean rose toward them. The ponies hit the waves one after another as the clouds tumbled around them, the castle falling apart. Then she was in the foam, and the waves crashed over her head, and the ponies had all disappeared, as if they'd dissolved into the surf. Water poured down her throat and—

She sat in a classroom. The teacher was at the blackboard. In chalk, he'd written: *You cannot escape.* Jumping to her feet, Sophie ran toward the door. She had to reach it before the teacher turned. Lunging for it, she yanked it open—

And there was nothing there. Vast emptiness before her.

A hand clamped onto her shoulder. She spun around, and the eyeless teacher opened his mouth wide. She screamed and threw her arms in front of her face—

14

A VOICE BOOMED IN SOPHIE'S EAR. "GOOD MORNING, Damsel! Or perhaps it's afternoon. Difficult to tell in this cave of yours."

Sophie pried her eyes open, and the winged pony blew air in her face.

Sophie's eyes watered. The pony's breath smelled like overripe strawberries. Slowly, as if swimming to the surface of the ocean, her brain woke, and she realized she was back in the Dream Shop. "It worked! You're here!"

"Of course I am. You are a damsel in distress, and I am supremely heroic. But before we begin our quest, I have a few complaints: I can't see the sun, the clouds are much too firm under my hooves" — he pranced, demonstrating, and his hooves rang like chimes — "and lastly, it . . . well, not to be rude, but quite frankly, this place smells. I think that's because it's infested with monsters."

Sophie shot up to sitting.

Beside the winged pony, Monster waved hello with his tentacles. Sophie relaxed. "That's my friend Monster." She pointed at Monster, then Ethan. "And that's Ethan. And my name's Sophie, not Damsel."

Eyes wide, a dazed Ethan raised his hand. "Uh, hi."

"Humph," the pony sniffed. "And *that* one?"

From beside the somnium, a man slinked out of the shadows. He had no eyes or nose, and when he opened his mouth, it stretched so wide that the skin curled back to where his ears should have been. Jumping to her feet, Sophie cried, "Watch out!"

The eyeless man inhaled, and the bottles tumbled from the shelves and flew into his gaping maw. Other bottles across the room rattled together.

"Get a dreamcatcher!" Monster yelled as he launched himself toward the man's legs.

Sophie threw herself at a counter and grabbed one of the nearly complete dreamcatchers. It lacked the feathers and ribbons, but the threads were all there. She clung to the counter as suction pulled at her. Her feet lifted off the ground.

"Sophie!" Monster released the man's leg and wrapped his tentacles around her, trying to pull her down. He wrapped two tentacles around the distiller table leg to anchor himself.

Both of them were pulled toward the man's overwide mouth, and Sophie felt her grip on the counter begin to slip. She screamed, and Ethan lunged for her. He grabbed her around the waist, and all three of them were lifted into the air.

Neighing as loudly as a trumpet, the winged pony charged from the opposite side. He pinned the man to the wall with his horn, piercing the man's shirt collar, close to his throat. Abruptly, the man closed his mouth.

Sophie crashed to the floor. Scrambling forward, she pressed a dreamcatcher against him. "Move away," she ordered the pony. "You can't be touching him."

The unicorn stepped back, and the man opened his mouth again. The wind howled in her face, but both Monster and Ethan held on to her ankles, anchoring her from below the gale. She felt the pull as if being sucked in by a tornado.

At last, the man faded and then disappeared. Sophie fell to her knees.

Releasing her, Ethan flopped onto his back. "What was *that?*" he panted.

"Not a nice monster," Monster said. "Curious. Or perhaps not. Sophie, were you afraid of him in the dream?"

"Of the terrifying vacuum-mouth man? Gee, let me think . . . Yes, obviously."

As if this satisfied him, Monster nodded. "So he came out as you expected him to. Like I did. You expected him to be terrifying, and he was. You expected me to be your friend, and I am."

"But why did he come out at all? I didn't want him to."

"Perhaps *he* wanted to. My theory still holds. I chose to come out of the dream, and so did vacuum-man and the obnoxiously sparkly pony."

Ethan rolled onto his side to look at Sophie. "Why did he disappear? What did you do?"

Sophie held up the dreamcatcher. "Changed him back into a dream."

"But . . . how?"

"You need to hold the dreamcatcher onto the dream creature for long enough for it to dissolve back into a dream. A single touch won't work, which is a good thing because otherwise, Monster would be in constant danger." She wrapped her arms around Monster, and he squeezed tightly with all his tentacles.

"So, do you do this all the time?" Ethan's voice was shaking, but she could tell he was trying to sound cool and unfazed. "Run around town, create and dissolve dreams, like some kind of superhero?"

Any second, he was going to bolt out of the shop screaming. Or lose it and start yelling at her. This was too much. Repression or not, he was going to freak out. "I've never done it before today," Sophie said as soothingly as she could.

"If you've never done it, how did you know what to do?"

Monster fluffed his fur and stepped in front of Sophie. "Her parents told her how to do it, when they taught her how to destroy me. They thought she needed to know in case my monster tendencies got the better of me." He bared his three rows of teeth.

Ethan backed up quickly. He thumped against the somnium table, and the glass tubes clinked as they bumped into one another. He jumped away from the table and then backed against a counter. "I didn't mean . . . Sorry. This is just, you know, new to me." His voice squeaked on the last word.

"And to me," the pony put in. "Quite frankly, I always imagined my first quest would be in a more majestic location with much more savory companions. Perhaps it would be best if I returned to my dream."

Sophie took a deep breath. It was too late for Ethan to flee or for the winged unicorn to change his mind. She'd already broken her most serious promise to her parents, and she was determined to see this through. She tried changing the subject. "What's your name?" she asked the winged pony.

"Glitterhoof."

Monster snorted.

Glitterhoof shot a look at Monster, then tossed his mane. Sparkles sprayed up in a cloud, dusting the Dream Shop in a fine layer of glitter. "It is an honorable and accurate name, Smelly Monster."

"Just Monster," Sophie corrected, trying to brush glitter off her shirt. It clung to her fingers. Ethan had glitter in his hair. Monster had dodged most of it.

Sliding closer to Sophie, Ethan said, "I'm sorry. Guess I didn't really believe you before." He lowered his voice to a whisper. "Just have a couple questions . . . Is he really . . . you know, real? Is he alive? Is he going to fade away? How long will he last? Will he go back to being a dream? When he's in the dream, does he exist when no one's dreaming him? Or is he, for all practical purposes, dead?" He lowered his voice on the last word.

"I'm right here, and I can hear you," Glitterhoof said.

Ethan blushed bright red. "Sorry. It's just . . . All this . . ." He raked his hand through his blond hair. "I mean, wow."

Glitterhoof tossed his mane, shedding glitter again. "I understand your wish to know more. I *am* supremely interesting."

Monster snorted again. "He also can't answer you, because he doesn't know. *I* can tell you that when I was a dream, that's all there was. We exist within the dream, like characters exist inside a book. The dream doesn't change, unless it's dreamed again. Like a book rewritten. You feel safe inside your dream. You know you belong there."

Sophie felt a little lurch in her heart. "You belong here, Monster."

He patted her with a tentacle. "I know I do. But at first, it feels strange."

She'd had no idea. He'd never said anything like

this before. "Monster . . ." She didn't know how to ask if he ever missed being in his dream. She wasn't sure she wanted to hear the answer.

"As for how long he'll last . . . Got me. I was told that I was an exceptionally vivid dream. The disco pony here, his dream was murkier. Who knows?"

"Again, you are discussing me while I am here. Highly rude." Wrinkling his nose, Glitterhoof sniffed and turned to Sophie. "You promised a noble quest. There is nothing heroically grand about a musty old cave filled with grumpy monsters."

"Right. Come on." She stood and checked the clock. Her parents certainly should have been home for dinner. They always ate dinner together. Yet more proof that they were in danger, not merely out running an errand. She tried to shove the last of her doubts aside. It was too late for second, or third, thoughts. Leading the way, she stopped at the stairs. "Um, can you climb stairs?"

Folding his wings on his back, Glitterhoof glared at Sophie. "I am not a cow."

"Yeah, I see that," Ethan said.

"Cows can't walk up stairs," Monster explained. "Their knees are backward. Also, they're stupid."

"Precisely." Tossing his mane, Glitterhoof marched on his four golden hooves up the stairs and then trotted through the bookshop. Craning his neck, he looked around the shop. He barely fit between the shelves. The tips of his wings brushed the spines of the books. "What are these things that clutter up your cloud?"

"Books," Sophie said.

"What are 'books'? Are they tasty?" Stopping, he nibbled at one, an old copy of *Jane Eyre* with a cloth spine.

Sophie rushed to stop him. "You don't eat them! You read them. They're written-down stories. You know stories?" Glitterhoof continued to chew, taking out a chunk of *Pride and Prejudice*. "Dreams! They're like dreams. But dreams that you have while you're awake."

"Oh my!" Glitterhoof spat bits of paper out on the floor. One hit Sophie's shoe, and she read the words "no compassion for my poor nerves."

Monster scooted past them, heading for the back door. "Can we move along?"

Ethan followed. "Are we really going to ride that?"

"I am not a *that*," Glitterhoof said. "I am a pegasus, direct descendant of Poseidon and foaled by the
Gorgon Medusa during the moment in which Perseus
decapitated her—which, by the way, was rude."
Swiveling his head, he fixed his sparkling eyes on
Ethan. "*You*, on the other hand, are descended from
dirt."

"Monkeys, actually," Monster corrected. Twisting
the knob with a tentacle, he pushed the back door
open. "And *you* were designed by a toy company."

Glitterhoof slammed the door shut with his hoof.

Spinning around, Monster bared his teeth.

Sophie stepped between them. "Not now. Please,
Monster. Glitterhoof, we're honored to have the help
of such a noble . . ." She hesitated, not sure what word
wouldn't offend him. She didn't have a lot of practice
flattering people. Or ponies. "I know this isn't what
you expected for your first quest, but there are people
in danger, and we really do need your help. You could
save the day."

Mollified, Glitterhoof lowered his hoof from the
door. "Very well. It is in my nature to be both heroic
and magnanimous. Forgiveness is a hallmark of great-
ness."

Shooting a warning look at Monster, Sophie turned to Ethan. "Ethan, can you show Glitterhoof the map so he knows where we're going?"

"Oh, right." Ethan pulled out his phone and showed the pegasus the map, switching it so it looked like an aerial view. After expressing amazement at the device, Glitterhoof studied the map.

Softly, Sophie said to Monster, "Try to be nice. He's here to help."

"He's not physically possible," Monster complained. "His wingspan cannot possibly support his body weight. A pigeon weighs about a pound, and its wingspan is a foot. Average horse weighs more than a thousand pounds. He'd need a thousand-foot wingspan. Besides, pegasi don't have horns. He's not a purebred pegasus; he's a mutt. And he's shedding glitter, which is weird."

Sticking his nose in the air and studiously pretending he couldn't hear Monster, Glitterhoof asked Sophie, "Would you prefer to travel by flight or rainbow?"

That wasn't a question she'd ever been asked before. "Uh . . . flight?"

"Then climb onto my back. We will exit quickly

and stealthily, and we will fly high above the clouds so we cannot be seen." He knelt his front knees on the floor. Sophie climbed on first, and Monster jumped up into her lap. Ethan swung on behind her and wrapped his arms around Sophie's waist. "Hold tight," Glitterhoof commanded. "If you must vomit, please try to aim away from my glorious mane."

"Can't believe I promised not to tell anyone," Ethan said. "This is awesome."

"Yes, indeed. I am pure, unadulterated awesomeness, not a toy or a mutt. I am going to fly so fast that the humans will not be able to see us." He bashed the door open, folded his wings tight to his sides to fit through, and squeezed out the opening. On the step, he paused as he gazed at the backyard with its aluminum shed, patchy lawn, and unweeded herb garden. "Ooh, so many colors!"

Sophie squeezed his mane. "Fly! Quickly!"

"My apologies, Damsel." The pegasus launched into the air. His wings flapped, and all the stray twigs and leaves in the yard swirled into the air. He shot through the debris toward the sky.

Sophie felt her stomach plummet. Wind battered her face, and she had to squeeze her eyes closed.

Monster dug his claws into her arm, and Ethan's arms tightened around her waist. The wind sounded like a shriek. She felt water droplets batter her face.

Steadying, the pegasus flew straight and even. Sophie cracked her eyes open and looked down. Clouds streaked the view below them. Cars looked like toys between the houses. Roofs made a patchwork, and the streets looked like black rivers. Pointing past her face, Ethan shouted, "There! Left! Go left!"

Tilting, Glitterhoof dived to the left. Sophie clung to his mane. Monster's fur was fully fluffed. His face was hidden in black fuzz.

Below, the park looked like it was made of green felt, and the playground was made of brightly colored toothpicks. Soon, they were soaring over curlicue neighborhoods with identical houses and abnormally green lawns. Each driveway had an SUV in it.

Sophie wished she could enjoy this. The dying sun felt warm on her back, and the wind blew in her face so hard that it felt like it wanted to blow away every worry, every fear, and every doubt she'd ever had — but it didn't work. She couldn't forget her parents were missing.

After the snarl of identical houses, the view

changed again, and the houses were more spread out with thick clumps of trees. Sophie hadn't realized they'd biked so far earlier.

"See that?" Ethan shouted over the wind. "Those trees! His house is the only one."

From up here, Sophie could see that Mr. Nightmare had no neighbors. There were thick wooded areas on all sides, which made it a perfect isolated location for a kidnapper. She could also see he had an above-ground pool and a deck, which didn't fit her image of a kidnapper. She wondered if she was wrong, for a second time. He could be 100 percent innocent, and she might be hoping too hard to see connections when there were none.

In front, tucked near the trees, were three cars: Mr. Nightmare's blue car plus two others. Maybe he had friends over? *Oh no, more people to avoid,* she thought. That could make this harder—or, if they were lucky, easier. With luck, the friends would distract Mr. Nightmare, and he wouldn't notice Sophie, Ethan, and Monster creeping around.

The pegasus spiraled down, circling the house. "There is a cave beside the dwelling. I will hide in it." Without waiting for a response, Glitterhoof flattened his wings to his sides and plummeted. The ground raced toward them, and Sophie clutched his mane. Her fingers dug into her palms. Monster hissed at the wind, and Ethan pressed against her back, holding on as tightly as a seat belt.

Glitterhoof shot into Mr. Nightmare's detached garage. He braked with his wings and landed gently. Even his hooves were silent on the concrete floor. "Speed *and* stealth."

"Yeah, very impressive." Monster slid off his back into a heap. On wobbling legs, he staggered away and then leaned against a lawn mower to pant. His tentacles hung as limp as cooked noodles. Sophie climbed off with Ethan. Her head was spinning, and she kept one hand on Glitterhoof's neck to steady herself.

"Do I earn an extra apple for that landing?" Glitterhoof asked, hopeful.

Sophie patted his mane. "It was a wonderful landing. Thank you. Definitely an extra apple. And if you stay hidden and wait for us, you can have as many apples as you want." She hoped she didn't sound as nervous as she felt. She'd never sneaked into a house before. They'd have to be very, very careful.

Glitterhoof whinnied (quietly) in approval.

Sophie felt Monster looking at her as he licked his fur flat. "What?" she whispered.

"You bribed him with fruit."

"So? He likes apples."

Monster sauntered past Sophie to the entrance of the garage. "Not a problem. I'm just happy you didn't tell him about the cupcakes."

Behind them, Glitterhoof cried softly, "What cupcakes?"

15

SOPHIE SCURRIED ACROSS THE YARD AND DUCKED
between the bushes that lined the house. Ethan and
Monster joined her. She listened for shouts or alarms,
but all she heard was muffled cheers. She guessed
someone—maybe Mr. Nightmare and his friends—
was watching TV, a football game or a boxing match.
They inched along the side of the house. Dropping to
her hands and knees, Sophie peeked around the corner into the backyard.

"Who's that?" Ethan whispered near her shoulder.

Lounging on a chair by the cellar doors was the
most enormous man she'd ever seen. He looked like he
ate pro wrestlers for breakfast. Muscles bulged from
his neck and were threaded with veins. His head was
so much narrower than his neck that it looked like

it might pop off. The lawn chair sagged underneath him. Maybe he was a friend of Mr. Nightmare's? One of the cars in front was probably his. "Let's not find out," Sophie whispered back.

She retreated, and Ethan and Monster backed up too. Branches scratched her arms. She halted when she bumped into Ethan, who had stopped. "Look," Monster whispered. He pointed at a basement window, covered in a mat of leaves. "I think I can unlock it."

Using his tentacles, he fiddled with the window until at last it popped open. Squeezing inside, Monster disappeared into the darkness. "Monster, wait," Sophie whispered. She flattened onto her stomach next to the window and tried to see in. It was as if the basement had eaten him. She couldn't see him, or anything else.

After several long seconds, he stuck a tentacle through the window and waved. "Come quickly."

"Mom and Dad?"

He poked his head out. "No, but you have to see this."

Ethan helped her pull the window open wider. She wriggled through and then dropped to the ground, landing with a squishing sound on a pile of wet towels. She heard the low buzz of several voices, men and women, their voices blending together into a steady hum— *The TV,* she thought, except it didn't sound like a TV anymore.

"This way," Monster whispered. He tugged on her hand with a tentacle, and she followed him around the corner, past the cellar doors that led to the backyard and the man with all the muscles.

It took a few seconds for her eyes to adjust to the dim, flickering lights. When they did . . . "Whoa," she breathed. She and Monster were on a balcony—a dark gray concrete slab with a railing that overlooked a sandpit.

Behind her, she heard a soft thump. Ethan. "Where are you?"

"Shh," both Sophie and Monster said, and Sophie added, "Around the corner."

Creeping closer to the balcony railing, Sophie looked down into the pit. It was a circle of sand surrounded by a chainlink fence that reached up to where they stood. Outside the fence, below them, were five people on a wooden bench. All of them were watching the empty pit.

"What's going on?" Sophie whispered. "What are they waiting for?"

"It looks like a gladiator thing. You know, from a video game. 'Two men enter; one man leaves.' Or is that from a movie?" Ethan pointed. "Look. Something's happening."

A man walked forward. His face was in shadow, but he held up a key. As he displayed it, right, then left, as if he were a magician about to do a trick, the people on the bench cheered.

He pushed a cage up to the door of the sandpit. Sophie couldn't see what was inside, but the cage rocked from side to side. Climbing onto the top of the cage, the man brandished the key again, and then with a flourish, stuck it into a lock and raised the door.

"This isn't good," Monster murmured.

"Behold, Specimen One!" the man cried.

Jumping to his feet, one of the onlookers punched his fists into the air. A woman stamped her feet and whistled, and music suddenly switched on. Heavy drumbeats thudded through the basement, and a guitar wailed as a monster charged out of the cage and into the pit.

Lit by the bulbs overhead, the monster was shriveled and bald. It blinked at the audience with six black eyes that looked like marbles stuck into its bulbous flesh. It had two squat legs and four muscular arms that sprouted out of its back.

"It's scared," Monster said.

The monster flexed its four arms and roared, and the watchers cheered louder.

"Or maybe angry," Monster amended.

Behind the four-armed monster, the cage slammed shut and so did the pit door. Roaring again, the monster pivoted and ran on its feet and knuckles like a gorilla toward the cage door. It grabbed the fence and tried to climb it.

"Correction: *very* angry."

The man in charge poked it with a pole, and as he twisted for another jab, Sophie caught a glimpse of his face—Mr. Nightmare.

"You were right," Ethan said. "He is a good actor."

The monster swiped at the pole, but Mr. Nightmare pulled it back fast. He poked again, and the monster fell backward onto the sand.

As the onlookers cheered again, Mr. Nightmare sauntered to the pit door. He shoved a second crate in position in front of it. Facing his audience, he raised his fist and the pole into the air, encouraging them to cheer even louder, and then he lifted the door to the second crate. "Specimen Two!" he cried. "Ready your bids!"

A second monster tumbled into the sandpit. This one had an elongated shark's mouth, a flat face, and spider legs. It was also coated in goo. As it saw the first monster, it hissed.

Sophie leaned forward to see it better. There was something familiar about it . . . and then suddenly she knew why the second monster looked familiar. She'd seen it before: in the somnium. "Monster, I think that's one of ours. Please, tell me I'm wrong."

He didn't say anything.

The first monster spotted the second one. Roaring, it charged.

The second monster opened its mouth and yellow slime spewed out, covering the first monster. The crowd fell silent for half a second, and then roared their approval.

"It *is* like a gladiator match," Ethan said.

"With monsters. *Our* monsters." Shuddering, Monster wrapped his tentacles around Sophie's leg. Below them, snarling and snapping, the two monsters in the ring tore at each other while the crowd howled louder.

16

Sophie BACKED AWAY FROM THE RAILING.

"What? What's wrong?" Ethan asked in a whisper. "Okay, yes, stupid question. Everything's wrong. But specifically, what's wrong now? You look like you've seen a ghost. Are there ghosts? What about vampires? Werewolves? Never mind. You can tell me later." He clamped his mouth shut as if he couldn't help the waterfall of words.

As Monster curled around her ankles, Sophie told herself fiercely to *think, breathe,* and *not panic.* At least she knew why all the bottles were stolen. And she knew for certain who stole them.

"He's making them, from the bottles he stole," Sophie said. "He's like me." She'd thought she was the only one who could bring dreams to life. Her parents said they'd never met anyone like her. She'd imagined a dozen times . . . no, a hundred times, or a thousand . . . what it would be like to meet someone like her—to know she wasn't alone; she wasn't a freak. But she'd never imagined anything like this.

Monster hissed and spat. "He's *nothing* like you. You'd never do this."

Kneeling, Sophie put her arms around Monster. He pressed against her, and she felt his heart beating as fast as a hummingbird's through his fur. "I mean, he can drink dreams and bring them to life. It's the only explanation."

"Not much of an explanation," Ethan said. "It doesn't explain why he kidnapped Madison and Lucy, if he did. Or your parents, again if he did. Or why we're still standing here, talking, when there are monsters fighting right down there, instead of running away as fast as we can." He pointed at the pit so hard that he stabbed the air, and then he pointed in the direction of the window, beyond the cellar doors.

Burrowing his face into her shoulder, Monster said, muffled, "The boy is right. We shouldn't be here. Sophie, this isn't a nice place."

Ethan nodded vigorously. "Exactly. This is not safe. We should go—"

"Not without looking for my parents." Releasing Monster, she stood. Below, the onlookers cheered, louder than the thudding music. One of the monsters wailed, a high-pitched screech that made prickles pop up all over Sophie's skin. The only good thing about this fight was that no one looked up to see Sophie, Ethan, and Monster on the balcony. "Mr. Nightmare's distracted. This is my chance to find them, or at least a clue to where they are."

She didn't wait for them to agree—or try to talk her out of it. She was afraid she'd lose her nerve. Slinking along the wall, she headed toward a door at the end of the balcony. It was gashed with claw marks. The knob had been broken off, leaving only a hole.

Below, one of the monsters howled. A cheer erupted.

Trying hard not to imagine what had made the gashes, Sophie opened the door. She jumped backward, but nothing leaped out at her.

Inside was a stairwell. It was lit by yellow, cobweb-coated lights, and it stank like a dumpster. It looked as if it went one flight up into the house and one flight down toward the fight pit. Up felt safer—there would be windows and doors and light, as well as furniture and carpet and kitchen appliances and other ordinary things. But she wasn't looking for ordinary. Down here was where the secrets were kept. And maybe her parents? Slipping into the stairwell, she crept downstairs. In the stairwell, the music was muffled.

"Sophie, you don't know what's down there," Ethan said, following her.

"That's kind of the point," Sophie whispered back. "Hey, didn't you say you wanted to be a hero?"

"Monster said that."

"Was he wrong?"

"Well . . . no."

"If it matters," she said, "I think you're brave."

He paused midstep. "Really?"

He'd had impossibilities shoved down his throat one after another for the past few hours, and he hadn't panicked once. He'd even cracked jokes. If their positions had been reversed, Sophie wasn't sure she'd have stuck around. "Yes, really."

Near the bottom of the stairs, the lights flickered, plunging the stairwell into darkness for a few seconds, then blinked back on. Sophie felt as if her heart was beating louder than the shouts from the pit.

The stairs ended in a narrow hallway. One wall was yellowed and stained plaster, and the other was chunky rock that looked like it had been gouged out by claws. She wondered if Mr. Nightmare had used the monsters to make this hall. There were two doors: one red, and one yellow. Both had windows in the middle.

Crossing to the red door, Sophie peeked through and saw the fight pit. Mr. Nightmare's back was toward her, and he was standing on the crate and shouting over the howls and cries of the fight and the wailing music. "Look at the speed and skill! Consider the detail, with the teeth and claws . . ." He continued describing the monsters, as if they were used cars he wanted to sell.

Sophie peered through the window of the yellow door. It was smeared with dirt, but she could make out what looked like a storage room. She didn't see any people. "Ready?" she whispered.

"You think I'm brave. Can't say no after that."

She opened the door and slipped in. The storage room was stuffed with cages, stacked one on top of another. The lights were dim and flickering, as in the stairwell, with just a few bare bulbs strung through the steel beams in the ceiling. Shadows crisscrossed the narrow cement corridors.

Monster stuck close to Sophie's ankles. "Sophie, this is *really* not a nice place."

Nodding, she walked forward between the cages. Most of them were empty. But a few weren't. One cage held a three-headed turtle with spikes on its shell. Beyond it was a half snake, half ostrich. Above it was a scarlet-colored monkey with eyes that looked like flames dancing inside his skull.

"Okay, interesting," Ethan said, his voice shaking. "Don't see your parents."

On the other end of the storage room was a thick steel door, like a bank vault door or a supermarket freezer. It had a metal bar across it, locking it, and a window like a porthole. "What do you think is in there?" Sophie whispered.

"Worse monsters?" Ethan suggested. "Come on, Sophie. This is well beyond freaky, and as someone with nightmare issues, I feel fully qualified to say that. Your parents aren't here. Let's look somewhere else."

"But we don't know what's in there." Sophie started forward.

As soon as she reached them, the monsters in the cages reacted. Screaming and howling, they bashed against their cages. The turtle-like monster roared, the ostrich kicked, and the monkey shook the bars so hard that the metal rattled like a thousand cans crashing together.

Sophie shot a look back at the yellow door that led to the stairs. For an instant, she was torn—stay or run? *You've come this far,* she told herself. She had to at least see what was on the other side of the steel door. If she didn't look and her parents were there . . . She hurried toward it, hoping the fight in the pit and the thunderous music were loud enough to drown these monsters out.

The monkey with flame eyes swiped at her. "Stop!"

She slowed. "You can talk?"

"Better than you," the monkey snarled.

She looked from the monkey to the turtle to the snake-ostrich. The other two quieted. "Are you from a dream?" she asked.

"Oh yes, I had a nice tropical dream with sandy white beaches, palm trees, and the scent of scared tourists for dinner, but I left it for the promise of tastier prey. But instead of the freedom to hunt, I was thrown into a cage like a . . . a . . ."

"Monster?" Monster supplied helpfully.

"You must let us out, before we're sold. Let us find our sandy beaches and our freedom!" He crooked his finger toward Sophie. "Come on, set us free, little girl."

"What do you mean, 'before we're sold'?" Sophie asked.

"You know what goes on out there! He drags us in, two at a time—the dumb brutes fight, and then he sells the winner to the highest bidder. We're his performing monkeys, parading our prowess on the auction block."

"He sells you? Who does he sell you to?" Ethan asked.

"Don't know. Don't care. But he lies to them. Oh yes, he lies. Tells them he created us in a laboratory. Trained us. 'Genetically engineered fighting machines,' he says. Good for defense. Or offense. Or whatever you need." The monkey twisted upside down inside his cage. "His customers want proven champions, he says. Winners command the highest prices. Losers . . . no one sees again. He calls it his fight club, as if it's all a game. But we have no choice. We fight in the pit or we rot in our cages."

Monster shuddered. "That's horrible."

"Precisely. But you can save us. You can free us!"

The turtle howled, and the ostrich kicked the cage again.

"Shh, if you want us to free you, we can't be caught!" Sophie whisper-cried.

The monkey snarled at the others. "Shut up, you idiots!" To Sophie, he said, "This lot is no brighter than animals. Can't even talk. Their dreams were short and blurry. Bad distillation," he said. "But I . . . *I* was made by the best."

Sophie rushed to the cage. "My parents? Are they here? Where are they?"

"Don't know. Don't care," he said again, sing-song.

"How about two kids? Two girls, one older and one younger?" Ethan asked.

"I said I don't know," the monkey growled. "Set us free."

Maybe her parents and the missing kids weren't the only ones who needed rescuing. These creatures had been lured out of their dreams, promised something better, and then suddenly, they were here, stuck in a basement, without light, without hope, waiting to be sold. She imagined if it were Monster behind these bars . . .

Ethan caught her arm and pulled her back, away

from the bars of the cage and the monkey's reach. "Sophie, tell me you aren't thinking of letting them out."

The monkey drew his gums back in a smile that looked more like a hideous grimace. "Oh, yes, let us out. Pretty please, let us out!"

"What will you do if I let you out?" Sophie asked.

The monkey bared his needle-sharp teeth. "Rend your flesh from your body and suck the marrow from your bones."

"And that was the wrong answer," Monster said. "Come on, Sophie." He scuttled across the storage room to the steel door. Rising up on his tentacles, he peered through the porthole window. He wasn't tall enough. Ignoring the curses and pleas of the monkey, Sophie scooped up Monster, and they both pressed their faces against the window.

Behind them, Ethan asked, "What do you see? Are they in there?"

It was too streaked with dirt to tell. All she saw was an amber glow, as if a light was on inside. She shook her head. "We have to open it." Twisting, she asked the monkey, "Do you know what's in here?"

But the monkey only whisper-howled, "Come back! Free me!"

"Let's look and get out of here," Monster said, "before he brings the entire audience."

Together, Sophie and Ethan lifted the bar that locked the door.

"Are you sure this is a good idea?" Ethan asked.

She glanced back—no one had to come to check on the noises yet. They must have been used to the monsters howling, or else the music drowned them out. "No."

"Be ready to run," Monster advised.

The monsters were watching them. Hanging upside down by his feet, the monkey licked his lips. Setting the bar aside, Sophie cracked the door open. Nothing leaped out.

Monster stuck his head inside. "Well, that's unexpected."

Sophie opened the door wider. "Oh. Wow."

Ethan pressed closer. "'Wow' what?"

Inside was a lavish, windowless bedroom. The walls were painted with images of castles, knights, and princesses, chased by dragons and gorgons and Cyclopes. The ceiling was blue sky with white clouds, a sun, a moon, and stars. One wall was lined with bookshelves stuffed with what looked like fantasy and horror novels. Three beds were piled high with pillows. A dreamcatcher hung from each headboard. Two of the beds were empty . . . but the other held Madison.

She was awake, and her eyes widened as they came into the room. She was tucked in with blankets and teddy bears around her. She was also bound and gagged.

17

ON THE BED, MADISON THRASHED, YANKING ON HER ropes. She was trying to talk, her voice a muffled *"Muph, murphle, mrph."* Sophie rushed to her side. Kneeling next to her, she pulled at the gag. It was too tight to slide off. She dug her fingernails into the knot. Squirming, Madison tried to break out of the ropes.

"Hold still," Sophie said.

Madison didn't listen. Stretching, she strained her arms.

"You're making the knots tighter," Ethan said, working on the rope around her ankles. Staring at him, Madison quit struggling. The whites of her eyes were bright and reminded Sophie of a frightened horse. Her nostrils flared as she breathed fast through her nose.

"Don't worry. We'll get you out of here." Continuing to work on the knot, Sophie said, "Monster, guard the door, okay? Shout if you see anyone coming." She saw Madison's eyes land on Monster as she glimpsed him for the first time, and her eyes widened even farther. If they widened any more, Sophie thought, her eyeballs were going to fall out of their sockets. "He's friendly."

"Usually," Monster amended.

At last, the cloth loosened. She pulled it quickly out of Madison's mouth. It left marks on her cheeks from where it had been tied too tight, and there was dried spit in the corners of her mouth.

"Get me out of here!" Madison cried. "There are monsters here!"

"Yeah, noticed that," Monster said. "Rather put out about it, actually. I liked being unique. Much of my identity, in fact, was wrapped up in my uniqueness." He peered out the door. "This place is a serious blow to my self-image."

Madison gawked. "It . . . it talks?"

"He likes to talk like a college professor when I'm upset or worried—thinks it's distracting or something." Sophie tried to sound casual, hoping that would keep Madison from freaking out. She set to work on the ropes around Madison's wrists. "He's just trying to calm you down."

"A talking mutant cat does not calm me down!" Madison tried to sit up and then failed, flopping back. "Look, it's very nice that you're saving me, if that's what you're really doing, but how did you find me? Why are you here? And what are you doing with *him?*" With each question, her voice grew more shrill, as if she was on the brink of losing it.

The knots were tight. "He's Monster. He's friendly."

"Not *that*. Him. Ethan, star basketball player."

Ethan looked up from the rope around her ankles. "Long story. Is there another girl somewhere? Lucy Snyder?"

Madison tried to jerk herself up to sitting. "Lucy!"

"You know her?" Sophie asked. "Do you know where she is?"

"They put us together at first," Madison said. "But then they took her upstairs. Said she was crying too much and they had to separate us. That's when he gagged me—said it was so I could practice not whining."

Ethan glanced at the ceiling. "Do you think she's okay?"

"Don't stop!" Madison begged. "Untie me! She's not okay; she's scared. They told her to sleep, and she wouldn't. Couldn't. How can we sleep?"

"Who's 'they'?" Ethan asked.

Madison was shaking as Sophie wiggled the knots in the rope around her wrist. Her fingers knocked together. *She's terrified,* Sophie thought. *Of course she is.* She wondered if Madison had been tied up the whole time. Did she know where she was? Or why?

"Two men," Madison answered Ethan. "One with bushy hair and scary eyes, and another with tons of muscles. Did you see them? Are they out there?"

Sophie thought of the man with the muscles in the backyard. He must work for Mr. Nightmare. They'd been lucky he hadn't seen them on the way in. "Have you seen my parents? I think they might be prisoners too." It was hard to keep her voice even, but Sophie managed to choke out the words.

Madison shook her head. "They weren't in here. Maybe upstairs with Lucy?"

"Okay, then upstairs next?" Ethan said to Sophie.

"No, no, we have to get out!" Madison cried. "Didn't you hear me? There are monsters here!" Jumping to her feet, she strode toward the door.

Spreading his tentacles, Monster blocked the door. Grabbing a book as if it were a bat, Madison barreled forward. She raised the book as if she planned to hit Monster with it. Monster hissed, "You idiot, someone's coming! Hide!"

"Back in bed," Ethan ordered. He seized Madison around the waist and hauled her away from the door. "Pretend you're still tied." He tossed the ropes at her. For a second, her eyes narrowed, and Sophie thought she was going to fight Ethan. Then she jumped into bed and stuffed the gag into her mouth. She bit it so it stayed, and she wrapped the ropes around her wrists.

Sophie ducked behind a pile of pillows. Ethan hid beside the bookcase, while Monster scrambled to the top and tried to squeeze himself into as tight a ball as possible.

At the door, the gray giraffe-man stuck his long neck inside and swung his head from the right to the left and back again. Sophie tried to pretend she was stone. *Don't see me,* she thought at it. *I'm not here. I'm no one. I'm nothing.* She imagined she was at school, invisible to everyone even though she was right there.

Peeking out from between the pillows, she watched

the giraffe-man saunter inside. His long arms with the razorlike claws swung by his sides. He prodded Madison, who whimpered.

Please, don't see me.

He was going to see her. She wasn't hidden well.

She scanned the room for something, anything, that could help. She met Monster's eyes. He looked deliberately above her then back to her again. Tilting her head, she looked up—and saw a dreamcatcher dangling from the headboard.

The gray creature plodded closer.

As he reached the pillows, Monster leaped from the bookcase. At the same time, Sophie tossed the pillows off, jumped up, and grabbed the dreamcatcher. Madison screamed as Monster landed on the gray creature's head. Springing forward, Sophie shoved the dreamcatcher against his gray skin, and Monster jumped away.

"Hold it on him!" Monster yelled, keeping his distance from the dreamcatcher.

The gray creature flailed, swinging his long arms in a circle. One connected with Sophie's stomach, and she was knocked back.

Ethan shot himself at the creature's knees. The creature wobbled and then tumbled over. Lunging forward again, Sophie pressed the dreamcatcher against his flat gray stomach.

He didn't cry out. He had no mouth.

Thrashing beneath them, the gray creature began to fade. First, it looked as if the color was leeching out of his skin. Then, the floor was visible through his body. And then Sophie and Ethan thumped to the floor as the creature melted away entirely.

Sitting back on her heels, Sophie held the dreamcatcher up. "It's done. Got him." She slid it into her pocket.

Madison jumped up. "What happened? Where did it go? What did you do? What was that? Is it gone? Can it come back?" Her voice was a shrill squeak, like a squeezed mouse.

Monster lifted his tentacles to point at her. "Explain later. Upstairs now."

He was right. The fight in the pit wasn't going to last forever. They had to get upstairs before Mr. Nightmare finished and came for more monsters to sell. Sophie led the way, out the door, past the cages. The monkey with flame eyes called after them, "Wait! Let us out!" All three monsters roared, howled, and shook their cages.

Sophie, Monster, Ethan, and Madison piled into

the hallway. Slowing by the door to the pit, Sophie looked through the window. In the pit, the fight still raged. Goo hung from the links of the fence. The sand was speckled with red. The muscled monster limped, dragging one of its legs behind him, and the shark-faced monster circled around him. The five men and women were still shouting, as if they were watching the Super Bowl—none of them seemed to have heard the noises from the storage room over the sounds of the fight and the pounding music. There was still time, right? She could search upstairs. "Take Madison out of here," she told Ethan as they hurried up the stairs toward the balcony. "I'll search for my parents and Lucy."

"I'm not leaving you here," Ethan said.

"I am," Madison said. "Where's the exit?"

They were nearly to the level of the balcony when the door to the pit opened below them. "Hey, what are you kids doing?" a woman shouted.

Above, from the kitchen, a door swung open, and the man with muscles came through. He was carrying a soda. He dropped it as soon as he saw them. "Stop right there!"

Sophie, Ethan, Madison, and Monster tumbled onto the balcony. They ran for the cellar doors and burst out onto the lawn. Sophie shouted, "Glitterhoof! Help! Get us out of here!"

Yelling, the muscle man emerged from the cellar doors after them.

In the time that they had been in the basement, the sun had set, and the sky had darkened to a deep gray blue. As the pegasus trotted out of the garage, he sparkled in the light of the street lamps. Slowing, Madison gasped.

"Don't stop," Sophie ordered, propelling her forward by the elbow. "Glitterhoof, fly us home!"

"You are too many for flight," he declared. Tossing his mane, he turned away.

"Glitterhoof, please! You can—"

He lifted his tail in the air—

—and out flowed a rainbow.

The rainbow arched into the night sky. As it hit the sky, it paled, nearly translucent—a moonbow. Sophie shot a look back and saw the muscle man had stopped. His mouth hanging open, he was staring at the sparkling pegasus and his night rainbow. Speeding up, Sophie propelled the others toward the moonbow.

"Climb it," Glitterhoof ordered.

Sophie didn't hesitate. She and Monster herded the others onto the rainbow. It looked pale and thin, but as soon as Sophie touched it, she could see it—the colors as bright as in the dream she'd swallowed. They scrambled on, hands and feet sinking into the glittering colors. It felt cool and wet, like mist, but also soft, as if they were climbing onto a damp pillow. Last, Glitterhoof stepped onto the purple band.

The man unfroze and began running toward them again. "Stop!"

"Step lively, little smelly ones," Glitterhoof said.

On hands and feet, they all scrambled up the rainbow. As they climbed, the colors dissolved behind them. Reaching them, the man leaped—and grasped at air. "Keep going!" Sophie shouted.

Clinging to one another, they climbed the night rainbow into the sky.

18

SOPHIE LOOKED DOWN — AND WISHED SHE HADN'T.
She squeezed her eyes shut as her head spun, and
then opened them again. Below, lights from houses
twinkled like stars. Above, the real stars shone by the
hundreds. She felt sandwiched between two skies, in a
narrow strip of nowhere.

The colors under her feet crept up her legs.
Madison was hip-deep in blue. Ethan waded up the
orange. And behind them, the rainbow faded into
empty air. She couldn't see Mr. Nightmare's house
anymore. It was blocked by a cloud.

Monster's tentacles were wrapped tightly around
Sophie's neck and waist. "I'm sorry, Sophie," he whispered. "We'll find a way to save them. I promise."

She hugged him back.

Ahead, Madison scooped up some of the purple.

It looked like cotton candy stuck to her hand. "Did he really just poop a rainbow? Seriously, did that just happen? Because I saw it happen." Her voice was shrill again, as if she was about to burst out laughing or screaming or both.

Only a few yards of the night rainbow were left before it curved down. Bathed in moonlight, the colors were soft and translucent. Climbing the green band, Sophie tried not to think about what would happen if she fell through. Her feet were buried in emerald-like dust.

Glitterhoof trotted past them. His horn sparkled in the moonlight. "Isn't this a glorious way to travel?"

Monster fluffed his fur. "Not the word I'd pick."

"Do not tell me that the ferocious monster is afraid of heights?"

"I am not afraid of heights," Monster said. "I simply don't trust your shiny collection of colorful water droplets. A rainbow is an optical phenomenon, not a mode of transportation."

"Why is the only one talking sense the thing with six arms?" Madison said, still shrill.

"Tentacles," Monster corrected.

"That's even worse."

"You'll get used to it," Ethan told her.

"I don't want to 'get used to it,'" Madison said. "I want to go home. Do you have any idea what it was like, grabbed by that gray thing, shoved in that basement? And when the fights in that horrible sandpit started, those two men tied me up. They didn't want me to scream for help . . ." Her voice broke. "How did you find me? And why you, with him?" She stopped at the top of the curve. Wind whipped her hair against her cheek. She pushed it back behind her ear. "Also, how do we get down?" She pointed at the spot where the rainbow pierced the clouds and then plummeted toward the earth.

"Simple." Glitterhoof came up behind her. "You slide." Using his horn, he prodded the girl in the middle of her back. She tumbled forward with a scream and slid face first. Ethan sat and slid next.

Sitting, Sophie wrapped her arms around Monster's stomach. Before she could think of all the things that could go wrong—or, rather, the one key thing that could go wrong, which would be falling to her death—she pushed off. The wind whistled past her ears and made her eyes tear up. Her clothes fluttered around her.

The rainbow bumped up, and for an instant, Sophie and Monster were airborne, then they crashed down again and kept sliding, faster and faster. Red, orange, and yellow cradled them. Below, the street grew larger. It seemed to expand, as if it were a balloon that was inflating. She saw her street . . . And there was her house . . . her roof . . . her windows . . . Above the street, the rainbow ended, the colors dangling in the air.

"Hang on!" Sophie shouted to Monster. She braced herself, and then they flew off the end of the rainbow and landed in a heap with Madison and Ethan behind the bookshop. Twisting, Sophie looked up at the rainbow—it was pale again. If she hadn't known it was there, she wouldn't have seen it.

"Ow," Monster said. "You're squishing my tentacles."

Glitterhoof stepped off the moonbow and pranced over the tangle of arms and legs. Behind him, the night rainbow vanished completely.

Squirming out of the pile, Sophie unlocked the back door to the shop and shooed everyone inside. "Quick, before anyone sees! Inside! Now, now, now!"

Sophie locked the door, then ran to the front and went from window to window pulling the shades shut. Dreamcatchers shook as she bumped into them. Across the store, Monster flipped on the lights.

Madison shrieked.

Sophie spun around—but she was only screaming at Monster.

Madison swallowed the scream. "Sorry. He looks worse in the light."

Miffed, Monster ruffled his fur. "So do you."

Tossing her hair as if she could erase her scream with attitude, Madison stomped over to the checkout desk. "I'm calling my parents. I want to go home."

"Wait, what are you going to tell them?" Sophie intercepted her. "You were abducted by a monster and rescued by a myth?"

Madison brushed past her. "You can't stop me."

"I don't want to. I just want you to have a plausible lie. My parents are still in there. And Lucy. You could endanger them if you say something stupid."

"I'm not stupid—"

At the window, Ethan interrupted them. "He followed us."

All of them ran to the door, crowding together to see. Sophie looked out between Ethan and Glitterhoof. A blue car with the license plate *MISTER N* was parked on the street in front of the bookstore. A familiar man stepped out of the driver's seat and stretched, as if he didn't have a care in the world. He crossed to the back door of the car and opened it. The red-eyed monkey leaped out.

"And he brought his monsters," Ethan said.

"We have to run!" Madison cried.

"Back door!" Leading the way, Sophie sprinted through the bookstore. She dodged piles of books. Behind her, she heard the others crash into them, and she thought of the books spilled upstairs—was this what had happened to her parents? Monsters came for them? Lunging past her, Ethan reached the back door first and yanked it open.

Howling, the flame-eyed monkey threw himself at Ethan. He slammed the door shut, and the monkey thudded into it. Spinning around, Ethan cried, "He's fast! Now what?"

"Down!" Sophie commanded.

At the front of the shop, the door rattled. It was locked, wasn't it? She heard glass break—the window! —as they ran through the store to the basement door.

Her hands shaking, Sophie grabbed the book with the key and unlocked the door. "Go! Fast!" Everyone piled through and thundered down the stairs, including Glitterhoof, who had to squeeze his wings against his flanks. Sophie shut the door and locked it, grateful her parents had put locks inside and out.

A second later, something slammed into the door. It rattled on its hinges. She ran downstairs. Madison was zigzagging back and forth like a bug caught in a jar. Ethan grabbed Sophie's arm. "Is there another door? A window?"

She shook her head. There was no way out.

"Then we have to try to block the door." Scanning the room, he grabbed a chair and carried it up the stairs. Grateful that he was thinking instead of panicking, Sophie took another chair and followed him. Together, they wedged the chairs up against the door. "It's not going to hold. We need more."

Hurrying back down, Sophie looked for something, anything else, that they could use. All the shelves and cabinets were bolted to the wall. The somnium was too fragile, and the distiller table was too wide.

"I will block the door with my body," Glitterhoof announced, "and save you with my life. Your valiant rescue of yonder maiden proves you are worthy of such sacrifice." He trotted up the stairs.

Monster followed him. "I'll help, minus the cheesy monologue."

Madison squeezed herself under the distiller table, trying to hide. "It won't work. They'll break through. I don't want to go back! I can't!"

Ignoring her, Ethan said, "We need something that will fill the stairs and not budge. Like a cement wall. Or a boulder. Or an elephant. Sophie, can you dream something up?"

She shook her head, hard. That was crazy! "Last time the man with the mouth—"

"Pick a different dream." He ran to the ledger. "Something large. Huge. This!" He tapped a number in the ledger and then ran to the shelf. Scanning it, he found the bottle and shoved it at Sophie.

"What is it?"

"Large. Dream it in the stairwell." He pointed.

She hesitated for only a fraction of a second. She wasn't sure it was the best plan, but at least it *was* a plan. She ran to the stairs. "Get out of the way," she ordered Glitterhoof and Monster. *Remember what you need,* she ordered herself. *Remember it's a dream.* She had to stay aware and control the dream this time. She didn't have time to be confused or wander around or mess up in any way.

The door shook and the hinges creaked. Cracks appeared in the wood as something thudded into it again and again. Sophie pulled the plug out of the bottle and drank it. It tasted like overripe melon. "Wake me if this works—or if he breaks through."

Sophie heard harsh cries and felt hot, thick air on her skin. Opening her eyes, she saw green. She was facing a leaf. A large, flat leaf. She looked right and left—enormous leaves were all around her. They even blocked the sky, tinting the light green as it filtered through.

For a moment, it didn't seem odd. She felt as if she'd been in this jungle all her life. She breathed in the heavy scent, as intense as fresh-baked chocolate chip cookies . . . And then she remembered: *Just a dream.*

She pushed the leaf aside. "Hello? Anyone here?"

She took a step forward, and the ground crumbled beneath her. Backpedaling, she clutched at the leaf and looked down. She was standing on a cliff. Before her, a waterfall plummeted thousands of feet down a rockface. Cries echoed through the air, and a pterodactyl winged across the cloudless sky.

Sophie backed away from the edge of the cliff— and into a cool, leathery wall. She looked up, and up, and up, to see a gray turtle-like face on a long neck.

Dinosaur, her brain helpfully supplied.

Every instinct said to scream and run, but she

forced herself to stand still. "Um, hi. I need help. But maybe . . . uh, smaller help?"

The dinosaur shifted her weight, and from between her legs, a young dinosaur poked his head out. He still towered over Sophie.

"Please, I need your help," Sophie said. "Can you come with me?"

He lowered his head in a slow nod and blew out his nose. His nostrils flared, and a stench like rotted lettuce rolled over her. She blinked as her eyes burned, and she coughed—then she woke to the sound of shrieking so high and loud that Sophie thought her eardrums were going to burst. She saw only gray.

Waking from this dream was worse than before. It felt like several long minutes before her brain detangled itself enough to recognize what she was hearing and seeing. Madison was shrieking. And the baby dinosaur was here, in the stairwell, wedged between her and the door. She'd done it!

Leaping up, Ethan punched the air. "It worked!"

"Anything else come out?" Sophie asked Monster. She blinked hard, trying to make her vision steady. She felt as if her eyes were covered in cobwebs.

"Just that," Monster said. "Isn't that enough?"

The dinosaur tried to shift, but he was crammed

too firmly between the walls. He filled every available inch, curved into a U shape with the bulk of his body toward the door and his head and tail pointed down the stairs. He craned his neck to look at Sophie. His droopy eyes looked sad.

"Nice dinosaur," Sophie said, patting his head. "Good dino."

"It looks like an apatosaurus," Monster said in his professor voice. "An herbivore that lived during the Jurassic period. Not to be confused with the brontosaurus, since those don't exist. Or more accurately, never existed." The dinosaur lowered his head and peered into the Dream Shop. "This has to be a young one. An adult would have demolished the house."

"Please, don't try to move," Sophie told the apatosaurus. "I promise I'll send you back soon." He nodded his head slowly, as if he understood her. His whole neck undulated. She guessed he couldn't talk. Maybe because he was a baby. Or because he was a dinosaur.

Plaintively, Glitterhoof said, "Could someone make the screaming stop?"

Crossing to the distiller table, Sophie knelt next to Madison. She patted her awkwardly on the shoulder. "It's going to be okay."

Gulping in air, Madison quit screaming and said

with a strained voice, "Nothing is okay about this. At all. And stop touching me."

Sophie retreated.

Trotting forward, Glitterhoof nosed the dinosaur's tail. It flopped down the stairs. "It is pleasantly large. I do not think even your enemy can dislodge him. Well done, Sophie."

Returning to the stairwell, Sophie called, "Go away! Leave us alone!"

"Oh no, my dear Betty. Or do you prefer Sophie?" His voice was the same civilized tone as before, with the hint of a British accent, as if he were inviting her to tea. "You've stolen something that belongs to me, and I'm afraid I can't leave without it."

"Does he mean me?" Madison said. "I think he means me." She tucked herself farther under the table, as if she could blend into the shadows.

"Yes, I mean you, Madison Moore. Or, more specifically, your mind." Drifting down the stairs, Mr. Nightmare's voice was like a purr.

Madison whimpered.

"And yours, Ethan Sandberg."

Ethan froze.

"Yes, Ethan, you were invited as well. I even sent

a friend of mine to escort you. He was most put out when you evaded him."

Monster wrapped his tentacles around Sophie's leg and bared his teeth. If he'd had laser eyes, they'd be shooting up the stairs. Sophie asked, "Your 'friend' wouldn't happen to be a gray creature who looks like a giraffe?"

"Indeed, yes. You've met him?"

Sophie didn't answer. She heard a snarl from upstairs—the flame-eyed monkey—and wondered if they knew she had the gray giraffe caught in the threads of a dreamcatcher.

"What do you want?" Ethan called.

"I thought that would be obvious. I want your nightmares. It's nothing personal, children. Merely business. You have such deliciously vivid nightmares."

I was right, Sophie thought. He did kidnap them for their nightmares. Was she right about her parents, too? She must be. He'd need a way to distill their dreams.

"I do owe Sophie a debt of gratitude for finding you," he said. "She has an excellent eye for troubled youth. If she hadn't given you dreamcatchers, I doubt I would have noticed you."

Sophie felt herself pale. *It's my fault,* she thought. She'd drawn his attention to Madison, Lucy, and Ethan. She glanced down the stairs to see both Madison and Ethan looking at her—Madison with fury in her eyes and Ethan with, oddly, sympathy. She wanted to say she was sorry.

But Mr. Nightmare wasn't done. "I've found kids like you before, with superb imaginations and unresolved personal or family issues. But they all learn to live with their traumas and outgrow their nightmares, and then begins the tedious process of finding more dreamers. So I've hit upon a brilliant solution: Don't let the nightmares die."

"You can't do that!" Madison shouted.

"You are mistaken, my dear. I can. Nightmares are my specialty."

At the top of the stairs, they heard a *thud, thud, thud,* as if something was pounding against the door. It creaked and splintered, and then they heard the wood shatter.

The dinosaur swung his head toward Sophie and let out a low moan like a cow. *They can't get through,* Sophie thought. "We're safe," she told Madison. "It will be okay."

"Safe?" Mr. Nightmare chuckled. "You aren't safe, my sweet dreamer. I know who you are. I know where you live. I know what you fear."

Madison shouted, "Leave us alone!"

"Oh, no, I cannot do that." His laugh died. "I need you. I need your mind. All of this resisting is pointless. You think Sophie set you free. But she didn't. She couldn't. You'll never be free."

And then the dinosaur began to fade. Through its translucent gray flesh, she saw Mr. Nightmare. He was holding one of the shop's dreamcatchers to the dinosaur's side. Next to him, the monkey with the fiery eyes jumped from foot to foot. It gnashed its teeth together, spittle dripping from its lips.

Mr. Nightmare wore a smile on his face as the dinosaur vanished. The monkey charged down the stairs. Screaming, Sophie and Ethan ran across the room toward where Madison cowered, but Glitterhoof stepped forward.

As the monkey reached the bottom step, the winged unicorn reared onto his back hooves and pinned the monkey down with his front hooves. He then jabbed his horn into the monkey's fur, securing him to the floor.

Passing them, Monster charged up the stairs. Sophie ran after him. "Wait, Monster, don't!" What was he thinking? Mr. Nightmare had dreamcatchers!

Launching himself at Mr. Nightmare, Monster buried his teeth into the man's leg. Mr. Nightmare howled and slapped a dreamcatcher onto Monster's back.

Sophie grabbed on to Monster. She yanked him away, and he released his bite. Blood welled from a long gash on Mr. Nightmare's calf. Sophie and Monster tumbled backward several steps, crashing against the side of the stairwell.

At the top of the stairs, Mr. Nightmare had dropped down to the floor, clutching his leg. "So your 'housecat' is your defender. Very nice. But it won't be enough."

"Looks like enough to me," Monster said.

Red stained his fingers, but Mr. Nightmare laughed. "You may think you've won, but you haven't. You can't save them. You can't even save yourself. Sooner or later, the Night Watchmen will hear about you . . . Perhaps sooner, if I make a little phone call . . . And once they do, they will come for you. They'll hunt you forever."

Sophie froze. Wrapping his tentacles around her,

Monster pressed against her, but she still felt cold inside and out. "You wouldn't . . ."

"Only way to be safe is to let me protect you. You can be part of my family. You can be with your parents again, and we'll all become rich together. How does that sound?"

Monster sniffed. "It sounds like a join-the-Dark-Side speech."

"Think about what I'm offering, Betty. A chance to be a part of something great! Your parents think of themselves as noble, easing the nightmares of others, but what they do is theft. What we do is art. We transcend the petty concerns of the ordinary dream trade by truly making something out of nothing."

"You're making killer monsters."

"For now," he said, his voice smooth, "but if you join me, we'll expand. There are buyers out there for the unique and beautiful. I happen to be fond of monsters, but the possibilities are endless, and the potential is immense. You can dream whatever you want, whenever you want. Think about it—the world of dreams, and you will be free to partake of any of it, without fear."

From below, Ethan called, "Don't listen to him, Sophie!"

"And what about them? Madison and Ethan? What about Lucy? Will they be without fear?" Sophie shook her head. She didn't believe him, not for a second.

"You can't trust them. If we let them free, they will tell the world about you, and the Watchmen will hear. They will come for you and your parents. Your family is inexperienced at hiding. But I can help you. I know how to disappear."

"You want to shove me in a cage, like your monsters," Sophie said. "You lied to them. And you're lying to me."

"I'll treat you and your parents like jewels," Mr. Nightmare promised. "As I will treat my dear little dreamers, *if* you all come willingly. Didn't you like your gilded cage, girl?" He directed the last question at Madison, who huddled with Ethan at the bottom of the stairs.

"You tied me up!" Madison yelled.

"Only because you squirmed."

"And gagged me!"

"Only because you screamed."

Madison had tears running down her cheeks, but her hands were curled into fists and she didn't wipe the tears away. She glared fiercely at him. "I'm never, ever going back!"

"Oh, I think you are mistaken," Mr. Nightmare said with a smile. "Once you have thought it through, you will come to the same conclusion. Let me help clarify your thinking: I have Betty's parents, and I have the little girl. And monsters get hungry."

Monster howled. He positioned himself in front of Sophie, protecting her.

"It is a simple choice, really," Mr. Nightmare said. "Come willingly and live in luxury, or come unwillingly and live with the monsters."

"That's a terrible choice," Ethan said.

"I will give you one hour to consider, and then I will return for your answer," Mr. Nightmare said graciously. "Don't try to run. Don't imagine you can hide. Don't think you're free. If you call the police, if you run to your parents, if you tell anyone . . . the monsters won't be hungry anymore." Struggling to his feet, Mr. Nightmare limped away from the stairs. She heard his footsteps as he crossed the bookstore. "One hour," he called. And then the bell rang as the door opened and shut.

PINNED TO THE FLOOR BY THE WINGED UNICORN, the monkey sneered at them. "Wherever you run, he will follow. Wherever you hide, he will find you. You can cry to your parents or wail to the police, but in the dark of the night, when there is only you and your nightmares, Mr. Nightmare will come."

Madison's face was flushed, as if she was about to scream or cry or both. Ethan was shaking. Grabbing another dreamcatcher, Sophie marched over to the monkey.

"Getting rid of me won't change anything," the monkey said. "He can make dozens more, and they'll come after you. You won't be able to stop him." He cackled. "Your life will become a nightmare, as your nightmares come to life."

Kneeling, Sophie held the dreamcatcher a few inches from him. "Tell me how to stop him."

"Three children, a pony, and a scruffy cat? You can't." He cackled again, as if he'd told the funniest joke in the world.

Ethan came up beside Sophie. "Why did you help him? You could have run for it. I thought you wanted to be free."

"He promised my freedom, if I helped him this once," the monkey said. "It was a no-brainer: my freedom, after revenge on the ones who left me behind. But it was I, I who was the fool for trusting him again. And you who will be the fool if you trust him now. He's a lying liar who lies. He won't wait an hour. He'll return, you'll see, as soon as he's conned more monsters into helping him."

Madison joined them on Sophie's other side. "He won't get away with this."

"Oh, you poor, deluded child with a penetrating voice, he already has. Unless you want to be responsible for that sweet little innocent girl becoming monster food. It's difficult to find good dreamers, but not impossible. He can replace you all, but he can't leave you to tell tales."

Ethan swallowed hard. "So he'll be coming back with more monsters."

The monkey fixed his flame eyes on Ethan. "Of course he will. He said as much. Haven't you been paying attention? He'll be back for you two. And you . . ." His gaze switched to Sophie. "The Watchmen will take care of you. Not to worry. In fact, I wouldn't be surprised if he's already informed them about you, despite what he offered you and despite his 'one hour' deadline. He does like to have all his loose ends tied up, and he has no real need of you."

Monster rushed over to Sophie. He had flecks of blood in the fur around his mouth. Sophie wondered how badly he'd hurt Mr. Nightmare. How long did they have before he came back? "I won't let them take you, Sophie. I swore to your parents—"

"Her parents belong to Mr. Nightmare now." The monkey cackled again. "You all belong to him! You'll never be free! Never, ever, never, ever—"

Sophie shoved the dreamcatcher into his red fur, and Glitterhoof stepped away, his horn low and ready to spear him again, if necessary. The monkey kept laughing his shrill, wild cackle as he faded and then disappeared.

Lifting his head, Glitterhoof shook his mane. Red fur clung to his unicorn horn. "How very unpleasant." He sniffed.

She stared at the spot where the monkey had been. He'd been telling the truth. Mr. Nightmare had them trapped as thoroughly as he had when the basement door was barred shut.

"He disappeared!" Madison's voice was a shriek. "How did you do that? You did it with the giraffe thing too. Are you a witch? What are you? What are they?"

Sinking onto a stool, Sophie kept staring at the floor. It was hopeless. He had her parents and Lucy. And he'd called, or would call, the Watchmen. Dully, Sophie said, "He was made from a dream. Well, nightmare, really. So this turned him back into one." She held up the dreamcatcher and braced herself, ready for Madison to shriek again.

But Madison planted her fists on her hips and glared. "I so don't understand. And you better explain everything right now, Freak Girl, or I'm going to start screaming and never stop."

Madison looked as if she meant it. Sophie felt like the monkey, pinned by her glare. She didn't know where to begin, or how much to say. If she'd never talked to Madison, Lucy, and Ethan, then Mr. Nightmare never would have known about them. If she hadn't given them dreamcatchers, he never would have guessed they had nightmares. They'd be safe.

Ethan spread his arms wide and answered for her. "These are dreams, caught in bottles. They're captured in dreamcatchers, then turned into liquid, bottled, and sold. If you drink a dream, you have that dream. If certain people drink one, the creatures in it become real. Sophie and Mr. Nightmare are those 'certain people.'"

Bristling his fur, Monster growled at Ethan. "You swore to keep her secret."

Sophie put a hand on his back. "It doesn't matter now." It was too late to worry about secrets. Mr. Nightmare was coming back, and there was nothing they could do to stop him. He'd already won.

"Sorry. But it was kind of obvious." Ethan waved his hands at Monster and Glitterhoof.

Madison was shaking her head as if that would shake apart his words. "Wait, wait, wait. Those dreamcatchers you gave me . . . You expect me to believe they really catch my dreams? And then you bottle them and sell them?"

Sophie shrank back. "Um, yes. I . . . I'm sorry." As she said the words, she realized that she truly was, for all of it. She shouldn't have taken their dreams and exposed them to this. She should have kept herself away from everyone.

"I always knew you were a freak, but you've taken it to a whole new level of freakdom. You sell our private dreams to complete strangers?"

"She also saved you," Ethan reminded her.

"Temporarily," Madison said. "You heard the freaky monkey. He's coming back! And if the monkey was right, he'll be back soon."

Ethan nodded gravely. "I think it's time to call the police. This is out of control."

"You can't!" Sophie cried. He had her parents! He'd threatened them! If they went to the police, he'd feed them to the monsters. And Lucy.

"You can't!" Madison echoed Sophie, to Sophie's surprise. "You heard what he said. We can't call the police. Or go home. He still has that little girl." She began to pace back and forth between the shelves of bottles. "This is all your fault, Sophie. You and your dreamcatchers. And I trusted you!"

"You never trusted me. You hated me."

Halting, Madison drew herself up, as if she'd just

been insulted. Her face was flushed as red as the band in Glitterhoof's rainbow. "I didn't—"

"And you were right to hate me. This *is* my fault. If I hadn't given you those dreamcatchers . . . If I hadn't wanted your nightmares . . . And I did want them." Sophie felt her eyes heat, and she blinked hard. She wasn't going to cry. She was going to say these words. She *needed* to say them. "I was jealous of you. Still am. You might hate that you scare yourself at night, but at least you can do it. You can take yourself on adventures. You can mix up the real and the impossible. You can have conversations that never happened. Live lives you never lived. Die a thousand times. And I can't!" Sophie took a deep breath, feeling the air rattle in her ribs. "I don't dream. I can't dream. I can never have a single nightmare on my own. But you, both of you, your minds are amazing. You make magic."

Stunned into silence, Madison stared at her.

"And you just wanted to throw it away," Sophie said.

In a hushed voice, Madison asked, "You think my nightmares are *amazing?*"

"Yes!"

"Oh."

Ethan shook his head. "You don't understand. It's one thing to have a vivid imagination when you're awake. Daydreams can be controlled. You always know they're just in your head. But at night, it's like being inside a pinball machine. All these thoughts hit each other, and you can't stop them. And when you're in it, really in it, you don't know if it's real or not."

Sophie looked at him, and he met her eyes— more serious and sad than she'd ever seen him, more than she thought he could be. For not the first time, she wondered *why* he had nightmares. "Believe me, Sophie," he said, "you aren't missing a thing by not dreaming. I'm jealous of *you*. There are so many terrible thoughts in my mind. At night, it's like my mind is the monster."

Sophie slumped on the stool. "*I'm* the monster. I'm the freak. All my life, I've thought I was the only one like me." Monster climbed onto her lap and curled up. She petted him. "And then it turns out I'm not, but the person who is most like me is worse than any dreamed-up monster." She couldn't see a way out of this. He'd left them no options. Sophie felt her eyes fill as she looked around the Dream Shop. This place had always been her sanctuary. She'd come here whenever she felt lonely or overwhelmed or bored or sad, whenever she felt ignored at school or separate from the world. But it had been invaded, and it didn't feel safe anymore. Half the bottles were missing—either stolen by Mr. Nightmare or sucked away by the man with the mouth. The others were toppled over. The unfinished dreamcatchers were strewn across the floor, several trampled. Up the stairs, the door was busted, and the chairs they'd wedged there were broken. Hugging herself, she wished she could disappear like a dream into a dreamcatcher.

"Enough," Glitterhoof said in his booming voice. "All this self-pity is making my hide itch. Please, stop. You are all very special in your own special way. If you'd like to sing a song about our specialness, I will sing along. But if you aren't going to switch to a more entertaining mode than simply moping . . ."

"I'm not moping," Sophie said without moving. "I'm explaining."

"Not very well," Madison snapped. "Let me get this straight. One, dreams are real. Two, you collect them and sell them without telling the dreamer,

specifically *me*. And three, Mr. Nightmare is . . .
Come on, someone, fill in the blank here, please."

"A very bad man." Monster shuddered, his fur
ruffling all the way to the tips of his tentacles.

Sophie hugged him as if he were a stuffed animal.
"He's a buyer. He came to buy dreams from my parents . . . but I guess he wanted more. His own direct
source. And he found it."

Madison was frowning, a crinkle in her forehead,
as if she were trying to force her brain to cooperate.
"So he's bringing our nightmares to life and using
them for prizefighting?"

"Monster Fight Club," Ethan said.

"It's not funny." Madison switched her glare to
him.

Ethan spread his hands to show his innocence. "I
didn't say it was."

"He wants you to dream up new monsters that he
can sell," Sophie said. "And I led him right to you, by
giving you dreamcatchers."

Glitterhoof whickered. "All of this is very interesting, and I'm pleased to see your friendship blossoming
through shared epiphanies and confessions of guilt,
but it doesn't change the fact that Mr. Nightmare will

be returning soon, and he'll most likely bring many more of his unpleasant creatures. We need a plan, if you don't want our quest to fail."

Sophie shook her head sadly. "There's no plan. He has my parents and Lucy. He'll hurt them if we tell anyone. He'll find us if we run."

Madison marched over to her and halted directly in front of her. "If you think I'm just going to meekly stay here and let him put me back in that room, then you don't know me very well." She poked Sophie in the shoulder. "There are things in this world that are stronger than you. Sicknesses you're born with. Things that can't be cured. But that doesn't mean you quit fighting them. That doesn't mean you don't try. My sister has been in and out of the hospital since she was born. She should have died when she was six months and again when she was two and then four and then six, but my parents don't give up. Even though it's hopeless because she won't ever get better. Even though it costs them everything else in their lives, they keep fighting because it might buy them one more day. And you're saying you want me to give up? Meekly go back? Not try? Uh-uh, Freak Girl. Think again. If we can't go for help, if you can't hide, then we're going to fight."

Sophie stared at her. She didn't know what to say.

"Very inspiring speech," Glitterhoof said approvingly.

"Thank you," Madison said. She looked as though she'd eaten something sour. "Now, stand up, Sophie. You know how to get rid of monsters. I've seen you do it twice. You're our best chance of stopping him."

Slowly, Sophie stood. Monster slipped off her lap. "You want *me* to stop him?"

Ethan put his hands on his head, as if squeezing his skull would make him think better. "We don't know how much time we have before he comes back—maybe he was telling the truth and maybe he wasn't—but we *do* know that he is coming back. What if . . . while he's coming *here,* we go *there* and rescue Sophie's parents and Lucy?"

"Yeah, and you zap all the monsters, and then it's over," Madison said. "He'll be just an ordinary man, and we call the police. It's brilliant!"

Sophie shook her head. "It's too dangerous."

"Agreed," Monster said. "It's my responsibility to keep her safe, and I can't fight all the monsters that Mr. Nightmare has, especially if he's off now dreaming up more."

Ethan spun in a circle, gesturing at the remaining bottles. "Then Sophie should dream up our own!"

Sophie held up her hands. "You want me to raise a dream army?"

Ethan nodded. "Sneak behind him with monsters of our own. How about more dinosaurs?" He raced over to the ledger.

Madison snorted. "You want to cross town with dinosaurs? Exactly how far do you think we'll get before everyone notices and stops us?" *Good point,* Sophie thought, *especially given the curfew.* The streets were being watched, and dinosaurs weren't inconspicuous at the best of times. Madison continued. "What we need are ninjas."

"Yes! Ninjas!" Ethan said. "Even better: ninja monsters with built-in throwing stars."

A tendril of hope began to sneak into Sophie. She did have the same power that Mr. Nightmare had, and she had a shop full of bottled dreams. "Fine, I'll do it, but we need to find someplace safe to hide you two."

Ethan shook his head. "We're safest with you."

"Basketball Boy is right," Madison said. "You're the Dream Girl."

Softly Monster said, "Sophie, you have to accept they're part of this now. We're all in it together." He laid a soft tentacle on her cheek. "Until Mr. Nightmare is stopped, they won't ever be safe."

"But . . ." But surely they hated her, or at least distrusted her. She wasn't like them. She didn't have dreams. She was a freak, as Madison said. She belonged on her own.

Glitterhoof trotted forward. He laid his head on her shoulder as if to comfort her. "Sophie, you must trust them. Trust will breed friendship, which will breed kindness, which may save you all. Friendship will be your strength. Men like Mr. Nightmare know nothing of it."

Rolling his eyes, Monster snorted. "Clearly, the glitter pony has watched too much TV. Still, the girl is right, and the boy has decent ideas."

Glitterhoof nudged her toward the shelves of dream bottles. Monster jumped up onto the counter next to the ledger. Sophie took a deep breath. "I'll have to work with whatever dreams we have left," she said.

Flipping through the ledger, Monster said, "He wiped out our entire collection of things with teeth and claws, and who knows what we lost to that thing with the vacuum mouth."

"How about this one?" Ethan picked up a bottle that swirled with sparkling blue liquid. It sloshed as he waved it from side to side.

Monster unfirmed a tentacle and plucked the bottle out of his hands. "Those are fragile."

Checking the number, Sophie compared it to the ledger. It was labeled *Forest variant, lots of fauna and waterfowl.* "It has animals," she said. Some animals were dangerous enough to fight monsters, or at least distract them. "Let's view it." Taking the bottle, she carried it over to the somnium. She dumped it in the top and put the bottle underneath to catch the dream when it finished. Madison and Ethan crowded next to her to watch.

"What are we looking at?" Madison asked.

"Just wait," Monster told her.

Images swirled in the mist as the sparkling blue dripped through the tube.

"Whoa," Ethan breathed.

An idyllic forest formed in the middle of the mist. Birds swooped through the air. A man in a suit and a woman with a parasol were having a picnic on the grass, and a rubber duck floated through the air past them, squeaking as it flew. And then without any transition, the man and woman were in a boat in the middle of a lake—the picnic was gone, and a baby moose stood by the shore of the lake. Rubber ducks flew in V formation overhead.

"Well, this makes no sense," Madison said.

"And is useless," Ethan said. "Rubber ducks can't fight monsters."

Sophie collected the bottle after the dream filled it again. She stoppered it and put it back on the shelf. She selected another from the same shelf and dumped it into the somnium. It was a different forest, with sunlight filtering through the trees and a stream trickling over rocks. A deer with magnificent antlers pranced across the stream, then paused to take a drink, while birds flew from tree to tree. She also saw a badger, a raccoon, and several rabbits. A few of the rabbits were wearing clothes, including top hats and gowns that stopped at their fluffy tails.

"Not seeing anything that can fight monsters," Madison said. "These are like the screen savers of dreams."

Glitterhoof snorted. "You do not have time to leisurely review your options. We've wasted enough time in chatter. Drink a dream, and then let's leave." *He's right,* Sophie thought. Mr. Nightmare could be back any minute. She ran back to the ledger and began flipping through before the dream in the somnium even finished.

"We need friendly monsters," Ethan said. "Like him."

"I'm not friendly," Monster said. "I'm just remarkably self-restrained. Sophie shaped me this way—the dreamer shapes the dream."

As the forest dream finished, Ethan picked up the bottle and stoppered it. "So if she dreamed something happy but wanted it to fight, would it come out ready to fight?"

Stopping, Sophie glanced at Monster. She knew that he was friendly because she'd dreamed him— she'd changed the dream the minute she entered it. Her parents had told her that was why they let her keep him. And Monster had thought the teacher with the vacuum mouth was frightening outside the dream because he'd terrified her in it.

"Theoretically?" Monster considered it. "Yes, I think it would."

"Okay, try for a vicious deer." Ethan tossed her the bottle.

"Fragile!" Sophie cried.

Monster caught the bottle with a tentacle. He handed it to her.

"Better yet," Madison said, "bring all the animals to life. We can have an army of forest creatures, like a Disney movie gone horribly wrong. If we're going to go for the crazy route, let's go all the way."

"Seriously, it could work," Ethan said. "Get that deer—it had sharp antlers. And a bear, if you can find one. Or wolves. Badgers. Porcupines."

"Ninja bunnies," Madison suggested.

Sophie laughed, in spite of herself, in spite of everything.

"You can do this, Sophie," Ethan urged.

"He's right," Monster said. "Do it, Sophie. Frolic through the forest and think pugnacious thoughts."

Sitting on the floor, Sophie leaned against the counter. She unstoppered the bottle and drank. She tasted fresh pine on the back of her tongue, and instantly she was in the middle of a forest. Birds chirped overhead. She was in a flouncy dress and carrying a basket. Whistling, she skipped through the trees, and then she stopped—she was supposed to find something. Frowning, she tried to remember what . . .

And then the memory slammed into her so hard that she staggered backward. *Animals,* she remembered. She was in a dream in order to find fighting animals. Bears, wolves, foxes, raccoons . . . anything with teeth and claws that could help against monsters.

The pine needles crunched under her feet. This dream had a smell. Pine. And flowers, sweet and heavy in the air. The forest extended a few trees in, then blurred into a generic green of "forest." This dreamer didn't have a very broad dream. Sophie reached the stream she'd seen in the somnium. Fish skipped over the rocks. She heard branches crack—and a deer trotted out from between the trees.

Seeing Sophie, the buck froze. He did have antlers—ten sharp points. *He's perfect,* Sophie thought. She pictured him tossing a monster into the air with those antlers.

Sophie didn't move. "Hi, I'm Sophie. I need your help saving my parents from a very bad man with a lot of monsters. Can you help protect us?"

He ran.

"Wait, please, come back!"

But he didn't come back.

She waited, but no other animals appeared. Walking along the path, she peered in between the trees, under the bushes, and up in the branches. She didn't see anything.

Sagging against a tree, she felt like crying. She was

both a freak and a failure. And now Mr. Nightmare was going to come back, and he'd capture all of them ... *Stop it,* she told herself. Every morning since September, she'd been climbing on that stupid yellow bus without a single friendly face to sit with. She'd been braving the halls by herself. She'd been facing down the cafeteria. And gym class. She was alone in middle school, life's shark pit. If she could survive *that,* she could wrestle this one ridiculous forest dream into helping her.

Pushing away from the tree, Sophie strode through the forest and into a clearing. Stopping, she scanned the view in all directions. If she couldn't have a vicious deer, maybe she could find a porcupine or a badger or even a bear, like Ethan said. She'd barely begun to look.

She heard a rustle of leaves in one of the bushes at the edge of the clearing and turned her head. A pink bunny with a white cotton-ball tail, wide black eyes, and a bow tie hopped out of the bushes. He sat and looked at her. Several more rabbits joined him. One held a teacup, as if she'd interrupted a tea party. A few of them wore top hats and aprons, as if they'd hopped straight out of a Beatrix Potter story.

"Uh, hi," Sophie said.

The rabbits stared at her. Even more hopped out of the bushes.

"Can you talk?"

They didn't answer.

"Guess not," Sophie said. "Any chance you'll help me defeat Mr. Nightmare?"

The pink bunny very clearly and very deliberately nodded.

Suddenly, they all vanished. "Hey, where are you? I need your help!" She hurried into the woods down a path, and it bucked and bent under her feet. She tripped over a clump of moss and sprawled forward, but her hands landed on nothing as the forest dissolved around her. She felt as though she was being pulled apart. She tried to cling to the images—she couldn't leave yet! She hadn't found her army! But her thoughts frayed, and her vision died in darkness.

And she woke.

This time, it hurt to wake, maybe because of the way the dream ended, shredding apart in her mind. She felt as if she were clawing her way through cobwebs. Her brain felt packed with fuzz, and her head throbbed as if her skull were too small. When she opened her eyes, Ethan and Madison were both staring down at her. Monster was perched on the counter by the ledger. Slowly, the pain in her head faded.

"Really, Sophie?" Monster said. "Bunnies?"

Pushing herself up to sitting, Sophie looked around the Dream Shop. It was filled with bunnies. Dozens of bunnies. The closest bunny—the pink one with the bow tie—stopped and rose onto his hind legs. "We might have to fight monsters. Can you do it?" Sophie asked.

The bunny twitched his nose. And then he launched himself at a chair leg. He dug his teeth into the wood and kicked with his hind legs so hard that the chair shook. Sophie, Madison, and Ethan scrambled back as the other rabbits flew at the chair. They attacked it with kicks and bites until the chair collapsed beneath them, gnawed and pounded apart.

Calm again, the pink bunny hopped back to Sophie, and then drew himself up onto his hind legs and saluted with one of his front paws. The other rabbits also rose onto their hind legs and saluted in unison.

20

"ALL THIS CUTE IS GOING TO MAKE ME SICK,"
Monster complained. Several of the rabbits skipped
around one another, taking turns sipping from the
tiny teacup that one of them held, in a sort of dance
around the Maypole without a Maypole. "Did you
tell them you'll send them back into a dream after this
is over?"

"I didn't get to that part," Sophie said.

"Humph." Monster raised his tentacles up as the
rabbits held paws and danced in a circle around him.
"Stop that. Shoo."

"No one will notice a few extra rabbits," Ethan
said as the pink bunny hopped over his feet. "Except
that one. People might notice that one."

Glitterhoof pranced from hoof to hoof. "We
should hurry. Time slips away."

"My Little Pony is right," Madison said. "Enough with the bunnies. He could be back any moment now, and we're fiddling around with rabbits."

Sophie watched the rabbits dance, and her heart sank. "Sorry. It's the best I could do." The attack on the chair was impressive, but they certainly weren't looking very vicious right now. She wished there were time to try again, though she didn't want to face that headache. She hadn't had a headache with the first couple of dreams—she wondered if she'd drunk the wrong type of dream, or too many too quickly.

"Come along, children and furry things," Glitterhoof said as he trotted up the stairs.

Sophie followed behind. The basement door was bowed out at the hinges and shattered in the middle, leaving a gaping hole. Gashes split the wood in multiple places.

"Wait, what if he's already here?" Madison asked.

Sophie laid a hand on Monster's shoulder. "Can you check and see if it's safe?"

"Stealth is my middle name." He slunk up the stairs and then paused. "Actually, I don't have a middle name. Wait here anyway." He then scampered into the shop.

Waiting on the stairs, Sophie listened as hard as

she could. She didn't hear anything—aside from the soft thumps of the rabbits as they hopped up the stairs. They weren't a match for monsters. Maybe they could serve as a distraction. It wasn't a nice thought, but if the monsters were indeed hungry . . . She glanced guiltily at the bunnies.

Monster poked his head around the corner of the doorway. "All clear."

"Take as many dreamcatchers as you can," Sophie told Ethan and Madison.

Gathering up dreamcatchers from the windows, Sophie stuffed them into her pockets and then filled her backpack with a bunch more. The others pocketed as many as they could too.

"Ready?" Ethan asked.

She surveyed the shop. Three kids, a winged pony, one monster, and a bunch of fluffy rabbits. It wasn't much of an army.

As if he knew what she was thinking, Monster said, "We may be little, but we are fierce."

All the rabbits stopped and looked at her—silently, solemnly, as if awaiting orders. A shiver chased over her skin. There was something in the weight of all their stares. Maybe, just maybe, they'd do all right.

"Okay, anytime now," Madison said.

Opening the back door, Sophie watched them all file outside. The backyard was dark, the shadows lit only by stray light from Ms. Lee's windows next door. Crickets chirped.

"Any chance we can fly?" Ethan asked. "It would be harder for them to see us."

Sophie turned to Glitterhoof. "I know you said three was too many, and now we have the bunnies, too, but you've been so brave and strong and . . ." She tried to think of another adjective.

"And sparkly," Monster supplied.

"And heroic," Sophie corrected. "Do you think you could try? Please?"

He preened. "But of course. Climb on."

The three of them climbed onto his back, squeezing together around the wings. Monster clung to the winged unicorn's mane. The rabbits climbed onto their laps and shoulders. Sophie felt as if she were wearing a fur coat. Several draped themselves over her shoulders and around her neck. Glitterhoof flapped his wings and rose off the ground.

Together, they flew up into the clouds and over the town.

★★★

Sophie felt wind in her hair. She tilted her head up and let the wind blow away her fear and doubt. She could do this. Droplets from the clouds sprayed into Sophie's face as they burst through. She saw the house below them, surrounded by dense clusters of trees. Lights were on inside, casting an amber halo on the lawn. It looked so innocent and ordinary from above; no wonder they'd been fooled. She wondered what was waiting for them down there. She hoped her parents were all right.

"Wait!" Ethan shouted.

Glitterhoof braked with his wings. They all lurched forward onto the pegasus's neck. He flapped, holding them at a steady height. "Ow, what—" Madison began.

"His car!" Ethan pointed at the street below as Mr. Nightmare's car pulled away from the curb. High above, they watched him drive away from the house and around the curve. The other cars were gone— she guessed the fights were over for the night. "Go now!"

The man with the muscles was still in the back-yard. Now she saw him for what he was: a guard. She didn't see any monsters with him, but that didn't mean they weren't there, lurking in the empty pool or behind a manicured bush or inside the barbecue grill. Leaning forward, Sophie pointed at him.

"Yes, yes, I *do* have eyes, you know," Glitterhoof said. "Bright and beautiful eyes, I might add, fit for captivating princesses."

Folding his wings, the pegasus dived for the muscle man in the yard. Sophie clung to his back as he flew silently, faster and faster. As if he felt a sudden rush of wind, the muscle man looked up, but it was too late. Glitterhoof slammed into him.

The man flew backward and landed flat. He opened his mouth to shout, and one of the rabbits hopped off of Glitterhoof's mane onto the man's face, pulled off his suit coat and top hat, and shoved them into the man's mouth.

"Nice," Madison said as she slid off Glitterhoof's back.

Ethan gave the winged pony a thumbs-up.

All of them dismounted and crept toward the house. Just because Mr. Nightmare was gone, it didn't mean the house was empty. It would be good if they could get inside unnoticed. "Monster, back door?" Sophie whispered.

Scampering ahead, he ran up to the back door and stuck his tentacles into the lock. In a few seconds, it popped open. The pink rabbit pushed past him and hopped inside, and then a stream of rabbits followed.

Sophie hurried to the door, but Monster stopped her, Ethan, and Madison with a tentacle. "Let the rabbits scout first," he suggested.

A second later, a rabbit hopped out and waved his paw, gesturing them inside.

They crept into the kitchen. It was dark—the light from outside fell in through the window across an ordinary sink, stove, and table and chairs. Lucy's backpack was no longer on the table. The only thing on the table was a newspaper and an empty glass. With the rabbits in the lead, Sophie peeked into the living room and dining room. "All clear," she whispered.

Ethan disappeared into the bathroom, and she heard the shower curtain shift. "Sophie . . . I think you need to see this," he whisper-called. She and Monster headed for the bathroom. "I don't know if this is anything, but it has lots of tubes and stuff, like the somnium, and . . ."

Sophie didn't hear the rest of what Ethan said. She stared into the bathtub. Sitting there, inside the tub, was the distiller.

It's here! she thought. *That means . . .*

Monster placed a velvety paw on Sophie's hand and voiced what she barely dared think: "If he has the distiller, then your parents must be here too."

Sophie felt herself beginning to smile. The distiller would be useless without Mom and Dad. If Mr. Nightmare wanted dreams distilled, then he'd have to keep them nearby. "Let's find them."

"I can tell you they weren't in my cell," Madison said. "Look upstairs?"

All of them headed for the stairs. The rabbits hopped up first, and the others followed. Upstairs was a dark hallway, lit only from the faint downstairs light. There weren't any windows on the hall. Sophie counted five doors. With the others in a semicircle around her, she tried the nearest door, bracing herself in case it wasn't empty. The rabbits filed inside, and she followed.

The first room was a bedroom. The sheets on the bed were rumpled, and a stack of laundry was falling off a chair next to a closet that was stuffed with men's shoes. This could be Mr. Nightmare's bedroom. It looked so . . . normal. A pile of books, mostly biographies, was on the bedside table, along with an alarm clock. The dresser surface had an electric razor plugged in and an assortment of ties and belts.

A dreamcatcher hung from the headboard. Monster pointed to it. "That's ironic," he whispered. "Mr. Nightmare doesn't want to experience his own nightmares."

The rabbits nibbled on the carpet as Sophie, Madison, and Ethan checked under the bed and in the closet and then gathered at the door. Monster pushed it open with a tentacle and poked his head outside. "All clear," he said.

They tiptoed back into the hallway. The next room was a bathroom, ordinary, with two toothbrushes, a tube of toothpaste, and a sliver of soap in the soap dish. The mirror was spotted with dried toothpaste, and there was a ring of mold around the drain in the sink. There was nothing monstrous. And nothing that indicated her parents or Lucy were here.

Next was a linen closet containing nothing more ominous than towels and a vacuum. "This isn't going well," she whispered. "Maybe they're—"

She heard footsteps on the stairs and cut herself off. Quickly, Ethan and Madison piled back into Mr. Nightmare's bedroom, while Sophie and Monster ducked into the linen closet, squeezing in next to the vacuum. She hoped the rabbits had the sense to hide somewhere too.

In the closet, Monster murmured, "Reminds me of where I was born."

"Shh."

She saw a shadow pass in front of the linen closet, and then she heard a growl. On the plus side, that didn't sound like Mr. Nightmare—he hadn't suddenly returned. On the minus side . . . "Guess the monsters aren't all in cages."

"Ready for our first one?" Monster asked.

"On three," she whispered. "One, two, three . . ." She burst out of the closet. She saw the monster—he was as gray as a rock and had multiple arms bulging from his back. Monster leaped for his head. The creature howled. His many arms flailed, but the rabbits swarmed him, leveling karate kicks at his body. Several jumped on each arm, pinning it down. He tossed a few rabbits against the walls, but they sprang back and ran for him again. Jumping on, the rabbits continued to cling to his arms, while Monster pulled him off balance with his tentacles. With rabbits all over him, he fell to the floor. Monster and the rabbits quickly backed away as Sophie sprang forward and pressed the dreamcatcher against his gray skin. He faded beneath her, and she thumped to the floor.

"Madison, Ethan," she called in a whisper. "It's safe. For now."

They crept out of the bedroom. One of the rabbits had lost his top hat, and the other had her apron askew, but everyone seemed okay.

"Nice job," she told the bunnies.

They nodded briskly at her.

There were two more doors on the floor. Sophie hurried to the next one and tried the knob—locked. Maybe, maybe, please, her parents would be behind it! She stepped back so Monster could open the lock with his tentacles. The lock unclicked.

All of them readied their dreamcatchers as Sophie swung the door open. The rabbits hopped inside, and the rest of them followed.

Inside was Lucy.

She was cowering on the bed, her knees tucked under her chin. Her face was red and splotchy, as if she'd been crying. Prowling around the foot of the bed was a lizard-like creature.

The ninja bunnies charged. They swarmed over the creature, knocking him to the floor. Wielding a dreamcatcher, Sophie threw herself onto its tail and pressed the dreamcatcher to his hide as the rabbits leaped off.

He swept his tail to the side, and she was tossed against the wall. Madison and Ethan rushed forward and both slapped dreamcatchers onto him.

The lizard thing flailed but then at last faded.

Sophie hurried to Lucy. "Are you okay?"

Lucy's lower lip was quivering. She nodded, then shook her head, lips pressed together as if she was too terrified to scream or cry. Several rabbits jumped up and climbed onto the bed. One sniffed at Lucy's feet. Another curled against her leg. A third—the pink one with the bow tie—hopped into her lap and snuggled.

She scooped the pink bunny into her arms and hugged him, crying into his fur.

"You're safe now," Ethan said. "We're here to save you."

Sitting on the bed, Madison put her arm around Lucy. "They saved me, and now we're saving you. But you need to be brave. We still have to—"

Lucy gave a hiccup-yelp and pointed toward the doorway.

Sophie turned to see another monster. Slinking through the door, it looked like a mix between a dog and an insect. Eyes covered its hairy body. A tongue shot out of its mouth, and then it widened its mouth and roared.

Monster and the rabbits ran toward it. The dog-insect snapped its teeth at Monster as he leaped over its head. From behind, Monster latched his tentacles around the dog-insect's neck, but the creature seemed not to notice. Circling it, the rabbits kicked and bit. The pink rabbit jumped off Lucy's lap and ran to attack the monster too. Dragging Monster with it, the dog-insect began going after the rabbits. It chomped one on the leg, and the rabbit squealed.

"No!" Lucy cried, speaking for the first time. "Don't eat the bunnies!" Jumping off the bed, she charged across the room, past Sophie, and leaped onto the back of the dog-insect. Sophie, Madison, and Ethan ran forward to help. As Lucy rode the nightmare, Sophie pressed a dreamcatcher to its side. Monster and the bunnies backed away as the dog-insect faded beneath the girl, and she collapsed on the ground.

Lucy lay on the carpet without moving or speaking.

"Lucy?" Dropping the dreamcatcher, Sophie knelt next to her.

"I did it!" Lucy lifted her head, and Sophie saw she was smiling. "I always run in my dreams, and I'm never fast enough. But this time, I didn't run away. And now it's gone."

Beside her, the rabbits tore the dreamcatcher into shards of wood and bits of string. Sophie moved to stop them—a dream was a dream—but she was too late. The dreamcatcher was shredded, and the monster was permanently gone.

Monster and Sophie stared at the ruined dreamcatcher. Kneeling too, Madison hugged Lucy, who hugged her fiercely back. "I didn't cry," Lucy said. "I didn't scream. It would have eaten me if I screamed. That's what he told me—the scary nightmare man, I mean. He wanted me quiet. Can I scream now?" Her voice sounded hoarse, as if she'd done a lot of screaming earlier.

"Not yet," Madison told her with another half hug.

"Why do you have rabbits?" Lucy asked.

"Don't ask," Madison said. "Trust me, you don't want to know. But they're friendly, and so is that fuzzy thing with tentacles."

Sophie wanted to tell the little girl how sorry she was that this had happened; how she'd wanted to help Lucy with her nightmares, not give her more; how it was going to be over soon and she'd never have to see Sophie again. "Do you know where my parents are?"

Lucy began to cry. "I want my mom and dad." The rabbits clustered around her. The pink bunny rose onto his hind legs and wrapped his paws around her ankle in a hug.

"We'll bring you to them," Ethan promised. "But we also need to find Sophie's parents. Have you seen them?"

Lucy shook her head.

Sophie felt her heart sink, but she told herself it didn't mean anything. Lucy had been locked up. It made sense she wouldn't know where the other prisoners were. There was still one door that they hadn't opened.

Crying harder, Lucy clung to Madison's arm. Sophie expected Madison to brush her off, but she didn't. She seemed uncharacteristically gentle with Lucy, and Sophie thought of Madison's younger sister, who had been born sick. Arm around the younger girl, Madison guided Lucy out into the hallway. Sophie, Ethan, and Monster followed.

"One door left," Ethan said.

Her parents *had* to be there. She was sure of it. She felt her heart pounding faster. Ethan reached the door first and pushed it open. The rabbits hopped in, followed by Monster.

Inside, a girl's voice said, "What is *that?* And why are there rabbits wearing clothes?"

"Whoa, another prisoner," Ethan said.

They all pressed inside, following the rabbits. Sophie squeezed past Ethan to stand between him and Madison. Lucy darted around them.

Inside was a bedroom covered in posters of the night sky. An unmade bed was in one corner, piled high with teddy bears and a stack of books. A girl with brown hair and brown eyes—about Sophie's age—in a pink T-shirt and jeans stood in the middle of the room. She was hugging a book to her chest, as if she'd just been reading. Her hair was stuck in a ponytail and bangs fell over her eyes. Sophie tried to squash her disappointment that it wasn't her parents.

Scurrying forward, Lucy grabbed the girl's hand. "Come on! Hurry!"

The girl resisted. "Who are you? What do you want?"

Forcing herself to smile, Sophie waved. "Hi. I'm Sophie. That's Lucy, and this is Ethan, Madison, and Monster. I don't know the rabbits' names. What matters is that Lucy's right. We have to hurry."

Pulling away from Lucy, the girl retreated across the room until her calves hit the bed and she had to stop. A teddy bear toppled from the bed onto the floor. Bending, the girl scooped it back onto the bed and dumped the book with it, all without taking her eyes off them. "But . . . How did you get here? You need to leave! It's not safe. There are monsters in this house. They're trained to attack strangers."

"Yeah, we noticed," Madison said.

Crossing to her, Sophie held out a dreamcatcher. The girl stared at it and then at Sophie. "Press it against any monster you see," Sophie explained. "Except that one." She pointed at Monster. "He's my friend."

"You're *friends* with a monster?"

"It's a little weird," Madison agreed, "but he's a nice monster."

Sighing as if he were long-suffering, Monster said, "I am *not* nice."

Sophie wondered who the girl was. She didn't recognize her, and the policeman had said there were two missing kids. Maybe she was from another town, or kidnapped at another time. Judging from the room, it looked like she'd been here for a while. Clothes were draped over a chair and bulging out of a closet. Crumpled pretzel bags filled the trash can. The rabbits sniffed at her shoes, and the girl skipped away as if afraid they'd bite. Gently, Sophie asked, "What's your name?"

"Christina."

"Christina, have you seen any other prisoners? Maybe a man and a woman who kind of look like me?" She tried to keep her voice calm and even. If Christina had been here a while, she might freak out easily.

"Her parents," Ethan clarified.

Christina shook her head slowly. *She must be in shock,* Sophie thought. She wondered how long she'd been walled off in this room. Weeks? Months? Sophie felt a surge of pity.

"Can we go home now?" Lucy sniffled.

Sophie held out her hand toward Christina and hoped she looked friendly and kind. She didn't have much practice with that. "We'll help you go home too. Come with us."

Still shaking her head, Christina was looking at Sophie as if she had sprouted tentacles. "But I . . . I don't understand."

Slowly and clearly, Sophie said, "We're rescuing you."

21

"YOU HAVE A PET MONSTER," CHRISTINA SAID.

"He's not a pet," Sophie said. "He's my friend."

At the door, Ethan said, "Guys, we should get out while we can." He retreated to check the hallway, and several rabbits hopped with him.

Christina looked at the bunnies at Sophie's feet and at Monster, wrapping his tentacles around Sophie's waist. She took a tentative step toward Sophie. "Are you . . . Are you like me?"

"Like you? What do you mean?"

Instead of answering, Christina scurried across the room to the desk. She yanked open a drawer and with shaking hands held up several empty blue bottles. "I thought I was the only one. But you have a monster and multicolored bunnies, and I didn't dream them."

Madison poked Sophie. "Hey, she's a freak like you."

"I can't dream my own dreams," Christina said, eyes fixed on Sophie, full of hope. "And when I drink someone else's dream . . ."

". . . you bring things to life." Sophie felt a lump in her throat, and her eyes felt hot. All her life, she'd thought she was the only one, and then Mr. Nightmare came . . . "Mr. Nightmare isn't the one like me. *You* are." He'd kidnapped Madison and Lucy to have dreams, her parents to distill them, and Christina to bring them to life—everything he needed to produce an endless supply of monsters to sell.

Sophie started walking toward Christina, and Christina walked toward her until they stood face-to-face, inches away, staring at each other in wonder.

At the same time, both of them began to talk. "How do you—" "What do you—" "No, you go first." "No, you." "I never—" "I thought—" And then they both began to laugh, covering their mouths to silence the sound. Tears leaked out of Sophie's eyes. It wasn't Mr. Nightmare! It was this girl!

"Very nice bonding moment," Madison said. "Can we leave now, please?"

Lucy tugged on Sophie's sleeve. "I want to go home!"

"Come with us," Sophie said to Christina. She held out her hand again, and this time, Christina took it with a tentative smile. Together, they plunged out into the hallway and hurried toward the stairs.

At the top of the stairs, Monster splayed out his tentacles to stop them. "Let the rabbits go first," he whispered. "Just in case."

The bunnies hopped past them and down the stairs.

After a few seconds, Monster nodded, and they all crept single-file down the stairs to the living room. Everything seemed quiet. The rabbits grazed on the carpet. Sophie peeked into the dining room, the bathroom, and the kitchen. All empty. Her parents must be in the basement—maybe there were more rooms like the one Madison had been in, or maybe they'd been moved into Madison's cell. Just because they weren't there before didn't mean they weren't there now.

Light swept across the living room. Pushing aside the curtain, Ethan looked out the window. "He's back! We have to leave!" He pointed to the kitchen. "Back door!" Madison, Ethan, and Lucy bolted through the living room to the kitchen.

"Not without my parents!" Sophie said.

"No choice," Monster said, tentacles flailing, propelling her into the kitchen. "I'm sorry, Sophie. We'll find a way to rescue them later."

Christina caught her arm. "Wait! There's a monster on guard."

Reaching the door first, Lucy flung it open. Outside on the patio, Sophie saw Glitterhoof had the muscled guard still pinned on the ground. The winged pegasus raised his head when he saw them and spread his wings. Seizing on the distraction, the guard spat the rabbit clothing out of his mouth with such force that the tiny top hat sailed into Glitterhoof's face.

Startled, the winged pony reared back, lifting his front hooves off of the man's shoulder. Roaring, the man punched his hands together, and his body began to expand like a balloon. His muscles bulged bigger, and his feet stretched.

Lucy began to scream, and Madison quickly shushed her.

The man's face contorted, bulging until it looked as if it were made of rocks.

"Other way!" Ethan cried, and they ran into the

living room—Ethan, Lucy, and Madison, followed by Christina, Sophie, and Monster.

Before they reached it, the front door was thrown open, and three lizard-like monsters with red scales and green tongues barreled inside, followed by Mr. Nightmare. Everyone retreated to the kitchen and ran again to the back door. Madison was fastest.

Glitterhoof galloped toward the house, and Madison tossed Lucy onto the unicorn's back. Before she could climb on as well, she was pulled away by the enormous muscle man. "Get her out of here!" Madison yelled to Glitterhoof.

With Lucy clinging to his mane, Glitterhoof took to the skies.

Sophie felt someone grab her arm and turned fast. It was Christina. "Quick, hide!" Christina said, and pulled her into a bathroom. Monster ran with them, as did the rabbits. Christina slammed the door shut and leaned against it, ear pressed to the wood.

In the kitchen, Ethan and Madison screamed. "Let go of me!" "Let me go!" "Get your hands off me!" "No!" And Sophie heard Mr. Nightmare and the muscle man shouting too, as well as the growls, hisses, and cries of the monsters. She wanted to run out and help them, but Monster wrapped his tentacles around her wrists.

"Stay safe," he whispered in her ear. "You can't help them if you're caught."

The rabbits huddled around her ankles. Pressed against the door, Sophie and Christina listened. Soon, it was quiet. Doors opened and then slammed shut. Sophie reached for the knob, and Monster again wrapped a tentacle around her wrist.

"There's someone still in the kitchen," Christina whispered.

Sophie heard a chair scrape across the floor.

"We have to wait until he leaves," Monster whispered.

Side by side, Sophie and Christina sank onto the floor of the bathroom. Still listening intently, Sophie didn't hear any sound from the kitchen. She hoped Lucy and Glitterhoof had gotten away. She didn't know where Glitterhoof would take her. Maybe they would go for help. Or maybe that was too much to hope for—he wouldn't know where to find help, and Lucy was most likely hysterical.

They sat in silence.

If there were a clock, she would be listening to

each second tick. As it was, she listened to each breath they took — first panting, and then slower. They breathed together, waiting, listening.

In a whisper, Christina asked, "How long have you known what happens if you dream?"

"Since I was six," Sophie said. "You?"

"About the same. My father used to find and sell dreams to dream shops —"

"My parents own a dream shop!" Sophie whispered back.

"I'd had a really bad day at school, I remember. I didn't have any friends because other kids were . . . not like me. You know."

Sophie did know. Oh yes, did she know!

"My dad snuck into my room and gave me a dream bottle. He'd bought it from one of the shops he worked for." Christina was whispering so softly that Sophie had to lean close to hear the words. "I think he thought it would cheer me up. Mom never would have allowed it. She was dead-set against anything to do with dreams. They used to fight about it all the time. Anyway, I drank it, and a monster appeared, and my parents freaked out."

Sophie nodded. "Mine freaked out also. But I drank it on my own. I was curious."

"I was curious too," Christina said. "Other people talk about dreams all the time. I thought it was like an enchanted journey, like to Narnia or Oz, and I wasn't invited. But it's not like that."

Outside the bathroom, a cabinet door creaked open and then shut. Sophie listened for another sound—footsteps, voices, the chair, but she heard nothing else. Climbing up onto the back of the toilet, Monster examined the window. It was frosted and small. He tapped around the edges. It wasn't the kind of window that could open. Even if it could, Sophie doubted she could fit. Maybe the rabbits could . . . But breaking the window would draw the attention of whoever or whatever was in the kitchen.

"You know what I like about not dreaming?" Christina whispered. "Waking up and feeling clear. I'm never confused after a dreamless night. But the times I drink a dream . . . It's like my brain feels fuzzy. It has to reorient itself. And it gets worse if I drink a lot of them. Imagine what happens to a brain if you dream every night!"

"I felt that way when I made them." Sophie pointed at the rabbits. "Felt like my brain was stuffed with fluff. And my head hurt afterward." She thought of all the monsters she'd seen here and wondered how badly Christina's head had hurt.

"Exactly," Christina said. "When you don't dream, you can see the world clearly. Your brain doesn't lie to you. You don't mix up memories and dreams."

Sophie nodded. She'd seen her parents mix up things like that—a conversation that one claimed to have had, an errand they dreamed they'd run. It must be scary to not be able to trust your own mind.

"Still always wanted to have a dream of my own, though," Christina said with a sigh. "Just one, and that would be enough."

"Me too." Sophie had never said these things to anyone except Monster. It felt like the words were pouring out of her, lightening her as they drained away. "You ever try not going to sleep?"

"Yes. You ever try to scare yourself so badly in hopes you'd have your own nightmare?"

"Yes!" Sophie had to fight to keep her voice to a whisper. "Did you read books right before going to sleep and imagine them as you closed your eyes, hoping you'd dream about it?"

"All the time."

"What were your favorites?" Sophie asked.

"*The Lion, the Witch, and the Wardrobe,*" Christina said.

"*Harry Potter.* All seven of them."

"Definitely. *A Wrinkle in Time.*"

The kitchen faucet was on. Water sloshed, a steady stream, and then shut off. Sophie heard footsteps again and held her breath, listening hard, hoping they'd exit the kitchen, but they didn't. She exhaled.

Christina whispered again. "When I was little, I thought maybe I did dream but just didn't remember it. I used to set the alarm clock at random hours, trying to catch myself mid-dream. Never worked."

"I tried eating weird food before bedtime," Sophie confessed. "Bananas with ketchup."

"Sometimes I left the TV on all night," Christina said. "I thought I'd hear the dialogue in my sleep and it would be my dream. Never worked either."

Climbing down off the toilet, Monster crossed the bathroom and squeezed between them to listen again at the door. Both Sophie and Christina fell silent, listening as well. Voices drifted from the kitchen, muffled by the door—two men. Sophie guessed it was Mr. Nightmare and the muscle man, who was actually a monster.

"Were you really kidnapped?" Christina asked.

"Not me," Sophie said. "That man, Mr. Nightmare, kidnapped Madison and Lucy and tried to kidnap Ethan because they have vivid nightmares, and he kidnapped my parents because they're really good at distilling dreams."

"But not you?"

"Guess he doesn't need me." Sophie didn't add, *Because he has you.*

"Then maybe he won't chase you if you run."

Sophie squeezed her hand. "I won't leave you here. Or anyone. We'll all escape." Beside her, Monster had perked up, interested, as if waiting to hear if Christina had an idea. She might, Sophie thought. If she'd been here a while, she might know about their captor and possible escape routes.

"You're friends with kids who dream?"

Sophie hesitated. "I don't know if they're really friends . . ."

"Dreamers aren't like us," Christina said, as if quoting a favorite saying. "They have weak, messy minds. When they sleep, their fear wins."

Sophie wasn't sure about that. Her parents weren't weak, and neither was Madison. After being bound and gagged in the basement, Madison still was brave enough to come back here—she even comforted Lucy, rather than falling apart, when they ran into more monsters. And Ethan seemed to think clearly even when presented with something he thought was impossible—he'd been the one who had the idea of dreaming up the dinosaur and of coming back. If they'd been a little faster searching the house, it might have worked.

In the kitchen, the chairs scraped again, as if the man (or men) were standing up. A door—the back door, she guessed—squeaked open, then banged shut. Sophie tensed. This could be their chance! But then she heard more footsteps, and the suction sound of the refrigerator door. "One of them is still there," Monster whispered.

"What if he doesn't leave?" Sophie asked.

"Or what if he has to pee?" Monster asked.

Christina stood. "I will distract him. You go."

"But what about you? And my parents? And Ethan and Madison?" She was *not* leaving them.

"I can't help them, but I can help you," Christina said. "And you're the important one. You're the non-dreamer. They're just ordinary people. Please, Sophie, don't argue. So long as I know you're free, that's enough." Stepping toward the toilet, Christina flushed it. She then gave Sophie a quick hug, unlocked the door, and strolled outside.

A chair scraped in the kitchen. "Christina? What are you doing down here?"

Sophie heard fast footsteps—Christina was running. She heard Mr. Nightmare shout, and then footsteps pounded on the stairs up to the bedrooms.

"Sophie, are we going to run?" Monster asked.

She looked at him, at the bunnies, and then at the distiller in the bathtub. *When they sleep, fear wins,* Christina had said. "No, we're not going to run," Sophie said. "I have an idea."

22

SOPHIE TOUCHED THE GLASS CURVES OF THE DIS-
tiller. "There was a dreamcatcher in Mr. Nightmare's
bedroom. It's hanging from his bed. Why?" She didn't
wait for Monster to answer. "He knows dreamcatchers work—I don't think he'd have one just for decora-
tion. I think he has bad dreams."

"And you want to drink his dream?" Monster
guessed.

She nodded. "When he sleeps, his fear wins—like
Christina said."

Monster clapped his paws together softly. "And if
we bring his fear to life, we win."

"Exactly," Sophie said. She knelt next to the rabbits. "Are you really ninja bunnies? Can you hop
upstairs and bring that dreamcatcher back without
being seen?"

In a semicircle, the rabbits were on their hind legs, at attention. The pink rabbit saluted.

She felt a stab of guilt, bringing them here and putting them in danger. "You could get caught. You could get eaten. You could be turned back into a dream. So I need you to be very careful. There are not-nice people and not-nice monsters out there. Only do this if you're sure . . ."

The bunnies hopped to the door and nudged at it with their noses.

"Guess that's a yes," Monster said.

She cautiously opened the door a few inches. Flattening against the wall, the bunnies slipped out. They scattered, slipping into the shadows. She shut and locked the door, and then she sat down with Monster to wait.

"Your parents weren't upstairs, so they must be downstairs," Monster said. "There must be more rooms like the one that Madison was in."

Sophie nodded. "So that's where we go, if we can, if this works." It *had* to work. Christina had bought her some time, but not forever. This was their best and only chance. Everyone else was captured. She was the only one who could save them—and if this worked, she could save all of them. "After we rescue my parents, Ethan, and Madison, we'll go back up and rescue Christina again."

"You don't know that he dreamed anything useful," Monster cautioned, "and without a somnium, we'll have no way to check the dream before you drink it. It could be useless or upsetting."

"At worst, it will distract him. At best . . . This will work, Monster." She checked over the distiller. None of the tubes looked broken. There were remnants of a dream on the bottom of the tub. It had been used here. Glittery yellow was caught in the drain.

"And the muscle man?"

"You saw him," Sophie said. "He's not real. We find a way to distract him too and then use a dreamcatcher on him. The rabbits will help." She looked around for a bottle and found some cups by the sink. That would do. She didn't need to store it; she just needed to drink it.

"You think we're 'not real'?" Monster's voice was soft.

Sophie stopped and knelt beside him. His tentacles were drooping. She petted one. "I didn't mean *you*. Of course you're real. You're my best friend."

He sniffed. "Old best friend. You looked like you'd found a new one."

Sophie poked him. "Monster, are you jealous? Of a human?"

"Never. But I'm not looking forward to the time when you don't need me anymore."

"I'll always need you!" It was hard to keep her voice to a whisper. What had gotten into him? It was *good* that she'd found someone like her. He'd seen her mope often enough about feeling alone and different.

"Children outgrow their imaginary friends."

"You aren't imaginary."

"I came from a dream. What other definition of *imaginary* do you want?"

Sophie glared at him, unable to think of the right words to convince him, and finally she reached over and pinched his ear on the tender spot under the furry flap. He yelped, softly. "*Not* imaginary," she said.

He glared back at her but didn't argue.

The wait was painfully long. She felt as if her ears were listening so hard that they hurt. There was someone in the kitchen again. She heard the kitchen sink turn on and dishes clatter. Someone—Mr. Nightmare or the guard—had come back to finish his dinner. The sounds were so ordinary. It was so strange to think that there were people imprisoned in this house, and that she was trapped in the bathroom.

At last, she heard little scratches at the door. She scrambled to her feet and inched the door open. Led by the pink one, the rabbits shot inside. They carried a pillowcase between them.

She locked the door behind them and opened the pillowcase. Inside was the dreamcatcher. "You are wonderful, amazing, the most brilliant rabbits ever."

The pink rabbit preened, and the others shook paws, as if congratulating one another.

She carried the dreamcatcher over to the distiller. She'd seen her parents do this a thousand times, but she'd never done it herself. Slowly, she tilted the dreamcatcher over the funnel at the top. "Monster, can you work the levers?" she whispered. Usually Mom poured and Dad worked the levers.

"On it," he said, taking up a position at the base of the distiller.

She couldn't see the dream on the threads, but as soon as Monster pressed the first lever, scattered droplets formed inside the funnel. Sophie tilted the dreamcatcher more.

"Gently," Monster whispered. His breath was hot on Sophie's leg. He pressed another lever, allowing the droplets from the dream to slide into the next tube. The liquid began to glow.

Her arms started to ache from holding the dream-catcher up and out over the bathtub. At last, no more drops formed. She laid the dreamcatcher down. "We can do this, right?"

Monster scooted sideways so Sophie could work the levers. "I'd cheer you on with pompoms, but they're not really my thing."

Watching the drips move through the tubes, she thought of all the times she'd watched her parents, memorizing their every move, practicing when they weren't looking. She mimicked what she'd seen them do. The key was to increase the sparkle, but to do it carefully . . . It would be very easy to accidentally lose bits of the dream. She had to watch it every second: when it dimmed, she had to make it turn; when it flickered, drop it down; when it glowed, guide it to a spiral. If she wanted a clear and complete dream, she had to do to right. Her parents always made the crispest dreams.

Concentrating, she raced through the levers, causing the liquid to veer faster down a tube, where it brightened as it sloshed, and then swerved to the left, where it dimmed. She hit another lever. The dream flickered as it switched direction, and then it flashed brighter again.

She continued to guide it through the tubes until at last, it dripped into the cup. Squatting next to it, she watched the shimmering blue liquid slosh inside. When the drips stopped, Monster turned off the distiller. Sophie gently removed the cup from underneath the spigot.

She lowered herself onto the bathmat and leaned against the cabinet. She didn't want to tip over and make any kind of noise when she fell asleep. She stared at the cup. It felt very wrong to sleep when Mr. Nightmare was right outside in the kitchen. She was making herself vulnerable at a bad time. But Monster would protect her and wake her.

Raising the cup to her lips, she hoped he'd dreamed something useful.

★★★

It was snowing fat flakes out the window.

She pressed her nose against the pane, and her breath fogged the glass. With this much snow, they'd cancel school. She'd better tell Mom and Dad. Slipping off the couch, she stood—and she didn't know where she was. This wasn't her living room. All the couches were red leather, and the rug was white. The shelves

319

were filled with glass figurines instead of books, and there was a coffee table made out of an old trunk. She'd never seen this room before.

I'm in his dream, she remembered.

There was a bowl of chocolate ice cream on the coffee table. The chocolate was piled several scoops high, and as she stared at it, it melted in front of her, pooling on the table and then dripping onto the white rug. When the melted chocolate hit the rug, it turned as red as blood. It seeped and spread until the whole room was red.

And then the red liquefied, and ocean waves lapped against the coffee table and the couch. Sophie climbed onto the back cushions. Sharks circled the sofa.

If a shark bit her in a dream, would it hurt? She clutched the cushions as the couch rose on a wave and smacked down on the other side. Water sprayed around her and then slammed into her. In the distance, a train whistle screamed, inexplicably, and then a jet engine roared, but then there was only the sound of wave hitting wave, hard smacks.

Water pummeled her, pouring over her head and face until she breathed water. It burned as it filled her throat, and then she was submerged. She swam toward the light above her, but it fractured. Her lungs felt shredded, and her skull felt as if it wanted to break apart. Spots appeared before her eyes, and then she was lying in darkness, her cheek pressed against a cool floor, and she was able to breathe again.

"Finally found you," a woman's voice said. "Did you really think you could run forever? You can't run, swim, or fly fast enough to ever get away from me." Sophie felt something rough and dry stroke her cheek. It felt like a stick.

A light switched on, and Sophie realized she was lying on a kitchen floor. Coughing, expecting water to come out of her mouth, she twisted to see who had spoken.

Sophie screamed.

A woman's face loomed over her. It was planted on top of the body of a massive brown spider. Her eight legs straddled Sophie. Her abdomen was the size of Sophie. Her face was as lovely as a model's, framed by lush black curls that cascaded down to her hairy arachnid shoulders. Her makeup was perfect, with bronze skin, deep pink lips, contoured cheekbones, and accented eyes. She frowned, a perfect upside-down rainbow frown. "You aren't Eugene."

"Hi. I'm Sophie. I borrowed his dream."

The spider woman lowered her face—all eight legs bending to bring her closer. Her breath smelled like overripe peaches. "Ahh, so this is a dream. That explains my shape. And you say you borrowed his dream . . . You must be a friend of his."

"No!" Immediately Sophie worried that the answer should have been yes.

"No?" The spider woman straightened her legs, and Sophie could see her entire spider body. She stepped backwards, allowing Sophie to sit up. "Why would he give you his dream?"

"I, uh, took it." In a burst, she told the spider woman about how Mr. Nightmare had kidnapped her parents and Madison and Lucy and how he now had Ethan as well, and Sophie was trapped in a bathroom . . . She petered out of words as the woman stared at her.

"So, he's taken more children."

"More? He's done this before?"

"He's done this to *me*. My child! Stolen away and fed a diet of lies." The spider woman skittered around the kitchen, her feet clicking on the floor. The kitchen was filled with shadows. A stove lurked in one corner. Half a sink was visible beneath a cloudy window. Crayon drawings were stuck to the fridge, the proud work of some small child, as well as photos, but they were blurry. Sophie wondered if she'd distilled the dream correctly. At least the spider woman was here, even if the room wasn't complete.

"He's doing it again," Sophie said. "Will you help me stop him?" As she asked, she wondered if it was a mistake to invite this spider woman out into the real world. Then she pushed her doubt down. If she believed this creature would help, then maybe she would. *Help us,* she thought as hard as she could.

And then she woke.

In the bathroom, she lay on the bathmat. Monster was around her. And the spider woman again straddled her, squeezed between the bathtub and the sink. Sophie tried to get her mind to stop spinning. Her head hurt even worse than after she'd dreamed up the rabbits. Squeezing her head with her hands, she concentrated on breathing evenly. She was here. Awake. Alive. Unhurt. Mostly unhurt.

"You brought a friend," Monster whispered in her ear.

"I hope so," Sophie whispered back.

Underneath the spider's abdomen, Sophie blinked hard several times, trying to clear the last of the fuzziness left over from the dream. The throbbing in her head had dulled to a faint ache. As it faded away, she pressed her ear against the bathroom door. There was still someone in the kitchen. She heard the squeaking of a chair, the shutting of a cabinet, the whoosh of the sink—one person, she thought. She hoped it was Mr. Nightmare.

Reaching up, she unlocked the door and twisted the knob. The spider woman lifted one leg and pushed the door open. She then shuffled out, carefully placing the tips of her eight legs silently on the floor.

"Creepy," Monster noted.

Clustering by the door, the rabbits crouched,

ready. Sophie laid her hand on the pink rabbit's back. "Wait until he sees the spider, then we'll go out."

In the kitchen, a glass shattered on the floor, and a man screamed.

"I'm thinking he saw her," Monster said. He darted out of the bathroom, and Sophie tiptoed behind him. From the hallway, she could see half the kitchen: the stove, the sink, and part of the table. It had a bowl with a spoon in it. He'd been eating.

"Aw, don't look so surprised, Eugene," the spider lady said. "You had to know I'd find you. Why else dream about me?"

Mr. Nightmare's voice shook. "You aren't her."

"I am close enough."

Dropping to hands and knees, Sophie peeked around the corner into the kitchen—the door to the basement was directly behind Mr. Nightmare. The back door to the yard was behind the spider woman.

Now the spider's many legs clicked on the kitchen floor. "I suppose I have you to thank for my appearance. Is this how you truly see me, Eugene?"

"It is what you are."

"Am I poisonous?" the spider lady asked.

"Just your words." He shuffled backwards, as if trying to inch away, and hit the sink counter.

"Interesting," she said. "Do I feature in all your dreams?"

His eyes were fixed on the spider woman. "Always."

"Then, in a way, I have already caught you. And this is only a formality." With a cry, the spider launched herself forward. Mr. Nightmare grabbed a skillet from the stove and hurled it at her head. It hit the side of her face, and she reared back.

"Inside, *now!*" Mr. Nightmare shouted.

The back door banged open, and the muscle man charged through and rammed into the off-balance spider lady. She crashed into the wall. A clock fell from the wall and smashed onto the floor.

"She needs help," Sophie said.

Brushing past her, the rabbits charged into the kitchen. They swarmed over the muscle man. Sophie stepped forward to follow, and Monster caught her leg with his tentacles. "How about a fire extinguisher?" He pointed beside the stove.

She nodded. If she ran fast enough, she could make it. He'd see her, but— Before she could complete the thought, Monster shot across the kitchen, keeping low, and leaped onto the counter. He plucked the fire extinguisher off the wall and aimed it at the muscle man.

He fired, and white foam sprayed out of the extinguisher and into the man's face. The man roared, and Sophie ran toward him. She pulled a dreamcatcher out of her pocket and pressed it against his back. The rabbits hopped away. Wiping foam from his face, the man spun and knocked Sophie sideways into a chair. She dropped the dreamcatcher, and it skittered across the linoleum.

The pink rabbit shot across the floor, picked up the dreamcatcher in his mouth, and ran toward the muscle man. He leaped onto his foot and pressed the dreamcatcher to his ankles.

Seizing the moment of distraction, the spider woman scurried toward Mr. Nightmare and caught him in her front legs. Mr. Nightmare screamed, and the muscle man turned to help him—then faded away, along with the pink rabbit.

Web shot out from the base of the spider's abdomen. Quickly, she began wrapping Mr. Nightmare in the threads, flopping him over as she wound the strands around his torso.

"Don't do this, Jasmine," Mr. Nightmare pleaded

with her. "You and me, we could be a formidable team, especially the way you are now. If you were to be my partner and help me showcase the monsters, prices would skyrocket. We'd be rich, powerful—everything you've ever wanted would be ours."

"I want my child," the spider woman said. "I want the moments I lost—the morning breakfasts, the walks to the school bus, the afternoons of homework, the bedtime books, the weekend cuddles, the laughter, the tears . . ."

Sophie wasn't sure what they were talking about, but she did know this was her chance. She stepped closer to Mr. Nightmare and the spider woman. "And I want my parents back. Where are they? And where are Ethan and Madison?"

Mr. Nightmare turned his head to face her. His arms were secured to his sides with threads, and he couldn't move his body, but he seemed suddenly more confident, now that he saw Sophie. "Ahhh . . . Betty! I assume I have you to thank for dreaming my Jasmine to life?"

"Where are my parents and the other kids?" Sophie asked.

He smirked. "Hidden, where you won't find them."

"Tell me, or I'll ask her to bite you," Sophie threatened.

The spider loomed over him. She wore a smile on her beautiful face. "He's not very tasty, but I do owe you. I'd be happy to oblige."

Mr. Nightmare matched her smile. "She plans to bite me anyway. She always does. I've had this dream before, and I can handle a few bites. So no, I don't think I'm going to tell you."

Monster began to growl, and the spider lady hissed. Spittle rained on Mr. Nightmare's face. He couldn't wipe it away, and he didn't flinch.

"You'll tell me or— " Sophie began.

"Or what? You can't keep me wrapped up forever, and she won't kill me," he said. The woman flopped him onto his stomach and then his back again as she continued winding him in thread. "You dreamed her up, which means she's your creation, and you don't have the heart for killing."

The spider woman stroked his cheek with one foot. "Do you really want to test that theory? I have my own free will."

His eyes were fixed on Sophie's. "You haven't won. You won't find them without my help, and I won't help you unless you send this atrocity back into a dream and free me."

Was it true? She refused to believe it.

"You have no other choice," Mr. Nightmare said.

"Actually, I do." Switching directions, she strode across the kitchen to the phone. She picked it up, and before she could reconsider, she dialed 911. "Hi. The kids you're looking for, the ones who went missing today, are at 263 Windsor Street, Eastfield." She hung up without answering any questions and then stared at the phone, not quite believing she'd done it. As the phone began to ring, she backed away. They'd come now, and then so would the Watchmen, but at least he would never kidnap anyone again. They'd stopped him; they'd won, almost. Squaring her shoulders, she marched past Mr. Nightmare to the basement door. She paused only to pick up the dreamcatcher that held the muscle man and the pink rabbit.

"Come back!" Mr. Nightmare yelled.

The spider lady wrapped his mouth in threads as Sophie and Monster hurried downstairs.

24

Monster cracked the door to the storage
room open and peered through. He drew back. "Ooh,
not good. Looks like Mr. Nightmare had your new
friend very busy."

"Do you see Mom and Dad? Or the others?"

He checked again. "I don't see your parents. But
Ethan and Madison are in the second cage on the
left."

Sophie peeked inside and stifled a gasp. The storage room was full of monsters. Every kind of monster:
one with a skull for a face, one lion man, the three
red lizards, a huge snake, an oozy ball of goo . . . She
spotted Ethan and Madison, huddled in the back corner of one of the cages. The other cages were empty,
and the monsters swung, climbed, and oozed around
the room. The dreamcatchers Ethan and Madison

had carried were strewn on the floor outside the cage, beyond their reach, and the monsters avoided them. It looked as if Ethan and Madison had tried to defend themselves, and the monsters had ripped away the dreamcatchers and tossed them on the floor. "If I could get those dreamcatchers back to them . . ."

The rabbits hopped toward the door.

Blocking them, Sophie dropped to her knees. "You saw what happened to the pink bunny. You can't touch the dreamcatchers. Let me do it."

"Sophie, you can't go in there. You'll be eaten like a cupcake." Monster clung to her, his claws digging into her jeans and his tentacles wrapped around her legs. "You aren't a cupcake."

"It's my fault they're here. If we hadn't come back—"

"He would have recaptured them. How about we search for your parents and let the police free Ethan and Madison?"

"The police won't know what to do." Plus she at least had the element of surprise. She could jump in there, a dreamcatcher in each hand . . . And then they'd eat her.

"Let me do it," Monster said, releasing her. "I'm like them. They'll think I belong."

"You can't touch the dreamcatchers either."

"I won't," he said, his voice calm and reasonable. "I'll pick the lock on the cage, and then Ethan and Madison can get the dreamcatchers themselves."

She wanted to say no, but he was right. If she went in there, they'd notice her instantly and probably tear her to pieces, but Monster could blend in. "Think you can pretend to be mean?"

"I *am* mean. I don't know why people keep thinking otherwise."

"Be careful."

Monster rose onto his tentacles as if they were legs, and he pecked her on the cheek. "In case things go disastrously wrong and I'm torn to shreds, I want you to know that you're the best friend a monster could ever have, and I count myself lucky to have had the chance to live beyond a moment of imagination and become not just a dream, but also a memory."

She felt a lump in her throat. "Wait. Don't go. We'll find another way."

"And waste that lovely speech? Don't be silly." Before she could reply, Monster scooted through the door. She pressed herself against the wall again, listening, afraid to watch because they'd see her. She heard Monster:

"Hey, guys. I'm new. Can I eat the humans?"

Growls. Barks. Hisses.

She didn't hear what else he said. Pressing her cheek against the door, she strained to hear. For a very long few seconds, everything was quiet and calm.

And then screams, shrieks, and howls split the air.

"Go! Help him!" Sophie shouted at the rabbits.

They didn't hesitate. As she threw open the door, the rabbits charged in. She took a step to follow, and Monster bounded through. Close on his heels was a slobbering mess of ooze, covered with hundreds of eyes. Monster ran for the stairs.

Behind him, the ooze monster left a path of gunk. Goo stuck to the steps and smeared on the walls. Sophie slapped a dreamcatcher on the creature as it ran past. The dreamcatcher stuck to its hide, and the monster faded before it could catch Monster.

Sophie stared at the gooey dreamcatcher. The threads had absorbed the monster itself, but leftover ooze still clung to the steps and the wall, where the monster had smeared its slime.

"Brilliant," Monster said.

Sophie pulled dreamcatchers out of her pockets and dumped them in the ooze. She then opened her backpack and dropped those dreamcatchers in the goo too. As soon as they were saturated, she scooped them up, ignoring the way the ooze stuck to her own skin. As the monsters came through the door, snarling and hissing and spitting, she threw the dreamcatchers at them, one for each. The dreamcatchers stuck to their fur and their hides. She backed up the stairs as they came after her—and one after another, they vanished.

She reached the top of the stairs, rubbed the last dreamcatcher in the goo from her shirt, and waited— ready. But no more monsters followed. Crouched on the top step, she listened. She didn't hear anything. No hisses, no snarls, no footsteps, no claws on the cement.

"Is that all of them?" Sophie asked.

"Maybe?" Monster said.

Cautiously, they crept back down the stairs.

Below, she heard the door creak open. She halted and crouched, the last dreamcatcher ready. Ooze congealed on her hand and dripped down her wrist. Beside her, Monster bared his teeth.

And then Ethan and Madison ran up the stairs, followed by a herd of rabbits.

Monster threw his tentacles around Ethan's leg in a hug, and Sophie, without thinking about it, hugged

Madison. As soon as she realized what she was doing, she jumped back. "Are you guys okay?" Sophie asked.

"The ridiculous rabbits rescued us," Madison said.

"After Monster unlocked the cage, the monsters went nuts," Ethan said. "But the rabbits fought them so we could get the dreamcatchers. We turned a bunch of the monsters into dreams, and it looks like you took care of the rest. Sophie, do you—"

"Are my parents down there?" Sophie interrupted.

At the same time, Madison asked, "Where's Mr. Nightmare?"

"Trapped by a giant spider," Sophie said as she hurried downstairs. Her parents could be in a cage that Madison and Ethan couldn't see, or in another extra room.

"A *what?*" Madison followed her down.

Sophie ran through the storage room, looking in cage after cage. There were no other rooms, except for the little bedroom with the painted walls. Maybe they'd been put there after Madison left? She flung open the steel door to the bedroom. It was empty.

MADISON MARCHED UP THE STAIRS TO THE KITCHEN. "Are all the monsters gone?"

"I think so." Pausing on a step, Sophie stuffed the used dreamcatchers into her backpack. She wouldn't be able to use them again—they were full—but she didn't want to leave them for anyone to find, and she couldn't bring herself to destroy dreams, even night-mares.

Madison opened the door at the top of the stairs, stuck her head into the kitchen, and screamed. She slammed the door. "Spider. Big spider."

"She's on our side," Sophie said. "I told you."

"Right. You said that. Sort of. More details next time, okay?" Madison cautiously opened the door again, and they all crowded into the kitchen.

Mr. Nightmare lay on the kitchen floor, swathed in spiderweb.

"Whoa," Ethan said.

"Friends of his?" The spider woman's feet skittered over the floor. Her body bobbed as she moved, and her spinner had a trail of thread hanging from it.

"Friends of mine," Sophie said quickly, and then wondered if that was true. *It can't be,* she thought. Given what they knew about her, she'd be lucky if they considered her the same species.

"Ah, very well, then." The spider backed away, allowing them to come up. Madison hugged the cabinets, her eyes glued to the spider. She was fingering one of the remaining dreamcatchers.

Sophie turned to Madison and Ethan. "I'm going to free Christina and ask if she knows where my parents are. She's been here the longest. She might know more about the house." She skirted the tied-up Mr. Nightmare. "Can one of you watch for the police and make sure they know he's the kidnapper, not a victim?"

Ethan caught her arm. "Wait, you called the police?"

"Yes, before I found you." She tried to sound as if it wasn't a big deal, as if it didn't make her feel like she was being wrapped in threads like Mr. Nightmare.

"But your family secret! You said—"

Sophie cut him off. "I said if we saw anything suspicious, I'd call." She stepped back, out of his grip. "You'd better call your parents. Let them know you're okay."

Madison picked up the phone by the fridge. "You're one hundred percent certain the spider won't eat me?" Backing against the sink, she evaded the spider's legs.

"I do not eat children," the spider said.

Her eyes on the spider woman, Madison dialed, while Ethan pulled out his phone and began texting. If the police weren't already on their way, they would be soon, Sophie thought. As if reading her mind, Ethan looked up. "If you find them fast, maybe you and your parents can be gone by the time the police arrive," he said.

She nodded. At least she could try.

With Monster on her heels, Sophie ran up the stairs and threw open Christina's door. Christina rushed out. "Why are you still here?" she cried, seizing Sophie's arms. "Are you okay?"

"Yes, everything's okay. You're safe. We turned all

the monsters we could find back into dreams, and we captured Mr. Nightmare. The police are on their way. Here"—Sophie gave Christina a dreamcatcher—"in case we missed any."

"You *what?* How? You called the police?"

Craning her neck, Sophie looked up and down the hall at the other doors. She'd already looked in all these rooms. "Christina, I haven't found my parents yet. Do you have any idea where they could be?"

Monster nosed at the wall. "Any hidden rooms? Secret passageways? Portals to other dimensions or what-have-you?"

Without answering, Christina pushed past them and hurried downstairs. Sophie and Monster followed close on her heels as she barreled through the living room.

Madison and Ethan had left the kitchen and were perched kneeling on the living room couch so they could see the street. "Good. You found her," Ethan said. "Does she know where—"

Christina sped toward the kitchen and then halted. Sophie and Monster nearly bumped into her. Retreating fast, Christina pressed her back against the living room wall. "What's *that?*"

"She's from Mr. Nightmare's dream."

Christina's face was pale, and she looked as if she was going to be sick. "Make her go away."

"Yeah, kind of felt that way myself," Madison said. "Don't worry. The police are coming." She waved at the window. "They thought the first call was a hoax, but they believed *me*. They're on their way now."

"The spider woman is on our side," Sophie told Christina. "She helped us."

Flattened against the wall, Christina looked petrified. "I don't care. Send her away. Please!"

"We probably should send her back into a dream before the police come," Ethan said. "They might not get that she's a *friendly* scary spider."

Spontaneously, Sophie hugged Christina. "It's almost all over. And then you'll be back with your parents, and everything will be fine! You'll see."

"Just please, get rid of her, okay?" Christina begged.

Sophie nodded and then went into the kitchen. The spider woman was busily adding more thread to Mr. Nightmare's wrappings. He looked like a plump mummy. "Um, hi. Sorry to interrupt, but I need to send you back into a dream before the police come. There'll be questions, and . . . it would be better."

To Sophie's relief, the spider woman nodded. "I

understand. I do not belong here. I can feel the air pressing on me, making me feel heavy. The physics of your world do not want me to exist. My true self is out there somewhere, in a body that isn't a spider. She will complete my work. For now, it is enough that even the memory of the woman I was had the opportunity to triumph over him."

"You were triumphantly triumphant," Monster told her.

"Thank you," she said gravely. Sophie had never thought a spider could be regal, but she was both grand and gracious. "You may send me now."

Reaching into her pocket, Sophie pulled out a dreamcatcher. It was her last unused one. The used ones were all stuffed in her backpack. With more than a little regret, Sophie used the dreamcatcher on the spider woman. She faded away with a contented smile on her human face and her spider leg resting lightly on Mr. Nightmare's encased chest. Sophie gently put the dreamcatcher in her backpack with the others and then called to Christina, "Okay, it's safe now."

Christina came into the kitchen and stopped when she saw Mr. Nightmare, trussed up on the floor. Emotions flickered across her face, too fast for Sophie to read.

Outside, sirens wailed in the distance.

"They're coming!" Madison cried from the living room.

Monster tapped Sophie with a tentacle. "Come on. We have to find your parents *now*. Ask her again."

"Christina, do you know—"

"He must keep them in the safe room," Christina told her, crossing to the basement door. "It's beneath the fight pit—there's a secret door in the floor. I'll show you." Together, they headed downstairs, passing the balcony and stepping over the ooze that clung to the stairs and dripped down the walls. Christina opened the red door to the fight club arena.

Sophie and Monster followed her in. The sand was still speckled with blood, and ooze had congealed on the fence. Various empty beer cans were under the benches.

Without hesitation, Christina led them into the fight pit. "The trapdoor is buried under the sand." She pointed. "Right in the dead center."

Dropping to her knees, Sophie began to dig. Inside, she was screaming, *Mom! Dad! I'm coming!* Sand filled her fingernails and flew into her eyes, but she didn't stop. Beside her, Monster used all his tentacles, flinging sand behind them.

Watching them, Christina asked, "Your monster . . . He's been with you a long time, you said?"

"Years. He's my best friend." It would be nice if they had a shovel.

"I didn't know they could be friends," Christina said. "I've never had any friends."

Pausing, Sophie looked up and smiled at Christina. "We'll be friends." *We already are,* she thought.

"Something's here!" Monster cried. Digging faster, he unearthed a handle. Sophie swept the sand clear of the trapdoor. She tugged on the handle—locked!

Christina took a key out of her pocket, knelt next to Sophie, and unlocked the trapdoor. She lifted the door and sand fell inside. Sophie peered into the darkness. "Mom? Dad?"

"Why do you have a key?" Monster asked Christina.

From below, Sophie heard familiar, wonderful voices: "Sophie?" It was them! "Sophie, run! Get out of here!"

"It's okay!" Sophie called. "We stopped Mr. Nightmare. You're safe!"

Key in hand, Christina backed away from the trapdoor. "I'd like to be friends, Sophie. But I don't think that's possible. You see, you've destroyed my

344

life. That's hard to forgive. In fact, I think it makes us enemies."

Sophie felt as if all her muscles had frozen. "What?"

"*This* is my life." Christina waved her hand at the fight club arena. "This was to be our future. My father's idea; my monsters. But you ruined it by bringing *her* back."

"Your father?"

"The spider . . . She wore my mother's face. The very first monster I ever created was a giant spider. My mother saw it, and she called the Watchmen. She said it was for my own good, that they knew what to do with people like me—but you and I both know what the Night Watchmen do with people like us. They hunt us. My father fled with me before they came. He saved me from them—and from her."

Sophie shook her head, as if that would make Christina's words make sense. It wasn't possible. Christina couldn't be a part of all of this. She was a prisoner! She was like Sophie!

"She chased us for years, but my father always kept me safe. This was supposed to be how we built our new life." Christina waved her hands at the fight pit and toward the storage room. "We were going to be rich. So rich she'd never be able to touch us. So rich the Watchmen wouldn't dare try to take me away. Then you came along."

"You were part of all this? Kidnapping Madison and Lucy and my parents?"

"We needed more monsters." Walking backwards to the door of the fight pit, Christina looked sad. "I was hoping for one to match the greatest monster I ever dreamed. We call him the champion. We were saving him until we had the right opponent for him. Guess you qualify."

Monster howled. "Sophie, it's a trap!" He ran toward Christina.

But Christina held the dreamcatcher—the one that Sophie had given her, the only unused one—in front of her and gave a sharp whistle. From the trapdoor, Sophie heard a growl, and her parents screamed at her to run.

Sophie's muscles finally obeyed, and she scrambled after Monster, toward Christina and the fight pit door.

But Christina's champion was faster. It burst out of the hole and lunged for Sophie. Swiping for her leg, it caught her ankle. She fell forward and slammed into the sand on her knees. Twisting to face it, Sophie screamed.

The champion bulged with muscles that popped over its arms. Its skin was fiery red and streaked with purple veins that glistened like snakeskin. Two curved bull horns crowned its head, and its face was dominated by a massive jaw full of fangs. Its tail was thick with spikes, and as it twisted, Sophie saw its back was covered in spikes too.

A foot from Christina, Monster snaked out a tentacle and ripped the dreamcatcher from her hands. He then pivoted and ran toward Sophie and the champion.

He flung himself onto the monster, wrapping his tentacles around its neck, and he pressed the dreamcatcher against its skin.

"Monster, don't! You'll disappear too!" Sophie tried to jump for him, to grab the dreamcatcher from him, but the champion swiped at her. Its claws raked her arm. Crying out, she clutched her arm and fell back again onto the sand.

Monster was fading, becoming translucent, along with the champion. She could see the sand through the champion's muscles. "Run, Sophie!"

"No, Monster! Throw me the dreamcatcher! Please!" Scrambling to her feet, she ran toward him. The champion's arm shot out at her, blocking her.

"Go, Sophie! Remember me!"

There had to be something she could do! Some weapon! She remembered the pole that Mr. Nightmare had used. It leaned against the pit outside the fence—

The champion clawed at Monster, pulled him off, and threw him against the side of the pit. Monster thudded against the wall, and the dreamcatcher fell out of his tentacle.

"Monster!" Sophie cried. She ran to him. He was half faded, limp, and breathing shallowly. Before she could reach him, the champion's tail swung around and knocked into her. She was tossed to the side.

Christina strolled in, picked up the dreamcatcher, and pressed it against the unconscious Monster.

"No!" Sophie screamed.

Monster vanished.

Christina ripped the threads of the dreamcatcher. As the droplets of the dream fell onto the sand, Sophie felt as if her heart had been ripped out of her chest. "Now you know what it feels like to be truly alone," Christina said. Then she ran out of the pit, slamming and locking the door behind her.

From the balcony, a horse whinnied.

"She's not alone." Ethan's voice came from above.

Sophie looked up. Ethan and Madison were mounted on Glitterhoof. He swooped down into the pit and kicked the champion with so much force that it flew backwards against the fence and slumped unconscious onto the sand.

Ethan and Madison jumped off Glitterhoof's back. Together, they pressed dreamcatchers onto the champion until it faded and disappeared.

26

ALL OF THEM GATHERED AROUND SOPHIE.

"I came to tell you I delivered Lucy to the bookshop," Glitterhoof said. "I'm afraid I was seen—a woman who introduced herself as Ms. Lee and said she baked those delicious cupcakes. She offered me a few and then agreed to watch Lucy until her parents could fetch her so that I could return to you and render assistance."

"Glitterhoof found us upstairs," Ethan chimed in. "So we all came looking for you . . . I'm sorry about Monster."

Sophie nodded, not trusting herself to speak.

"Send me back to a dream," Glitterhoof said, "before anyone else sees me. You must keep your secret, if you can. You can owe me those apples."

"The police are outside," Madison said. "They

had just parked their cars when Glitterhoof arrived at the back door. They'll be inside any minute now."

Sophie knew she should say goodbye, or thank him, but she felt numb, as if her skin weren't her skin, as if she was looking at everything and everyone through a thick sheet of cellophane. Someone passed her an unused dreamcatcher. She held the dream-catcher to the pegasus.

She then added that dreamcatcher and the one holding the champion to the backpack. She wanted to tear the champion's dreamcatcher to pieces, but she didn't. It wasn't the champion's fault that Christina had made it what it was. Monster had said once that the dreamer shapes the dream—that's why all of Christina's creatures were terrifying monsters.

"She escaped?" Sophie asked, though it wasn't really a question. Christina had had plenty of time to escape while they fought her champion. Upstairs she heard heavy footsteps in the living room—the police must have entered the house. Soon, they'd find Mr. Nightmare, wrapped in spider threads.

Madison nodded. "Saw her run out the cellar doors, but the monster—"

"I know." Standing, Sophie crossed to the trap-door.

"Do you think there are any more down there?" Madison asked. "Because I am tapped out. Done with monsters."

Ethan elbowed her.

"Oh, sorry, Sophie. You know . . . except him."

Sophie told herself not to cry. She'd do that later, when she was alone. Right now, she still had to free her parents, before the police explored the basement. She lowered herself through the trapdoor and dropped down.

It took a second for her eyes to adjust to the dim light. When they did, she saw a cement-walled room with a jail door that cut through the middle. There was a vat for water and one for food, and the room stank of pee. The stench made her gag. She breathed through her mouth as she looked around—and then she saw that the jail door hadn't been holding the champion *in*. It had been keeping it *out* of the cage that held her parents.

"Sophie!" her mother cried, running toward the bars.

"You're all right!" Dad said.

Sophie ran to the jail door, and her parents reached through the bars to touch her hands, arms, and face. "How do I get you out?" Sophie asked.

Dad pointed to the wall. "The key!"

Hands trembling, Sophie fetched the key from a hook. She tried to unlock the door. Her hands were shaking too hard. Taking a deep breath, she tried to steady herself.

"I'll do it." Madison reached past her and unlocked the lock. Sophie hadn't realized that Madison had come through the trapdoor. Dimly, she was aware that Ethan had followed her too.

Sophie ran inside. Mom and Dad both pulled Sophie to them. Sobbing, they held her. Sophie didn't cry, but she held them both as tightly as she could. She felt as though there was something missing inside her.

As her parents cooed to her, she led them to the trapdoor and looked up. There wasn't a ladder. How were they —

A woman's face appeared in the opening. "Is anyone hurt down there?"

"Ms. Lee?" Sophie said.

"Jia?" Mom said, just as shocked.

"Who?" Madison asked. "What's going on?"

Leaning over the opening, Ms. Lee, the baker, held out her hand. "Come on. We have to hurry and get you out of here. The police will have a lot of questions, and it will be best if the three of you aren't here when they search the basement—they're already upstairs."

None of them moved.

"Who *are* you?" Dad asked.

"I'm your neighbor," Ms. Lee said. "Will you accept that I'm here being neighborly?"

Clutching Sophie, her parents shook their heads.

Ms. Lee sighed. "I am from an organization that watches for abuse of dreams. I was assigned to observe your family's shop and monitor your customers."

"You're a Night Watchman," Dad said flatly.

"Yes, I am," Ms. Lee said.

Sophie's parents hugged her tighter.

"What's a Night Watchman?" Madison asked.

"I wish I could have intervened sooner, but we didn't have enough information on who was responsible." Ms. Lee sighed. "It took the arrival of a pegasus with that little girl before I was able to track you down. Come, we need to hurry."

"I don't understand. *You're* a Watchman?" Sophie tried to match her memories of Ms. Lee—sweet, insecure, smelling like cupcakes—with her image of the Watchmen—shadowy and terrifying. She couldn't make herself think of Ms. Lee as terrifying.

"We trusted you," Dad said, echoing Sophie's shock.

"You can still trust me," Ms. Lee said. "I'm here to help you."

"But the Night Watchmen hate us," Sophie said. "They want to destroy dream shops."

Ms. Lee shook her head. "You've been misinformed. We have no problem with dream shops. We have problems with people like Mr. Nightmare, who misuse dreams."

Sophie felt rather than saw her parents exchange glances and knew they were communicating in that look.

"In fact, we are grateful to you," Ms. Lee said. "You've all been instrumental in bringing down one of the worst dream-creature traffickers that we've seen. Now, please, we have limited time. Come with me."

Another exchanged glance.

"Very well," Mom said heavily.

Ms. Lee helped pull them out and onto the sand of the fight pit. She was surprisingly strong. On the sand, she smiled at them—the friendly, reassuring smile that Sophie knew so well. Sophie felt as if everything was turned inside out and upside down. Monster was gone, and the Watchmen weren't evil? Two of the constants in her life had disappeared in seconds.

"Ambulances are outside," Ms. Lee said to all of them. "The EMTs will check the two kids over, and the police will take your statements. They've already taken Lucy's. You will tell them you were kidnapped and held in the basement. Do *not* mention monsters or pegasi or dreams, do you understand? Regular police do not need to hear that. They *do* need to hear that Mr. Nightmare is guilty of kidnapping. If you stick to that fact, then he will be in jail for a very long time."

"But . . ." Ethan began.

"I am sorry to put this burden on all of you, but you *must* keep this secret."

"Why?" Madison asked.

"Explanations later," Ms. Lee said to Madison and Ethan. "We need to get you two back where you belong. Your parents will be overjoyed to see you. Remember what I said: if you want to be believed, leave out the impossible." She turned to Sophie's parents. "We'll send medical professionals to check you out. And later, I will be speaking to you both about your failure to disclose Sophie's abilities. She needs to be registered, and she needs training so that nothing happens to her—or to anyone else. You've seen what damage a rogue nondreamer can do."

"She's just a child," Dad objected.

"So was Christina, and she . . ." Sophie couldn't make herself say the words. It would make it too real. "Monster . . . Monster saved me." Her voice broke.

Mom stroked her hair. "You can't take her from us!"

"Why would I want to do that?" Ms. Lee asked. "She's your child. Whatever you were told about the Night Watchmen, we aren't ogres who take children from their parents. We aim to stop people like that. We're the good guys."

"Are you with the police?" Madison asked. "Secret branch of the government?"

"Secret agents?" Ethan asked.

"All you need to know for now is that this kind of situation is an aberration," Ms. Lee said. "After the immediate crisis is over, I will be available to answer all your questions." Turning to Sophie and her parents, she said, "Come with me, quickly."

"Wait, what about the distiller?" Ethan asked. "And all the dreams still in bottles? He stole dozens. We saw the empty shelves."

"Our shop can't function without the distiller,"

Dad said. "If you don't intend to put us out of business, we'll need it back."

"I'll ensure it's returned," Ms. Lee said.

"There are also rabbits," Ethan said. "Lots of them. Some are multicolored."

Ms. Lee paused. "Multicolored rabbits?"

"In clothes," Madison said. "And they're kind of ninjas. It's weird."

"Everything will be taken care of," Ms. Lee said. Guiding Madison and Ethan to the stairs to the kitchen, she then led Sophie and her parents out the back cellar doors.

Sophie was surprised to see it was still night outside. She had no grasp of what time it was, what time she'd lost Monster.

While the others were brought to ambulances to be examined, Sophie and her parents were driven home in an unmarked white car. No questions were asked.

27

Sophie slept through most of the next day. She heard her parents check on her a few times, tiptoeing in and then out, shutting the door softly behind them. Every time they came in, she kept her eyes shut and her breath even, until at last she was too hungry to stay in bed anymore.

She opened her eyes. Her bed felt cold. Stretching her legs, she didn't feel Monster's heavy warmth at the foot of the bed. She sat up. It was quiet. She didn't hear his voice, demanding that she go back to sleep or that she fetch him a cupcake. She was alone in her room for the first time in years, and suddenly she wanted to be anywhere but here.

Standing up, she slid her feet into slippers. They didn't make her feel warmer. She padded down the stairs to the kitchen, hoping her parents would be in the bookshop. But no such luck. Both her parents were sitting in the living room, as if they'd been waiting for her. Both of them had circles under their eyes so dark that they looked like bruises. She wondered if they'd slept at all.

Her mother stood up from the rocking chair but didn't move toward Sophie. "You were very brave," she said. "I want you to know that."

Sophie noticed that the fallen books had all been restacked and that the stacks were pushed against the walls, leaving a clear path to the kitchen for the first time in ages. She'd forgotten that the floor was wood. It glowed in the sunlight that poured through the window. Her parents must have dusted, too. Everything shone.

Her father was sitting on the couch with an unopened book on his lap. She had the impression he'd been sitting there for hours, without touching the book. "Do you want to talk about it?"

Sophie tried to summon up enough energy to answer, but she felt as if she were swimming through sludge. She shuffled to the refrigerator and opened it.

"Are you hungry?" Ditching the book, Dad popped to his feet. "I can make you something. Grilled cheese and tomato?"

"Okay." It was easier to agree than to think of any particular thing she wanted. She wanted Monster. Just Monster. She saw extra cupcakes on the counter, and her eyes felt hot. She turned away and was certain she'd never eat a cupcake again.

"We miss him too, sweetie," Mom said.

"I know." It was hard to say the words, and her voice felt distant and small. She was not going to cry. *Not* going to cry. Monster used to hate it when she cried. He'd complain she got his fur wet. She sat down at the table while Dad heated up a skillet and smeared butter on two slices of bread. She watched him for a while, and then she asked, "What did Ms. Lee mean, about registering me? And training me?"

Mom and Dad exchanged glances, the kind of look that implied entire unspoken conversations. "You aren't the only one with this . . . gift," Dad said.

"Yeah, I figured out that much." Thinking of Christina, she felt her stomach churn. She suddenly wasn't hungry anymore. "How many more are there like me?"

"No one knows," Mom said. "There could be just a few or there could be hundreds. Most people don't ever encounter liquid dreams, so no one knows how many nondreamers there are."

"That is one reason why what you can do needs to stay secret, and why the Watchmen keep an eye out for people like you," Dad said. He added a second sandwich to the skillet and glanced briefly at Sophie, as if to check on how she was taking this news. "If all the nondreamers knew and could access dreams ... Imagine thousands of people drinking dreams and bringing them to life, all across the world."

"Monsters, demons, vampires, werewolves, every kind of bogeyman could spring up everywhere, faster than anyone could stop them." Mom sat at the table, across from Sophie. Her voice was gentle, her eyes kind, which made her words all that much worse.

Sophie felt herself start to shake. "But good things, too. There could be good dreams, the kind that could help the world." Monster was good.

"Yes, but the Night Watchmen believe the bad would outweigh the good," Mom said. "According to Ms. Lee—"

"She was here?" Sophie asked.

Dad nodded. "While you slept, she came to visit."

"Being able to dream things to life ... It's a rare and dangerous ability," Mom said. "There are consequences to what you can do."

Dad sighed heavily. "We didn't want you to have to bear that kind of burden. We thought we could keep you separate from all of it. No drinking dreams equals no danger. You knew the rules. We thought that was enough."

"I'm sorry," Sophie said in a small voice.

Mom's smile was sad. She reached across the table and touched Sophie's hand. "We aren't mad at you, Sophie. What you did . . . You did the right thing, with the knowledge you had. You thought you were alone. You didn't know there was anyone who could help you, and frankly neither did we. We'd always believed that the Night Watchmen were our enemy. Regardless, we should have told you more."

"Will you now?" Sophie asked.

"Yes," Dad said, after exchanging another glance with Mom. "Ms. Lee is right—you should be trained. She can help you find a mentor who will teach you everything you need to know. She says there are dangers to drinking dreams for people like you, and if you aren't trained, you could hurt yourself or others."

Sophie thought of the headaches that she'd gotten after the last few dreams and wondered if that's what Ms. Lee meant, or if she meant something worse.

"Sophie . . ." Mom stopped as if searching for

the right words. "You should know that from here on out, for the rest of your life, you will be watched. Ms. Lee and others like her . . . The Night Watchmen are aware of you now." Mom hesitated. "They might not be our enemies as we thought, but that doesn't necessarily mean they're our friends. You'll need to be careful."

Without Monster, it was hard to get worked up enough to care. "I'm always careful," Sophie said.

"Even more careful," Mom said. "We may have been wrong to fear the Watchmen so much—and to make you fear them—but as nice as Ms. Lee is, she doesn't necessarily have your best interests at heart."

"Keep your friends around you," Dad said, and Mom nodded. She fetched a plate from the cabinet as Dad cut a tomato.

"I don't have any friends," Sophie said, pushing back from the table. She headed for the stairs. She could feel the tears coming now.

"Hey, Sophie?" Dad called. "What about the sandwich?"

"I'm not hungry."

Sophie ran up the stairs and threw herself onto her empty bed. Alone in her room, she finally cried.

The next morning, Sophie woke to sunlight streaming through the curtains. She sat up, alone, and didn't want to curl up in bed again. She went to the bathroom, showered, dressed, and trudged downstairs. Her parents were again in the kitchen. Her mother's eyes were overbright, as if she'd been crying too, and Dad looked as if he hadn't slept in days.

"I forgot to set my alarm," Sophie said. "Did I miss the bus?"

"You don't have to go to school today if you don't want to," Dad said. "We can call in sick for you if you want to rest some more."

"I don't want to rest anymore, and I can't stay here." Every room had a million memories. She kept expecting to see Monster out of the corner of her eye, to hear his dry voice as he commented on breakfast or her homework or . . .

Mom nodded. "It will be good for you to start a routine again."

"Can I make you breakfast?" Dad opened the fridge without waiting for Sophie to answer. He examined the date on a container of yogurt and tossed it.

"Not yogurt. Cereal? Pancakes? Waffles? Come on, let me make you the finest waffles you've ever seen, with strawberries and whipped cream . . ."

"Dear, we don't have any strawberries or whipped cream," Mom said.

"She's going to say no anyway," Dad said. "Let me at least imagine whipped cream."

Sophie felt her mouth want to quirk into a smile, but it didn't actually move. She wondered if she'd ever smile again. She supposed she would, but it would be wrong, without Monster. "Cereal is fine." She went to the cabinet for a bowl and the box. Sitting at the table, she poured the cereal. Her father poured the milk, and her mother handed her a spoon.

As she ate, both her parents hovered over her as if they expected her to explode. She had to leave. School would be a welcome relief. Everyone there would ignore her, and she could go back to pretending that she didn't exist. She finished her cereal in record time, got her backpack, wondered what homework she'd missed, and headed downstairs to the bookshop.

Her parents followed her like lost puppies.

"Love you, Pumpkin," Dad said behind her.

Sophie hesitated, her hand on the door handle. She was supposed to say "Love you, Zucchini," and then Mom would pick another fruit or vegetable and then Monster would mock them by calling out the names of every other vegetable he could think of. But without Monster, the words stuck in her throat. "See you after school."

She went outside and walked to the bus stop without looking back.

★★★

Everything at the bus stop seemed ordinary. The mother with the toddler tried to talk to her again, but Sophie ignored her. The boys shoved one another off the curb. The two girls gossiped and laughed and never even glanced at Sophie. When the bus came, she climbed on and sat by herself.

At school, she walked through the hallway without meeting anyone's eyes. She passed the bathroom where she'd let Monster out to climb into the ceiling, and she avoided the music room, where they'd fought the gray creature. At her locker, she traded her textbooks for her notebooks. There were no happy birthday notes, no missing dreamcatchers, nothing unusual at all, and she told herself that was a good thing. The danger was over, and life was—at least on the surface—back to normal, except for the way her heart hurt every time she breathed.

In class, she kept her head down and eyes on her notebook. She half listened to what the teacher said, writing down a few scattered words but not really letting them compute. She drifted through several classes that way, and then it was time for lunch.

After dropping her notebooks off at her locker, Sophie let the stream of students sweep her toward the cafeteria. She got in line and ignored how the line grew in front of her as kids cut and then cut the cutters. She stared at the chocolate milk. Was everything going to remind her of Monster? Was it going to be this way forever? Sophie picked up a few items at random and then slinked over to an empty table. She set her food down and stared at it, not hungry.

Two trays were placed on the table. She noted their arrival and wondered why their owners didn't pick an empty table.

"Hey, Dream Girl, snap out of it," Madison said.

Sophie looked up.

Madison sat across from her. Ethan was next to Sophie. "You got shepherd's pie again," Ethan said. "On purpose?"

"Obviously not." Madison reached across the table and swapped Sophie's shepherd's pie for an egg sandwich. "Eat this instead."

Sophie picked up half the sandwich. "Uh, thanks. Um, why are you guys sitting here? And being nice to me?" She eyed Madison, then the sandwich, and wondered if it was poisoned or filled with spit or something. Just a couple of days ago, Madison would have rather showed up to school naked than talk in public to Sophie.

"Believe it or not, fighting a pack of imaginary creatures after being kidnapped by a creepy guy is surprisingly bonding," Madison said.

Ethan shrugged. "We can't talk about this with anyone else."

Sophie put down the sandwich. "I really don't want to talk about it."

"Then we'll talk around you," Madison said merrily. Leaning forward, she asked in a conspiratorial whisper, "Do you wonder what happened to the rabbits? Do you think they caught them all?"

"Maybe. Or they could have slipped out of the house. Where do you think Christina is?" Ethan asked. "Was Mr. Nightmare really her dad? Makes my own parents seem not so bad. I'd rather uninterested than evil."

"Seriously," Madison agreed.

"I wouldn't be surprised if the Watchmen already found her," Ethan said.

Sophie looked at them both, talking so casually about things that not so long ago they would have considered ridiculously impossible. But now they sounded . . . excited and weirdly happy. "Aren't you guys mad at me? I mean, you wouldn't have gone through all that if not for me."

They looked at her, and then they exchanged glances in a way that reminded Sophie of her parents. She realized they'd been talking without her. Or about her.

"Yeah, we know." Madison reached into her pocket and pulled out a dreamcatcher. She laid it on Sophie's tray. "We want a commission. We'll come by after school to work out the details, but we think it's only fair. And if it turns out the dreams have too many personal details, we expect your parents not to sell them."

Ethan handed Sophie his dreamcatcher. "This one isn't for sale. This one is for you."

Sophie felt her face flush red. "I . . . uh . . . I don't understand."

"We like you, Sophie," Ethan said, "even if you don't want us to."

"Not that we think you're suddenly cool or anything," Madison said. "I don't want to be BFFs. But yeah, after school today. Your place."

Madison and Ethan both nodded.

Sophie felt herself almost smile.

28

AFTER SCHOOL, THEY MET IN THE DREAM SHOP.
Sitting on the stairs, Ethan was tossing a ball into the
air over and over. Next to the somnium, Madison was
filing her nails.

Sophie, with her father guiding her, was distilling
Ethan's dream.

She chased the light through the tubes as it shimmered with flecks of gold. Her father whispered in
her ear, "That lever. Yes. Now that one, fast. Good.
Excellent." She guided the liquid through another
tube, steering it so that the flecks of light brightened
into a steady glow. "You have a good eye for this."

She didn't answer, instead concentrating on sending the liquid light through the next spiral of tubes.
Dad reached across her and hit another lever, which

sent it shooting into a tube to the left. It sparkled brighter.

"Get a bottle," Dad said.

Scurrying to the shelves, she fetched an empty blue bottle. She placed it under the spigot. Drip by drip, it filled with Ethan's dream. When it was full, she carried the bottle over to the somnium, where her mother waited.

Catching his ball, Ethan stood and crossed to stand beside Sophie.

A moment later, the others all crowded around. Sophie watched the clouds in the somnium swirl. She saw the school music room, and Monster standing in front of Ethan, defending him from the gray creature. And then they were on the bus ride home, with Monster in her backpack, and then the bike ride where he was seasick. Sophie felt tears on her cheeks.

The dream shifted to show the night rainbow. She saw herself holding Monster in her arms as they slid toward the bookshop. And then another shift, and there was Mr. Nightmare's house—first the garage, then the bushes, then through the cellar doors, above the sandpit. The champion was in the ring, and Sophie saw herself fall on the sand . . . She began to turn away. If Ethan had dreamed about what happened next, she didn't want to see it. She'd replayed that moment in her mind over and over again, wondered if it would have been different if she'd been faster, if she'd been less gullible, if she'd . . .

"Sophie, wait," her father said.

Reluctantly, she turned back. She didn't know why Ethan had insisted she see it. It was more a string of memories than a new dream, and she didn't want to remember. She certainly didn't want to relive it. As Sophie hugged her arms, the dream collected again in the bottle.

Her mother picked up the bottle carefully and held it out to Sophie. "Drink."

Her friends were all smiling at her, hope in their eyes. And Sophie suddenly realized why Ethan wanted her to have this dream:

It had Monster in it.

Monster, alive, with her.

Hands shaking, she tilted the bottle to her lips, and drank.

Sophie was in school, in the music room, with Monster, Ethan, and the gray creature, and the feeling of déjà vu was so strong that she couldn't move . . . until she remembered this was a dream.

She walked up to the gray creature and pulled a dreamcatcher out of her pocket. She wondered briefly how it had gotten in her pocket and if it would work within a dream, and then decided it didn't matter if it *should* work so long as she believed it *would* work. Without a word, she pressed it against his hide. The gray creature swiped at her with his claws and missed. She continued to hold the dreamcatcher to him until he faded.

The dream-Ethan was curled by the piano. She didn't talk to him. Instead, Sophie went directly to Monster and knelt in front of him. "Is it really you?" she asked.

"Am I dreaming?" Monster asked. "I feel like I am. I can remember all the things that are going to happen, or, more accurately, have already happened— like that nauseating bike ride."

"Technically, Ethan is dreaming. Or was. And now I am."

"Ooh, sweet. So you're going to dream me to life

again, and then I'll have a clone? Hey, that means one of us can be the good twin and one can be the evil twin, and anytime I do anything bad, I'll blame the evil twin."

"No twin," Sophie said. "Just you."

"Oh. Why?"

"Well, you . . ." She swallowed a lump in her throat. "You're gone."

Monster craned his neck to see his stomach and back. He waved his tentacles in the air experimentally. "Funny, I don't feel gone. Hey, is it that scary 'champion' thing in the sandpit? Is that what gets me?"

"Actually, it's that girl Christina."

"The one you greeted like long-lost family?"

"*You* are my family," Sophie said. "And I want you to come home." A horrible thought occurred to her. "Unless you don't want to come?" He was back in a dream, where he belonged. "You said once that the dreamer shapes the dream . . . Would you rather stay here? Be yourself?" It hurt to say the words, but she had to ask. She couldn't force him.

"Everyone, whether they're born in a dream or out of a belly, is shaped by the people they love. That's not necessarily a bad thing."

"So you want to come?" She had to hear him say it.

"Of course, Sophie. You're my best friend," Monster said. She hugged him, and he added, "Besides, you feed me."

She grinned.

Monster wrapped his tentacles around her neck. "Okay, let's wake up before we have to relive the scary parts. You know, I don't like scary dreams."

"Really?"

"Deepest secret. Don't tell, okay?"

Sophie laughed and then her laugh faded as another thought occurred to her. "But are you really *you?* I mean, this is Ethan's dream. He's only known you a little while."

"This is *your* dream now," Monster said. "You are dreaming, Sophie, no matter where the dream came from. Your mind is here. Your heart is here. And Sophie . . . whether I am in the world or not, I will always be with you, in your mind and in your heart. It's where I'm meant to be—where I *choose* to be."

"Promise?" Sophie said.

"Nothing that's loved is ever really gone." With

one tentacle, he touched her forehead. With another, he touched her heart. "Believe that, Sophie, even if it sounds like a fortune cookie . . . Speaking of which, I'm hungry. Can we wake up now, Sophie? It's snack time."

And with that, Sophie woke up.

Opening her eyes in the Dream Shop, she saw everyone in a tight circle around her, peering down at her. She lay on a pile of pillows, and for an instant, she didn't know if she was awake or still asleep. Curled up with her was a warm lump of fur. Blinking hard, she looked at him.

Monster lifted his head up. Out of the side of his mouth, he said, "Sophie, why is everyone staring at me? Did I sprout horns?"

Dad knelt next to Sophie and Monster. "Monster? Do you remember us?"

"Um, yes? Is that a trick question?" Snuggling closer to Sophie, Monster whispered, "Sophie, is your father all right?"

"He's just worried because you've been dead for a while." Her voice cracked. She felt like crying. Her eyes felt hot, and her throat was tight.

"Dreams can't die," Monster said.

"But they can be lost." Sophie wrapped her arms around him.

He threw his tentacles around her. "And then found again."

Mom and Dad exchanged glances, and then Mom asked, "Monster, if I told you there was a small child for you to eat, what would you say?"

Monster perked up. "I'd say, 'Where's the ketchup?'"

Mom smiled. "It's him."

Everyone crowded closer, patting Sophie's shoulder and Monster's head, and talking all at the same time.

"Wow," Monster said. "This is like a party. Are we having a party?" He looked hopefully at Madison. "Just to be clear . . . that was a joke, right? About the ketchup?"

"Yes," Sophie, Mom, and Dad said.

"Of course, just a joke." He patted Madison, looking a bit disappointed. Confused, Madison scowled, and Sophie tried not to laugh. "Are there cupcakes?"

Sophie hugged him. "All the cupcakes you want."

Acknowledgments

I'd like to thank the monsters under my bed, in my closet, and in my basement, for all the support and inspiration, as well as for not eating me. You guys rock. I owe you imaginary cake. I'd also like to thank my fantastic agent, Andrea Somberg, and my magnificent editor, Anne Hoppe, as well as my wonderful publisher, Dinah Stevenson, and all the other amazing people at Clarion Books and Houghton Mifflin Harcourt, for bringing this dream to life. Many thanks and much love to my family, and especially to my husband and my children, who are better than any dream and make me happy to be awake.

BUBBLES

TABLE OF CONTENTS

· · · · ·